W9-BQB-299

TANGLED UP IN BLUE

JOAN D. VINGE

TOR®

A TOM DOHERTY ASSOCIATES BOOK
NEW YORK

This is a work of fiction. All the characters and events portrayed in this book are either products of the author's imagination or are used fictitiously.

TANGLED UP IN BLUE

Copyright © 2000 by Joan D. Vinge

Edited by James Frenkel

A Tor Book
Published by Tom Doherty Associates, LLC
175 Fifth Avenue
New York, NY 10010

www.tor.com

Tor® is a registered trademark of Tom Doherty Associates, LLC.

ISBN: 0-812-57636-5
Library of Congress Catalog Card Number: 00-026835

First edition: July 2000
First mass market edition: October 2001

Printed in the United States of America

0 9 8 7 6 5 4 3 2 1

Raves for
Tangled Up in Blue

"Vinge's *Tangled Up in Blue* makes for a triumphant return . . . This is an exceptionally well-told tale by one of the enduring stars of science fiction, a writer of grace as well as imagination." —Charleston SC *Post and Courier*

" . . . the foreground is well occupied by pain and romance, mystery and slaughter. This one will not disappoint Vinge's many fans, and it should awaken new interest in her older titles." —*Analog*

"*Tangled Up in Blue* has it all: a fast-paced plot that won't let go until its thrilling conclusion; clever ideas drawn from science; romantic interludes; and a plot with more twists and turns than the exotic alleys of Carbuncle. Vinge has written another winner." —Catherine Asaro, *SF site*

"Joan D. Vinge is a brilliant writer. Her novels are infrequent, but always worth waiting for. *Tangled Up in Blue* is complex, filled with intrigue, and impossible to put down. Rarely does a follow-up book garner the same awards as its progenitor, but I wouldn't be surprised to see Vinge cop another Hugo for this one."
—Robert J. Sawyer, Nebula Award-winning author of *Calculating God*

"I really enjoyed *Tangled Up in Blue*. It was exciting to be back in Tiamat, and to see it from such a different point of view. Joan Vinge's voice remains unique in science fiction, drawing for us a rich and vibrant world full of fascinating characters involved in a dark and intriguing mystery." —Sarah Zettel, author of *Fool's War*

"*Tangled Up in Blue* is compelling reading, the kind of SF adventure that keeps your eyes glued to the page and transports you to its world, so that you miss your train stop in this one. I liked it a lot."
—David G. Hartwell, editor of *Year's Best SF* series

(turn the page for more enthusiastic response
to Joan D. Vinge's novels)

Joan D. Vinge's *Snow Queen* Cycle

The Snow Queen
Winner of the 1981 Hugo Award for Best SF Novel

"I think this is a future classic—I was enormously impressed. . . . It has the weight and texture of *Dune*. Hell of an achievement."
—Sir Arthur C. Clarke

"A triumph for a fine writer . . . massive and exciting. . . . There are memorable characters here and a complex, suspensefully orchestrated plot that builds with steady inevitability to a symphonic finale . . . A sure award contender."
—*Publishers Weekly*

"A timeless story of the corruption of youth and redemption by love."
—*Chicago Tribune Book World*

"Ms. Vinge has one of the most wished-for gifts any writer can have—the ability to make the strange come wholly alive."
—Andre Norton

"It is almost impossible to lose interest in this book, for it is one of the more notable feats of storytelling on the grand scale in science fiction since Frank Herbert's *Dune*."
—*Booklist*

"Joan Vinge's *Snow Queen* is a book I wish I'd written . . . a splendid novel."
—Anne McCaffrey

"The best science fiction book I have read this year . . . succeeds in everything it attempts, and it attempts just about everything. Her world comes to life, and her characters will always be with me."

—John Varley

World's End
A Nebula Award Nominee

"Shows an unusually high level of stylistic sophistication."
—*Newsday*

"This is science fiction of a most refreshing sort—based on human values and the development of recognizable characters, and thus an attempt at serious literature, rather than being just another interplanetary shoot-'em up. It is no surprise that Vinge is being hailed as one of the bright new voices in the genre."

—Clarus Backes, *The Denver Post*

"Sure to captivate more subjects for one of the reigning queens of science fiction." —*Publisher's Weekly*

"A satisfying extension of the themes introduced in *The Snow Queen*. An important purchase for any collection serving older students and sophisticated science fiction readers." —*VOYA*

The Summer Queen
A Hugo Award Finalist

"As large and splendid as its predecessor."

—*Chicago Sun-Times*

"Fascinating . . . full of drama, conflict and tragedy. . . . Vinge is at the top of her form. [*The Summer Queen*] blends complex characters and mythic resonances with the sweeping grandeur of an interplanetary saga."

—*Publishers Weekly*

"Vinge has written a book which is a true sequel to *The Snow Queen*, and it's a winner. *The Summer Queen* is more complex, richer, and in the end more rewarding than *The Snow Queen*. Totally satisfying. This is the kind of book that could only be science fiction: the kind of book we're all richer for having in our field." —*Locus*

"Monumental. . . ." —*Washington Post Book World*

"The long-awaited sequel to Vinge's enormous *The Snow Queen*. All in all, an absorbing and sastifying performance." —*Kirkus Reviews* (starred)

BOOKS BY JOAN D. VINGE

THE SNOW QUEEN CYCLE
The Snow Queen
World's End
*The Summer Queen
*Tangled Up in Blue

THE CAT BOOKS
*Psion
*Catspaw
*Dreamfall

*Heaven Chronicles
Phoenix in the Ashes (story collection)
Eyes of Amber (story collection)

*denotes a Tor Book

Dedicated to all those men and women,
in or out of uniform,
who understand that Justice is not blind—
she is blindfolded, by choice.

*It is only with the heart that one can see rightly;
what is essential is invisible to the eye.*
—ANTOINE DE SAINT-EXUPERY

ACKNOWLEDGMENTS

Time and tide wait for no one—publishing deadlines and carpal tunnel surgery are hardly more accommodating. So, a brief but heartfelt THANK YOU to all those who inspired, encouraged, guided, sheltered, and made me laugh while I was writing this book. If there is any justice in this world, then you do know who you are. . . .

As flies to wanton boys are we to the gods;
They kill us for their sport.
                    —SHAKESPEARE, *KING LEAR*

The policeman's lot is not a happy one.
                    —W. S. GILBERT

1

"You two! Patrolmen! Wait a minute—"

Hegemonic Police officer Nyx LaisTree stopped at the exit of the station house, his hands already pushing open the windowed doors. He turned, along with his partner, to see a Kharemoughi sergeant gesturing them back toward the dispatch desk. "Damn!" Tree muttered. "It's Gundhalinu."

"Relax." His partner, Staun LaisNion, laid a reassuring hand on his shoulder. "He's a Technician; he doesn't even know our names. It's probably nothing." Grudgingly they reentered the obstacle course of work stations, and backtracked through the human gridlock created by the evening's shift change.

They halted at last in front of Gundhalinu. "Sergeant, we just got off duty," Staun said, somehow keeping his face expressionless and his voice respectful. Gundhalinu didn't deserve their respect any more than he deserved to be a sergeant, not when he was barely old enough to spend his pay in the kinds of places they'd just spent their shift policing.

Tree glanced over at Haig KraiVieux, the duty officer observing their interaction from his seat at the dispatch desk. KraiVieux had been a Blue longer than Gundhalinu had been alive, and he was still only a sergeant. But then, he was a Newhavener, not a Kharemoughi. Most of the force stationed here on Tiamat were from Newhaven; but Kharemough, Gundhalinu's homeworld, was first among equals in the Hegemony. Members of Kharemough's aristocratic Technician caste tended to advance rapidly within the Hedge's bureaucracy. They dominated the highest levels of its foreign service, including its paramilitary peacekeeping force, the Hegemonic Police.

"We had plans—"

"They'll have to wait." Gundhalinu cut Staun short with the unthinking arrogance of every Technician that Tree had ever met; and he had met a lot of them since joining the Hegemonic Police. The more of them he knew, the less he liked about them. "We need extra men working tonight."

"Why, Sergeant? Is there some kind of trouble?" Staun asked.

Gundhalinu shook his head. "The Snow Queen has requested extra security at the palace. She's having a party."

"Another one?" Staun said glumly. "Why do we have to do guard duty at these things? She's got all of Carbuncle's city constables, plus her own private security force."

"The Winters are celebrating another successful *mer* hunt, I suppose," Gundhalinu said. "Since the Queen controls our access to the water of life, it's in the Hegemony's best interest to humor her."

Tree grunted in disgust. Tiamat's seas were a fountain of youth, from which only the richest and most privileged could afford to drink. The most convenient way of obtaining the extract that humans euphemistically referred to as the "water of life" was to cut the *mers*' throats and let them bleed to death.

It didn't seem to bother the human users that what it all came down to was drinking blood. What was the life of an animal, compared to their own? The kind of people who were willing to pay anything for eternal youth would probably cut their neighbors' throats and collect the blood in a bucket to get it.

Tree had no doubt at all that the Snow Queen would do it. The water of life was the only resource this godforsaken planet possessed that was valuable enough to make Tiamat worth the Hegemony's trouble. And besides, the Queen herself used the drug every day, for free. She had ruled for nearly a hundred and fifty standard years; she didn't look a day over twenty.

All of which had nothing to do with him personally—but everything to do with the fact that he and Staun were stationed here in Carbuncle, and suddenly faced with the prospect of standing guard at the Snow Queen's palace all night, after patrolling the streets of Tiamat's starport capital all day. He remembered the last time they had pulled this duty: how they had been forced to watch the Queen's favorites drink the water of life in front of them and then smash the crystal vials at their feet . . . rubbing their noses in the fact that two Hegemonic patrolmen wouldn't earn enough in both their lifetimes combined to taste even a drop.

"Hey, you slugs!" Gil MarDesta came in through the double doors of the station house shouting in their direction. "Get your fubar butts in gear. Sud-Halek's waiting—"

Tree shrugged helplessly. He looked back at Gundhalinu as Staun repeated, "Sergeant, we had plans—"

"We've already got a party to go to," Tree said, frowning.

Gundhalinu scowled as their eyes locked. "Your plans have changed, Patrolman."

Tree glanced pleadingly at KraiVieux, the duty sergeant. "We already signed out, Sarge. Can't you get him somebody else? It's SudHalek's nameday party at RedFutter's Tavern."

KraiVieux looked chagrined as Gundhalinu snapped, "I'm in charge of this assignment, Patrolman, not Sergeant KraiVieux. It's up to me to decide who goes."

"Then find somebody else, Gundhalinu. You've got a whole station house full—" Tree felt Staun's warning hand on his arm. He shrugged it off and started back toward the exit where MarDesta stood waiting.

He heard Gundhalinu order him to stop; heard Staun call his name, and KraiVieux saying something he didn't listen to.

"What's the problem—?"

It took a woman's raised voice to stop him in his tracks. Staun reached him and hauled him around just as Inspector Jerusha PalaThion came down the hallway from her office.

"Shit," Tree muttered, before his eyes even registered her face. PalaThion was the only woman on the force. And since Gundhalinu was her assistant, he'd probably been acting on her orders. "We're dead."

"Shut *up*," Staun said, his sudden tension surfacing.

"What's going on, huh?" MarDesta trailed after them, typically oblivious to context, as they retraced their way through the milling chaos toward Pala-

Thion. She waited, arms folded, at an intersection they could not possibly avoid passing. Her gaze was fixed on Staun's face; Tree made himself as unobtrusive as possible in Staun's shadow.

"Inspector PalaThion," KraiVieux called suddenly. "Can I speak with you, ma'am?"

Looking surprised, PalaThion turned toward him, and nodded. With a final warning glance in their direction, she went on to the dispatch desk.

Tree glanced longingly over his shoulder at the exit. But Gundhalinu's stare was still fixed on them like a targeting beam; reluctantly, they followed PalaThion back to KraiVieux's station.

A pair of Blues coming in off duty shoved their way past Tree, ignoring his protest as they forced a path through the foot traffic ahead of them. The two men squeezed up to the counter in front of PalaThion, who frowned.

KraiVieux's matching frown at their show of disrespect became a smile of sudden inspiration. "Gilles-Fort and TierPardée—just the pair I wanted to see. This is your lucky night; you're going to the Queen's ball."

"Aw, Sarge. . . ." TierPardée groaned, raising his gauntleted hands in despair.

"Enough of that!" KraiVieux said. "You both need the overtime, to pay off your gaming tabs. These men will do the job for you, Sergeant Gundhalinu." He gestured; the same motion signaled Tree and Staun away from the desk again with subtle urgency.

Tree saw his own profound relief mirrored in Staun's face as they swung around and headed back toward the exit, somehow avoiding even eye contact with either Gundhalinu or PalaThion.

Herding MarDesta ahead of them, they made it

through the doors and out into the street without being called back again.

"Inspector—?" KraiVieux said again.

Inspector Geia Jerusha PalaThion turned back from watching the two relieved patrolmen scramble for the exit like truant schoolboys. Gundhalinu went on glaring at them until they disappeared through the station house doors. Jerusha saw him throw a brief, annoyed look KraiVieux's way, before he began to give instructions to the men who had replaced them.

She leaned on the dispatch counter, wondering wearily whether the men had been more eager to avoid the Snow Queen's company or her own. There was hardly a Newhavenese Blue on the force who would look her in the eye when he spoke to her. And even if any of them did, she knew the kinds of things they called her when she turned her back. "The Warrior Nun" was the least humiliating . . . and probably the most accurate, considering the state of her social life. She glanced over her shoulder a last time at the station doors, and kept the sigh to herself.

"What is it, Sergeant?" she said to KraiVieux. The unexpected somberness of his expression kept her tone neutral.

"It's Sergeant Gundhalinu, ma'am . . . there's been a death in his family." KraiVieux kept his voice down, glancing in Gundhalinu's direction as he produced a message transcript. "I just received this file from the starport data center. I thought, since you're . . . that is, you're his superior officer, well, I figured you would be the best one to give him the news." He looked down as he pushed the transcript at her, avoiding her startled gaze.

Ordinarily she would have expected KraiVieux to deliver a message like this one himself. He was a veteran officer; the Newhavenese Blues who patrolled the streets all trusted him, because he was one of them. That generally made him better at helping them deal with their grief than some counselor called in from down at the Med Center.

But Gundhalinu was Kharemoughi. He wasn't one of them, any more than she was. She might come from the same homeworld, and even the same city, as most of the men on the force—in her own family, wearing the blue uniform of the Hegemonic Police had been a tradition for generations. But it was a tradition for sons, not for daughters. The women of her family didn't wear the uniform, they married the man who did. They kept the home fires burning, raised the children, tended the sick and the injured. . . .

They comforted the bereaved.

With a final glance at KraiVieux's averted face, she began to read the transcript. It contained a brief, impersonal message saying that Gundhalinu's Technician-caste father had died, that his oldest sibling was now head-of-family, in possession of all estates and properties. It was signed by one HK Gundhalinu, the aforementioned oldest sibling, and included a copy of their father's will.

During the time he had been her aide, BZ Gundhalinu had been reticent to a fault about his personal life. She had observed that it was a Technician trait; even when they were with other Techs, men they had known for years, they always seemed to be among strangers. The transcript confirmed the few assumptions she had made about him based on reading his personnel records, and from studying his face with its classically Technician features: He was a third son from an aristocratic family, forced to leave home and make some kind of living on his own because he had no inheritance rights under the laws of primogeniture that bound Kharemough's upper classes. Joining the Hegemonic Police was one of the few honorable—meaning respectable—career choices open to a younger Tech sibling.

"BZ!" she called, raising her voice over the general clamor as Gundhalinu finished giving instructions to TierPardée and GillesFort. She gestured him down the hallway that led toward her office, where they could find respite from the crowd of officers and civilians, the bookings-in-progress, questions, demands, and loud obscene protests.

As he approached she heard him muttering, "Well, at least *I* don't have to attend the damn thing, thank the gods. . . ." His expression turned guarded as he looked up and saw her face.

"There's a message from home for you, BZ." She held out the transcript; said, with painful awkwardness, "I'm . . . afraid it's bad news."

Suddenly his eyes were empty of expression. He put out a hand, supporting himself against the cold, featureless wall, as if the world had abruptly tilted out from under him. When he took the transcript from her, his fingers were like ice. Without even glancing at the message, he said, "My father is dead."

"I'm sorry," Jerusha murmured, speaking Tiamatan, as they all did here. And then in her own tongue, she said, "May he live forever in the space of a thousand hearts."

Gundhalinu's head jerked slightly, as if it was the only acknowledgment he had the strength for. He looked down at the actual message; read it, and crumpled the transcript into a wad, as though he wanted to crush it out of existence.

He opened his hand again; the sheet sprang back

into perfect form and drifted to the floor. A crowd of patrolmen herding rowdy offworlders toward the lockup trampled it underfoot.

"BZ . . ." she said quietly. When he did not respond, she put her hand on his shoulder and said, more clearly, "Sergeant." She felt his muscles tense, as if the contact had startled him. "Why don't you take the rest of the day—"

"No, Inspector." He turned back, his eyes registering her again. He shook his head. "I'm all right. My father—my father's been dead for more than two years." It had taken that long for the news to reach him, with the sublight time gaps at either end of the hyperspace wormhole that linked Tiamat to Kharemough. "There's nothing I can do about it now." The words were as empty of expression as his face was.

Jerusha frowned. "You can take the time to let yourself feel something."

"I don't want to . . ." he murmured, glancing away. "What?"

He drew himself up. "I don't want to—to inflict my personal problems on you, Inspector. I can grieve on my own time, if that's necessary."

Gods give me strength. Jerusha glanced ceilingward in exasperation. *Kharemoughis*—"Then the rest of the day is your own time. That's an order, Sergeant."

"Yes, ma'am." He pressed his fist to his chest in a salute, helpless to do anything but obey.

She leaned down, picking up the transcript. He took it from her hand. "Thank you," he mumbled absently. She thought he said something more as he moved away, but it was lost in the echoing din from the main room.

Shaking her head, she went back into her office and shut the door. Relieved of both the noise and

the unwelcome duty, she sat down at her desk/ter-
minal, letting her mind take refuge in the rituals of
mundane procedure, the simple, straightforward task
of processing right and wrong.

2

"**F**uck *me*. That was too close." Tree shrugged the tightness out of his shoulders as they headed down Blue Alley toward the street.

"Gods bless KraiVieux," Staun murmured. "May he outlive us all."

MarDesta snorted. "I don't believe this. Does PalaThion have both you boys completely whipped?"

"You ass, MarDesta—" Tree said irritably. "Did they hold your head underwater too long on your name-day, or were you born stupid?"

"Hey," MarDesta said, aggrieved.

"The point Tree is making, Mardy . . ." Staun glanced behind them, lowering his voice, "is that PalaThion almost got a look at our datapatches. She'd probably bust us if she realized we're related. You know that."

"Oh." MarDesta gave himself a sharp rap on the head. "Right."

"I guess I should be glad that brasskisser Gundhalinu has never even bothered to learn our names." Tree flexed his hands. "What's our target after the party tonight? Gods, I really need to bust something up—"

They were passing the Judiciate complex; Staun elbowed him hard in the ribs. "Keep your voice down. And don't *ever* forget why we decided to do this." He gestured at Tree's uniform.

Tonight, when the nameday celebration had run sufficiently late, a smaller, private party of Blues would end their own night by raiding an off-limits warehouse, destroying a cache of contraband they couldn't legally touch when they were on duty. "You're not thirteen anymore, Nyx." Staun looked searchingly into his eyes. "This is not some stupid game of smash-and-grab."

Tree glanced down, away from the past. "I know," he said sullenly. "I'm sorry." He raised his head again. "I knew what I was promising when I swore to 'serve and protect.' This uniform means as much to me as it does to you. Believe it or not."

"Right." Staun sighed, and glanced away.

Tree frowned; his hands tightened at his sides. "It's just knowing that as long as we play by the rules, we can't ever win, but if we don't—" He drew a finger across his throat like a knife blade. "It gets to me, sometimes."

"Yeah, I know," Staun said wearily. "Somehow, when I pictured 'service above and beyond the call of duty,' becoming a vigilante wasn't what I had in mind, either."

"They ought to give us medals, not kick us off the force, for what we're doing," MarDesta muttered.

Staun laughed. "Just don't go in and ask the Chief Inspector to give us one, okay, Mardy?"

MarDesta winced, and grinned, and shook his head.

The first time they had raided a warehouse full of illegal goods, it had been an unpremeditated act. A nameday celebration had run late; too much of the locals' kelp beer, plus too much frustration, had led to a midnight crate-smashing spree.

But in the sober reflection of a new day, the Blues involved hadn't regretted it; instead, they'd decided to do it again . . . and to keep on doing it. The Nameday Vigilantes had been born, to flout the self-defeating restrictions laid on the Hegemonic Police by the Hegemony itself. In its lust to get its hands on the water of life, the Hedge capitulated to the Snow Queen's every demand, effectively hamstringing its own police force; until, in Carbuncle, the only way to be an honest Blue seemed to be to do it outside the law.

The vigilantes had let only their most trusted friends in on their plans; and they had sworn a solemn oath that they would never let things get out of hand, or spread too far. . . .

"Saint Phimas wept! Get a full fix on that." MarDesta pointed toward the Judiciate complex, either changing the subject or already oblivious to it.

Tree followed his gesture and saw Special Investigator Jashari, of the Judiciate's Internal Affairs Division, standing outside the courthouse entrance with his arms around a stunning Kharemoughi woman. Tree watched the woman lean in to give Jashari a long, deep, completely outrageous kiss. Jashari bowed formally to her, and kissed her hand as she left him. "Is that his wife?"

MarDesta guffawed. "He's got a wife, but that ain't

her. She's back on Kharemough, minding their estates."

"Talk about your Internal Affairs . . ." Staun said, grinning. "I guess it figures. You'd have to be a fucking hypocrite, to do his job."

"Saint Ambiko, change my life!" Tree lifted his hands in an utterly sincere prayer gesture. He couldn't take his eyes off the woman as she walked away. The fluid motion of her body made him think of the sea. "Damn, I know dead men who aren't as cold as that rat-squad bastard. How the hell did Jashari get himself a woman like her? She's even Kharemoughi—"

"And where did he *find* her, out here?" MarDesta said.

"They'd find you, if you had his rank and credit line." Staun gave a grunt of disgust. "This place has always been a crossroads; Tiamat's the closest world to a Gate. And the Queen lets the scum of the Hegemony hide behind her skirts, as long as they give her what she wants in return for giving us hell."

"That's the truth on a platter, with a side of greens," MarDesta said feelingly.

"You serve here in Carbuncle long enough and you'll see everything, including yourself walking backwards."

Tree shook his head. "I've never seen a Kharemoughi woman who could move like that."

"She's not Kharemoughi," Staun said. "She's a shapeshifter. She could be anyone you wanted; anything . . . even Newhavenese."

"She's a 'shifter—?"

"She's wearing a sensenet?" MarDesta echoed Tree's disbelief. "How can you tell?"

"Because her hair just changed color, Mardy."

"You were looking at her *hair*, 'Nion?"

Staun smiled wistfully. "That, too."

They slowed as they reached the Records annex, the last building before Blue Alley spilled into Carbuncle's one and only Street. MarDesta went inside to fetch SudHalek; Tree and Staun leaned against the wall to wait, basking in the sourceless light of Carbuncle's artificial day.

Carbuncle was an entirely enclosed, self-contained city, a relic of the Old Empire. It lay like a cast-up shell on the shore of the world-encompassing ocean that Tiamatans worshiped as Mother, Goddess, and Provider, for its omnipresence in their lives. The Street spiraled down from the Snow Queen's palace at the city's peak to the artificial harbor beneath it, making a widening gyre through the honeycomb of alleys where its inhabitants lived and worked.

The unchanging light that bathed them all shone ceaselessly, part of a closed system as constant as a mother's womb. Beyond Carbuncle's transparent storm walls, the twin suns of Tiamat rose and set, marking the days, years, centuries. But Carbuncle never slept, just as it had never changed down through the millennia since the Old Empire's fall.

On the wall above Tree's head, a faded sign preserved Blue Alley's original name, *Olivine*. He had heard once that the alleys were named for the colors of gemstones, although he had no idea what gems, or in what languages, or even if it was true. This was Blue Alley now, even to the natives, and would be for as long as the Hegemony remained here. The entire government complex was located in Blue Alley, but it was the blue-uniformed Police who patrolled the city's streets, the interface where onworlder and offworlder met, and frequently collided.

Staun pulled out the small, battered notebook that he usually had with him, and scribbled something in it with a stylus. He had been doing that for as long as Tree could remember; but it was the one thing Staun had never shared, even with his brother. Tree looked away again, having been taught long ago not to read over Staun's shoulder.

He watched the shapeshifter turn the corner and disappear, heading uptown. "Where do you think she's going?"

"Probably to the Queen's ball," Staun said, and laughed.

"Maybe we should've taken that duty after all." Tree sighed, looking back toward the Judiciate complex. He swore suddenly under his breath.

"What?" Staun asked.

"Gundhalinu." Tree pointed with his chin. Gundhalinu was coming up the alley toward them; alone, with an expression on his face that Tree couldn't peg.

"Be more careful what you wish for," Staun muttered, stuffing his notebook into a pocket as Gundhalinu approached.

But the sergeant passed on by without even a glance their way, as if they had morphed into the wall.

"What the hell?" Tree frowned.

Staun relaxed into a slouch again, shaking his head. "Kharemoughis . . . who can ever figure them out?" He pulled a tin of bitterroot out of his sleeve pocket. Taking a chew for himself, he handed one to Tree.

Tree put it in his mouth, chewing gamely until his tongue finally went numb. Bitterroot chews were a poor man's stress relief; they tasted worse than shit. After eight years on the force, he knew exactly how many other, better things, legal or otherwise, were available to help an officer ease the stress of his job. But Staun had an unshakable loyalty to bitterroot; he claimed it was all that had saved his sanity in the hard years after Ma died.

The first time Staun had given him a chew of bitter-root, when Tree was ten, it had made his tongue bleed. It still made his tongue bleed. After all these years, he didn't see much point in complaining about it. He glanced toward the Street again, studying the passersby. Now that Gundhalinu was safely out of sight, his thoughts drifted back to the shapeshifter they had watched leave the alley. *Anything he wanted . . . even Newhavenese?*

"Staun?" he said.

"What?"

"You ever think about Tarina anymore?"

"Tarina?" Staun glanced over at him. "Where the hell did that come from?"

"Who's Tarina?" MarDesta asked, emerging from the Records building with Baine SudHalek in tow.

"Girl I used to know, back home," Staun said non-committally. "We talked about getting married once."

"What happened?"

"She didn't want to live in Buttfuck, Tiamat, for ten years."

SudHalek grunted in sympathy. "Who would?"

"She made great kassock pie," Tree said. "And she never burned the tapola."

Staun looked back at him. "You're thinking of Ma."

Tree shook his head. "Tarina cooked like Ma did."

"I never thought about it."

"Maybe you should have. Maybe she would've said yes."

"Yeah, well." Staun looked away. "I guess I had too much else on my mind back then."

"Like helping your kid brother get through the academy, and getting his orders changed, and making sure the transfer got through . . . ?"

Staun shrugged. "I couldn't very well leave you behind, now could I?" He smiled suddenly. "What is all this about me and Tarina? You think I regret the choice?"

"You could've had a family, a real life—"

"I have both," Staun said, giving him a look. "And my timeline's got plenty of string left to unwind. I'm your brother, not your grandfather." Abruptly he cuffed Tree's helmeted head. "I know what your problem is. I think you need to get laid, partner."

Tree frowned, pulling away. "That's not—"

"Hey, yeah," MarDesta interrupted. "SudHalek, you lucky perverts over in Vice always know some ladies who owe you a favor, right?" SudHalek shrugged modestly. "We've got time before the festivities start at RedFutter's. Can you get us some dates?"

"Sure." SudHalek grinned. "It's my nameday; how could they refuse?"

Frowning and silent, Tree followed the others as they set off into the Maze, Carbuncle's wide-open heart, where any and all forms of entertainment could be found at any time of the day or night.

They passed a boy playing a flute on a street corner, heard the calls of food vendors, the dickering of customers and store owners, a dozen more kinds of music echoing off the walls down the narrow alleyways. Buyers and sellers and curiosity-seekers from eight different worlds, speaking a hundred different tongues, engulfed them. The heady input of sights and sounds and smells rebooted Tree's mood; his restless dissatisfaction flowed back into a shared eagerness for the evening ahead.

"Gods . . . now I really have seen everything," Staun muttered, glancing over his shoulder at the couple they had just passed in the crowd.

"What the fuck was that?" SudHalek whispered. "Was that even human?"

"What?" Tree glanced behind him, seeing only a heavyset man in a hooded cloak, and a woman whose body was completely hidden beneath layers of *shadoudt* veils. He heard the tinkling of countless tiny bells on her clothing, wrists, and ankles; their faint, sweet music was almost lost in the street noise. "What? They're probably Ondinean."

"His face." SudHalek screwed his own face into a grimace. "Didn't you see it?"

"No." Tree shook his head. Growing up in Miertoles Porttown, he had learned early to watch a crowd for certain kinds of motion, telltale body language. As a Blue, he rarely let himself be distracted by irrelevant details.

"Remember that corpse we found last year, with all his guts hanging out?" Staun asked.

"Yeah. . . ." Tree looked back at him.

"It was a match."

Tree mimed gagging. "By the Boatman! There goes my appetite."

"Five to ten she's as ugly as he is, under the veils," MarDesta said, to sniggers of laughter.

"How'd you like to wake up next to a face like that in the morning, laddo?" SudHalek waved a hand behind him.

"You're a twisted son of a bitch, Suddy."

"What do you suppose they're doing here?"

"Going to the Snow Queen's ball, to drink the water of life," Tree said sourly.

"Yeah, that's Carbungle for you."

"That's *life*, laddo," SudHalek murmured.

Staun shrugged, with a final glance over his shoulder as the couple disappeared into the faceless crowd. "I guess there really are some fates worse than death."

"Spit in your hand!" Tree spat in his palm and tightened his fist in a warding gesture. "That's bad luck. Don't ever say that, damn it!" He glared at his brother, wiping his hand on his pants.

"Tree . . ." Staun frowned, and shook his head.

"Do it!" Tree said fiercely. "You know where we're going later tonight."

The others stared at him. Finally, Staun spat into his own fist, with a look that said it was done just to humor him. Reluctantly, the others followed, one by one.

3

Devony Seaward stopped just inside the doorway of the private meeting room, spellbound by its beauty, as she always was. The room's nacreous walls and ceiling made her feel as though she had entered the heart of a polished shell; and this was just one of half a hundred rooms inside the Snow Queen's palace at the pinnacle of Carbuncle—that relic of a civilization which had been ancient before Tiamat's history even began.

She glanced across the room, to find the Snow Queen herself waiting there. Millennia telescoped into a moment, and Devony forgot her surroundings entirely.

She bowed, with all of her considerable, practiced grace. "Your Majesty."

Arienrhod nodded in acknowledgment, and gestured her forward to stand in front of the baroquely carved imported desk. "Devony." The Queen's smile and voice were warm, almost welcoming, but her eyes were as cold and distant as the icebound peaks of the interior Devony remembered from her youth. Arienrhod's eyes were always like that; Devony no longer took them personally. "What news have you charmed out of the offworlders this week?"

The Queen never made small talk. Devony wondered whether it was because she had too many other things on her mind, or whether, after nearly a century and a half, the Queen had simply had enough of it. In either case, she was honored just to be in the Snow Queen's presence, holding Arienrhod's complete attention, and knowing that the Queen found her information useful.

Devony prompted the memory feed of her sense-net and began to speak from the notes she had made for herself. She had become an excellent listener over the past few years, and with a little encouragement, her clients were at least as interested in talking about themselves as they were in having sex. When she combined their conversations with the idle gossip and casual remarks of her numerous offworlder acquaintances—including Berdaz, the employer whose sense-net she wore—their pillow talk told her far more than they ever suspected.

Other Winters who worked for and with the offworlders also brought news they had overheard to the Queen. Their first loyalty was always to Arienrhod, the ruler of all the Winter clans—of all Tiamat, for as long as the Black Gate remained open. But the offworlders who came through the Gate to this world weren't loose-tongued fools, for the most part, and few Winters got the kind of intimate opportunities that came to Devony for learning things the Queen found useful.

She knew as well as any Tiamatan that the end of the Snow Queen's reign was coming soon, along with the end of the planet's century-and-a-half-long High Winter. In less than five years of standard time, the increasing gravitational stresses created as the Twins, Tiamat's binary sun system, approached the perigee of their orbit around the Black Gate would render the Gate's space-time wormhole unstable, and make travel through it impossible. Before that happened, the offworlders would abandon Tiamat.

The Hegemony called it the Departure. Tiamatans called it the Change . . . and everything would change then, for the worse.

The Black Gate would not reopen, the Hegemony would not return again, for another century. Few, if any, Tiamatans who witnessed the Departure would live to witness the Return.

That would hardly be a tragedy, except for one thing: when the offworlders left, they took progress with them. Tiamat would slide back into primitive stagnation under the rule of the mer-loving, technology-hating, superstitious Summer clans for a hundred long years.

The Summers were already migrating north from their scattered island homes, as increased solar radiation from the increasingly unstable Twins caused rising temperatures worldwide, and made their insular lives untenable. By tradition, Winters and Summers would share the slowly expanding strip of arable land along the east coast of Tiamat's single continent throughout High Summer; they would be forced to endure each others' unwelcome presence face-to-face in Carbuncle itself.

The new Summer Queen would be chosen . . . and the Snow Queen, along with her consort, would be sacrificed to the Sea Mother. They would be drowned together in a ritual as ancient as it was barbaric.

Any technology left behind by the Hegemony would go into the sea with them. There would be no more mer hunts, and no more water of life; the mers, held sacred by the Summers, would have a century in which to renew their depleted numbers.

All of which suited the offworlders perfectly. The Hegemony wanted Tiamat to remain in a perpetual technological dark age, so that when they returned, bringing a new Snow Queen to power, the Winters would be desperate for their high-tech bribery, eager to let them exploit Tiamat's resources—rather, its single, singular resource: the water of life.

During the century and a half of her rule, Arienrhod had come to recognize the pattern as clearly as the Hegemony did; and she had determined to make this Change a real one, a permanent one—a change for the better. Throughout her reign, the Queen had been acquiring proscribed technology from the offworlder criminals whose presence here she tolerated and facilitated. But she distrusted them as much as she despised the Hegemony; which was why, she had explained, she spied on all factions equally, constantly, for her own sake and the sake of her people.

Some Winter courtiers whispered that by now she spied on them more for her own perverted amusement than from any urge for justice or need for protection; that she had come to crave the act itself as if it were the water of life. But the Queen's deeper motivations were of little concern to Devony Seaward, because they had so little impact on her own life.

On the other hand, if the Queen was successful in her plans, the rest of Devony's life would continue to be lived in comfort and pleasure. While if the Queen failed, her new life would turn back into the old one, which she had hated so much.

She knew only two ways of dealing with difficulties: either you changed the difficulties, or you changed yourself to endure them. She liked her new life, and who she had become. Before she was forced to surrender either one, she would do anything in her power to help Arienrhod change the Change.

Even as she spoke, the corner of Devony's mind that always stood apart, observing, analyzing, watched Arienrhod as intently as Arienrhod watched others. It registered the Queen's striking coloring: her mass of milk-white hair, upswept and braided, interwoven with strands of pearls; the almost translucent paleness of her skin; the strange fog-agate color of her eyes.

Arienrhod was already dressed for the reception she was hosting tonight. Devony noted the deceptive simplicity of the Queen's imported gown and robes, how they set off her features to stunning, ethereal effect. She admired the clothing's sophisticated lines, the sensuous beauty of the fabrics, the crown of spun silver set with moonstones.

Devony recorded every detail of Arienrhod's appearance in the artificial memory of her sensenet. She had long since added the Queen's personal mannerisms and way of speaking to her own performance repertoire, with the uncanny precision of a born actress and mimic.

In the beginning, when both the sensenet and her use of it were new, she had been surprised by how many clients had wanted Arienrhod for a lover. That no longer surprised her at all. Arienrhod was power incarnate—a woman who had ruled for nearly a hundred and fifty years, yet seemed never to age, thanks to the water of life. Arienrhod alone, out of all the people in the Hegemony, could afford to use the drug every day. She controlled this city, this entire world. Just to be standing in her presence was an achievement that Devony had never imagined in her wildest fantasies while growing up in the outback—a goal as unattainable, for most people, as the water of life itself.

There was an exquisite and absurdly expensive liquor named for the water of life. Devony drank it with the clients she entertained, while wearing her exquisite and absurdly expensive re-creation of the Queen's persona, almost as often as the real Queen drank the real thing. She had come to realize that an imitation of the one was as necessary as an imitation of the other; and in its own way, nearly as rewarding.

". . . even though I spent the entire afternoon with Special Investigator Jashari." She sighed. "His lunch hour seems to be quite flexible, unlike his personality. If only certain of his body parts were as rigid as his opinions—"

The Queen laughed. "So your affair with Internal Affairs revealed no . . . unusual quirks, or exploitable vices, when the Special Investigator finally let his hair down?"

"His hair is very short, I'm afraid." Devony's smile was genuinely spiteful. "The only thing I can say with any conviction is that as a lover, he has no gifts . . . and, I might add, after we had sex he badgered me about whether I actually came or only pretended to. Calling me a liar aroused him more than having sex did . . . and then he began to call me a bitch, and a slut; and he actually pushed me down on the bed and tried to force me—"

The Queen's eyebrows rose. "He preferred to rape you?"

Devony shrugged. "If it was just a kink, at least it would have been a little exciting. But when I saw his eyes . . . I'd become a *thing* to him. I wasn't even human anymore." The Queen leaned forward but didn't interrupt, as Devony frowned faintly. Devony's gaze was hard and clear as she looked up again, and murmured, "Perhaps he forgot he wasn't at work. . . . So I pretended to cry, and told him he was hurting me, and called him *eshkrad* to remind him of his precious Technician 'honor.' That shriveled him up."

Her smile came back, widened with satisfaction. "He was so humiliated afterward that he actually gave me this, in apology." She held out her hand, displaying the fine filigree of gold that joined four jeweled rings to a jeweled bracelet circling her wrist.

"A beautiful piece of work," the Queen said, her laugh acknowledging more than simply the jewelry.

"A family heirloom, he claimed. I'm sure his wife will never miss it." The edge on Devony's smile as she glanced up again was honed to perfection. "I don't expect I shall be seeing the Special Investigator again. . . . And that is absolutely *everything* of any interest, Your Majesty."

Arienrhod nodded, with another laugh. "Thank you, Devony. As usual, most entertaining, as well as instructive."

Devony bowed.

The Queen rose and moved past the corner of her desk. "My guests are starting to arrive; I must go and greet them. . . . Would you like to come to the party?" Unexpectedly, she extended a hand in invitation.

Devony's jeweled fingers pressed her throat. "I would be honored, Your Majesty."

"Good, then." The Queen's smile widened. "I'm sure you're bound to make some new friends. . . ."

"Here is the palace, my lord Humbaba." Bells chimed softly as Mundilfoere exposed a delicate, night-black hand from beneath her veils. She gestured across the pristine spiral of alabaster pavement that marked the courtyard at Street's End.

"At last," her husband said, his voice muffled by the hood of his cloak, and tinged with impatience. He studied the massive, carven doors they were approaching. Two members of the Snow Queen's guard stood on either side of the entrance, in their costumish imitation of offworlder Police uniforms. "I had expected . . . more," he murmured, and shook his head. "I confess, Carbuncle as a whole is so much *less* than I had imagined it would be, from the legends. How does it strike you, my jewel? Is it disappointing?" He reached up to caress her cheek through the layer of dark, semitransparent cloth. His large blunt-fingered hand was perfectly normal, unlike his mutilated face, and he had never raised it against her in anger.

She shrugged slightly, making the bells sing. "I find it . . . both less and more than I had expected, my lord." The traditional *shadoudt* robes she wore hid her striking features from curious eyes far more effectively, and purposefully, than his hooded cloak disguised his elaborate facial scarring. "On the surface, it is most disappointing: its shabbiness, the provincial ignorance. But I sense that so much lies hidden. . . ." She glanced up at her husband's face, masked by cicatrice.

On his homeworld, Tsieh-pun, ugliness symbolized strength, power . . . *i-shin* scarring such as his had come to be regarded as a unique form of beauty. That uncommon cultural perspective was obviously lost on the citizens of Carbuncle. "You have seen how the Source remains here—centers his entire sphere of influence here," she added, "and not simply because it is convenient to him."

The massive palace doors opened, and a Winter

noble greeted them. The pale, elegant woman led them down a corridor muraled with scenes of ice and snow; her mannered disinterest scarcely betrayed her hidden disgust.

"That fact alone leads me to wonder about so many other things." Mundilfoere went on expressing her thoughts aloud, confident that no one they passed could even identify the language they were speaking. "For one, how did Carbuncle survive, and why does it still thrive, this long after the end of the Old Empire? It must hold secrets no one can imagine, not even the Source. Perhaps he senses that, and that is why he remains here. . . ."

She did not mention that Carbuncle had recently, quite inexplicably, chosen to surrender one of its secrets: an Old Empire artifact that was potentially of incalculable value. That information had been offered to only a handful of individuals at the highest levels of the ancient, hidden order known as Survey. The chosen ones included Mundilfoere herself—and also Thanin Jaakola, the monster of corruption who called himself the Source.

Survey's inner circles did not include Sab Emo Humbaba, and never would. Nor, ironically, did they include the Snow Queen. Arienrhod could never be allowed even a glimpse into Survey's hidden world, even though she must become their ally in obtaining the artifact—because, more ironic still, she alone had access to it. Which meant that she must eventually also become Survey's pawn.

"The Snow Queen was nothing but a peasant girl when the Hegemony reopened Tiamat, a century and a half ago. But she has ruled Carbuncle, and dealt with offworlders, successfully for nearly a hundred and fifty years." Mundilfoere went on musing aloud as Humbaba made no comment. "What are her

strengths, after so long, and what are her weak-
nesses?" *And how best to make certain that Arienrhod never
came to suspect she held the future itself in her hands?*

"It is fascinating, my lord, is it not, when one thinks
of it? And in any case, the Source certainly has the
influence to provide you with a new Head of Research, and the additional equipment you will re-
quire, so that you can expand your operations when
we return to Ondinee. Your time here will be well
spent." Her husband's trade was dealing in illegal
drugs, a line of work that became more profitable
with the introduction of each new escape hatch from
reality that his researchers provided—although for
her own part, she still found that the most powerful
mind-altering substance of all was simply the truth.

"Yes . . . all that is quite true, my jewel." Humbaba's
massive arm curved contentedly around her. "You
have peeled away the superficial, as always, until the
naked body of the truth lies revealed. . . ." He ran his
hand along her side, exploring the hidden mysteries
of her body, barely concealed beneath the layers of
gossamer cloth.

"You flatter me, my lord."

He made a sound that might have been laughter;
their guide walked a little faster, up ahead. "I am
many things, wife, but I have never been a flatterer,"
he said. "And you have not been my First Wife, or my
most trusted advisor, for this long because you are
one, either."

"No, my lord," she murmured. "Of course not." Beneath her veil, a faint smile formed.

They fell silent as a deep moaning sigh filled the
air: They were approaching the Hall of the Winds.
Mundilfoere had tried to prepare herself and Humbaba for this trial by air, which everyone who entered
the Snow Queen's presence was forced to endure.

Well before their arrival, she had studied everything it was possible to learn about Carbuncle without actually being in the city.

But there were some things that not even the resources of Survey could fully prepare one for.

The Hall of the Winds had no floor. The center of the chamber, called the Pit, was a vast well separating the uninvited from the upper levels of the palace. She knew that its open shaft dropped through the city's heart all the way down to sea level, and that it was in fact a service well, giving access to Carbuncle's self-sufficient operating plant. The city's Old Empire technology had not needed servicing, as far as anyone knew, during the entire thousand-year history of the Hegemony's relationship with Tiamat.

Spanning the Pit was a railingless bridge, wide enough to be crossed easily in quiet air. But a constant, powerful updraft rose through the hollow core of Carbuncle, bringing with it the smell of the sea, and a moaning like the voice of an elemental being.

And high above their heads, the city's transparent storm walls stood open. Everywhere else in Carbuncle those same walls, visible at the end of every alley, sheltered the inhabitants from Tiamat's pitiless weather. All of them were perpetually closed . . . except here. In this one spot, the winds of the open sky were allowed to run wild, sucking the breath out of the city's subterranean hollows.

Suspended high overhead, panels of some fluid, resilient material billowed like sails, creating treacherous crosscurrents and backflows in the relentless winds above the Pit. Unless the winds were somehow stilled, crossing the bridge would be suicide.

The Winter noble wore a small whistle suspended from a cord around her neck. She raised it to her lips as they drew near the bridge, and glanced back at them; Mundilfoere saw her eagerness for a taste of their fear. The woman looked away again abruptly, as if she had forgotten what she would find instead.

"Stay close together," the woman muttered. "Don't lag." Gathering herself, she sounded a note on the whistle and stepped onto the bridge.

Mundilfoere followed, suddenly as hungry for what came next as a hunting cat that had scented prey. Humbaba followed close behind her, less eagerly, she knew, but with the stolid lack of fear that was both his greatest strength and his most dangerous limitation. The shrill notes of the Tiamatan's whistle created a zone of quiet air around them, barely large enough to encompass them all.

As they crossed the span, Mundilfoere looked up in fascination, watching the wind curtains reposition themselves high above: somewere, the deft progression of notes being played by the Winter woman was activating automated controls. The noblewoman strode forward, sounding one tone after another with complete confidence, seeming never to doubt either her ability to play the precise sequence of notes at precisely the right intervals, or the millennia-old system that diverted the winds for their protection.

Mundilfoere exhaled in pure exhilaration as she reached the far side of the span; the Winter noble glanced back, frowning. She led them onward without speaking, up the glacial flow of stairs that lay ahead.

Mundilfoere's fascination only grew as they entered the vast, arching space where the Snow Queen held court, and she caught her first glimpse of Arienrhod. The still-sparse gathering of guests had scattered like multicolored jewels across an imported carpet as white as a field of new snow. At the center of the

room, and, more subtly, at the center of their attention, the Queen sat on a throne that seemed to be
made of crystal, or even of ice.

The Tiamatan people were pale-skinned and pale-
eyed to a degree Mundilfoere rarely saw: the result
of inbreeding among their original, long-isolated genetic stock. But the Snow Queen herself, dressed in
white velvet, crowned in silver, was so fair that the
title might have been created to describe her alone,
and not simply her position as ruler of the Winter
clans.

"I was not aware that this was a costume party,"
Humbaba murmured disparagingly, as he glanced toward the throne.

At the Queen's side, leaning against the throne's
high back with the desultory arrogance of a spoiled
pet, was a man dressed from head to foot in black.
Even his face was masked by a helmet of black
leather; the effect was made all the more striking and
barbaric by its rack of silver-spined antlers.

If the calculated effect of the Queen's icy, ageless
beauty was to make her seem Elemental Winter per-
sonified, then her consort was the avatar of Winter's
age-old companion, Death.

"He is called Starbuck, my lord," Mundilfoere said,
with a hidden smile. "He is not only the Snow
Queen's consort, but her Hunter. He oversees the
blood harvest of the mers, and shares in its rewards.
The mask is a holdover from the time when the
Queen was worshiped as the Goddess Incarnate, and
her consort was a kind of shaman. He wore a magic
mask while in her presence, so that he could look
upon her without being destroyed."

The tradition still served a purpose; the purpose
had simply changed. The position was always held by
an offworlder now, his real identity a secret known

only to the Queen. That way, unmasked, he was free to roam the city among his former associates, supplying the Queen with intelligence about their activities as faithfully as he supplied her with the water of life.

The mask of Starbuck served the Queen in the same way that the veils of *shadoudt* served Mundilfoere's purposes . . . although the difference between the worlds to which those masks gave them access was as vast as the distance between the stars.

"I will present you to Her Majesty," their guide said abruptly, and started across the hall.

"Go with her," Humbaba said, gesturing indifferently. "The Queen is your concern, not mine. I will observe the gathering."

"My lord," Mundilfoere demurred, taking hold of his hand, lightly but insistently. "You must come with me. It would not be seemly for me to go before her unaccompanied."

Humbaba acquiesced without protest. She knew from his manner as they crossed the room that secretly he was pleased by her gesture of subservience— as pleased as she was by his willing embrace of the *shadoudt*'s oppressive patriarchal tradition. No one who ever met her while she was accompanied by Sab Emo Humbaba could even think of ignoring her. . . .

Arienrhod glanced up as they approached, and her gaze lingered. There was no revulsion on her face, as there was on Starbuck's when Mundilfoere looked into his eyes. Visible through the slits of his mask, his eyes were dark and long-lashed. She guessed that his face was probably handsome, but there was nothing besides disgust that she could identify as human in his stare.

Her gaze dismissed him and her attention moved back to the Queen. The Queen's eyes were the color of moss agate, and Mundilfoere saw in them the same kind of hunger for new experience that had filled her own as she entered the Hall of the Winds.

Arienrhod rose to her feet, extending a hand as they bowed before her. "We meet at last," she murmured, raising Mundilfoere up with a touch. "I was told by our mutual acquaintance that you would be attending tonight."

"Your Majesty," Mundilfoere said, smiling behind her veils. "The pleasure is truly all mine. . . ."

4

"Tree! Pass the pitcher down. Suddy needs refueling!"

"By the Boatman, SudHalek," Staun said. "Didn't you get a bellyful of that klee-piss on your own nameday? I heard it corrodes ceralloy."

"Hell, that was a . . . um, three months ago, already," SudHalek slurred indignantly. "*Seems* like a lifetime. . . . You want me to get stinkin' drunk only once a year?"

"Beer," Staun muttered, propping his chin on his fists. "It's not just for breakfast anymore."

"Yo, LaisTree! Wake up and pass that tanker!"

"He's gone south. I got it—"

Tree caught his half-full mug with a reflexive grab as the pitcher of kelp beer *skreek*ed past him along the table full of off-duty Blues. He stood up, staring across the sea of shadowy figures in the dimly lit club, his gaze like a compass needle drawn to magnetic north.

"Hey, 'Nion, what hit your partner? His brains are hangin' below his belt."

"He's lost in thought." Staun shrugged.

"Uh-oh. Unfamiliar territory. . . ." Laughter.

"It's the shapeshifter," Staun said finally, when Tree didn't rise to the bait but just went on staring, transfixed, at a point across the room. "She's why he wanted to come here."

"So *that's* why we're not still at RedFutter's?"

"Forget it, loverboy. You don't make enough in a year—"

"Hey, screw you. It's *his* nameday! Go for it, partner." Staun gave Tree a push, staggering him slightly. "Put that Motherlover's-courage you've been swilling to some use."

"Yeah," somebody yelled, "flash your badge and tell her it's your nameday. Maybe she'll give you a freebie—"

"Get stuffed." Tree drained his mug and set it down.

". . . More than you'll get!"

Tree flipped him an obscene gesture, grinning as he started away from the table.

Staun reached up to catch his arm as he passed. "Just remember, we've got plans later . . . when the call comes, we're on it. We need you to be there."

Tree looked back at him, meeting his eyes, and nodded once.

Hoots of encouragement propelled him out into the open room like a physical shove. People were actually dancing; sitting with the others, he hadn't even been aware of music. He concentrated on walking a straight line through the random motion on the dance floor, not doubting his sense of balance as much as he doubted his resolve.

The woman watched him from the booth where she was sitting, alone for the first time all night. She wore an enigmatic smile that suited her face, her body . . . everything about her, because none of it was real. During the course of the evening, he'd watched her talking, eating, and drinking with an ever-changing series of companions; watched her fey features become darker, fairer, older, younger . . . changing like a dream, but never anything less than beautiful.

He'd seen a lot in the eight years he'd been a Blue, most of it in the five that he'd been stationed here in Carbuncle. But he'd never seen a woman in a full-body sensenet playing with her skin.

He saw her begin to change again as he approached—the tone of her skin shading toward the color of his, her eyes becoming brown, upslanting, her shining black hair shot through now with deep glints of auburn—until by the time he reached her table, she had become his own secret fantasy of the perfect woman.

He came to a dead stop two meters short of her private booth; stood paralyzed by indecision, while his body reminded him with painful hunger of how long it had been since he'd seen a woman who looked anything like that . . . since he'd spoken more than a dozen words in a row to any woman at all from his homeworld.

Ever since SudHalek's nameday, when he'd watched the shapeshifter walk away down Blue Alley, he hadn't been able to get her out of his mind. For the last three months, he'd found himself looking for her as they patrolled the streets, daydreaming about her when he was alone, dreaming about her at night.

He had no idea if this was even the same woman, beneath the sensenet's veil of illusion, although she could be, since there were probably only a dozen 'shifters in all of Carbuncle.

Not that it really mattered, because it was all make-believe anyway. And this was his nameday, Saint Ambiko's Day—the one day he could let himself believe that entire worlds lay in the depths of her eyes, and that a single word from her could transform his whole world, making it infinite with possibilities.

It struck him suddenly that he could be facing a moment of humiliation so total that he would never live it down, in front of a dozen witnesses who would never, ever, let him forget it. And all because somewhere in a dream, her changeling smile had whispered to him that *all lies must come true somewhere, if only for a moment* . . . daring him to redefine the limits of his life, to admit that one step beyond the boundaries of his very ordinary days there lay something more, something extraordinary.

"What do you want . . . officer?" The woman rested her chin on her palm; her smile turned amused as she gazed back at him.

Officer. His mouth quirked. He wondered if she'd heard them, clear across the room. All he could hear now was the blood singing in his ears.

"What would you Blue boys like to know: 'How do I do that?' 'Does it feel as real as it looks?' Or how much it would cost you to find out?"

He glanced away over his shoulder, back again, helplessly. "Do you . . . like to dance?"

He saw her hesitate, as if he'd actually surprised her. And then her face changed again; her smile became radiant. "Well . . . I thought you'd never ask." She rose from her seat in the booth to join him; her acceptance seemed to defy gravity as well as logic. A single piece of scarlet cloth wrapped her body in flame. He offered his hand; her touch felt warm and real as she clasped it.

As they reached the dance floor her arms circled his waist, tendrilling up his back like vines on a trellis. She closed the space between them, the slight but sensual pressure of her body inviting him to make himself equally familiar with her own. The club's music was fluid and slow, almost subliminal. He wasn't much of a dancer, but then the handful of other couples on the floor were barely moving, anyway. Lost in their own pocket worlds, they were fused against each other as if dancing was what came after foreplay.

He looked toward the table where his friends were sitting. He knew they were watching him, probably even yelling encouragement, considering how much they'd drunk. But his brain seemed to have shifted nexus points: their faces had become formless ovals of light; their voices dissolved into the ambient music. The distance he had walked across the room to reach her seemed measurable in light-years. Somehow, she was in his arms instead, and he was in hers, and her hair smelled of blooming sillipha, like a warm summer night on Newhaven. "What's your name?" he murmured, breathing the past in her perfume.

"Whatever you want it to be," she whispered, her lips brushing his ear.

"No. . . ." He drew back, breaking the hypnotic contact of their bodies. "What's *your* name?"

She bent her head at him. "I don't kiss and tell . . . and that would be telling. But I can tell you your name, Officer Nyx Ambiko LaisTree. And that you were born twenty-six years ago, in Miertoles lo Faux on Newhaven, and you have—"

"My friends call me Tree."

"Tree. . . ." She smiled, and he smiled, letting her

draw him back into the motion of the music that still moved her body. "Is that what you want—to be my friend?"

"It's all I can afford," he said, "on a Blue's pay."

"Then you must be an honest one."

He glanced away at the others, looked down.

As he raised his head again her smiled softened, as if she'd thought he was only being modest. He could feel the heat radiating from her . . . or maybe the body heat was his alone.

"I've never danced with a Blue before," she said, almost to herself; as if accepting his invitation had been as unexpected for her as offering it had been for him. "Behind Closed Doors isn't exactly a Police bar. What brought you here tonight, and off duty?"

He shrugged, smiled. "I just felt like we should . . . broaden our interests."

"This is certainly the place for that." Her hair flowed across her shoulder as she nodded toward the shadowed walls. "But you seem to be the only one brave enough to try something new—?"

"Yeah, well, it's my nameday. Ambiko's supposed to be the patron saint of change." He laughed. "And the others know what they like, I guess."

"Happy nameday, then," she said, smiling. "And a long life, filled with many more."

He blinked as he realized suddenly that she had spoken to him in Klostan—as if she really were New-havenese. He glanced away and back again, letting himself slide deeper into her uncanny dimension. "So," he murmured, racking his brain for another topic of conversation, "what else do people do in a place like this?"

"Get to know each other better. . . ." Her shoulders moved in an insinuating shrug. "They make connections."

"And you . . . work here?"

"Not exactly." She shook her head. "I come here to meet the kind of people who . . . want to know me better. I've met people from all over the Hegemony. There are a lot of lonely people in Carbuncle." She looked up into his eyes again; her body closed the fractional space between them.

Over her shoulder he saw what the couple behind them were doing. He exhaled in disbelief and took a long, slow breath. "So," he said again, inanely, "I guess your sensenet's got, what . . . an ID scanner, and datanet access built in?" *Gods, he sounded like an idiot . . . worse, like a Kharemoughi.* But it was better than the multiplication tables. "And . . . some kind of galvanic response reader? Lets you know when the solidographic imager's getting it right for your client?" His hand moved down, coming to rest in the hollow of her back; but it was his skin that got goose-flesh.

She raised her eyebrows. "Yes. Yes. And yes. . . ." She smiled, but her smile wasn't about what he'd said. "I take it you have experience with sensenets?"

"No—" He shook his head; the heat rose into his face again. "Uh, no, not really, just studied the specs. It's part of what we do. That's about all we ever do, here in Carbungle." He gave it the name the street Blues used, when the brass weren't listening. "Look, but don't touch." He resettled his hand higher on her back, looking away across the room again.

"That must get frustrating, when you care about your job."

"Yeah. It does." He tried to guess from her expression whether she meant that, or was just humoring him. Maybe it didn't matter, anyway. It was his problem, not hers, and he'd be dealing with it, later to-night. . . .

He blinked as his memory downloaded a final piece of data. "The sensenet's wired directly into your nervous system, isn't it? And it would be EM pulse-sensitive?"

"Yes." She drew back. "Why?"

He shook his head. "Nothing."

"That's not a casual question, Tree. Are we dancing, or are we—?"

"Dancing," he whispered, and pulled her closer, until her mouth was almost on his, and the music they moved to became the song of his yearning: a plangent prayer of love and loss that soared and fell in a language he had never heard before, yet somehow understood, instinctively, completely.

Hardly believing his courage, he leaned in and kissed her. He felt her begin to kiss him back, feeding his hunger.

"Excuse me. . . ." A stranger's voice, speaking Tiamatan without an accent.

"No," he murmured, eyes closed. "She doesn't want to dance with you." He felt her smile.

A hand fell on his shoulder. "Excuse me—"

He shrugged it off as he slid his ID from his pocket. He flashed the badge, barely glancing up at the pale-eyed, pale-haired stranger. "Hegemonic Police, Motherlover. Get lost, or I'll run you in for assaulting an officer."

"*Officer LaisTree*—" the voice dripped acid. "Point one: I own this club. Point two: I am a Tiamatan citizen, and not under your jurisdiction. Point three . . . your friends are leaving. Your partner wants you to leave with them. And so do I."

Tree looked directly into the club owner's glacial eyes. "In a minute." He held the man's gaze until finally the Tiamatan turned and walked away. Tree turned back to . . . *who?* She'd never given him her name . . . any name at all.

But her cinnamon-skinned arms still circled his waist; her smile, her expectant eyes evaporated his will like fog . . . and he wondered whether he was stupid, or crazy, to be taking them at face value. He looked toward the club's exit. The others were already heading for it. Somebody gestured impatiently at him.

"Damn it," he muttered, to no one in particular. He looked back at her and shrugged in resignation. "Thanks, for the dance—" he said, his voice husky. He reached up, gently touching her face. "I . . . listen, where do you live? You live around here?"

"I live uptown, near the palace." Her arms released him, reluctantly, but not her eyes. "Why?"

"Shit. . . ." He broke her gaze, frowning. *Trust your gut,* Staun always said. Raising his head again, he murmured, "You should go home now. Go straight home." He let her go, and turned away.

"Why?" She blocked his path to the exit, her changeling hands planted solidly on his chest. Her entire body seemed to exert a sourceless pressure on him, even though they were barely touching now.

"Tree!" Across the room, Staun had stopped by the door as the others went out one by one.

"Something's happening tonight." Tree pushed his hair back from his eyes, glancing down. "Maybe it could affect you . . . your sensenet. So just go home. You'll be safe there."

"Thank you," she whispered.

He looked up, and was surprised by the expression on her face. Her hands gripped his shoulders; she kissed him lingeringly on the mouth. "And will you come by later . . . to see if I am?"

For a moment, he couldn't answer. "Yes," he murmured, hearing his own disbelief, "I will . . . later." He watched her fade out of reach as she let him go. Then he headed toward the door, and the waiting night.

"Hey, partner, thought we lost ya." Staun slung his jacket at him, propelling him outside into the alley.

"Tree, you fuckin' pullover—!" The others' envious laughter dragged him the rest of the way back into reality.

"Eat your heart out, MarDesta." He squinted as the inescapable glare of Carbuncle's artificial day dazzled his eyes after the darkness of the club. Staun claimed the word "Carbuncle" meant both "jewel" and "festering sore." Tree felt as if that ambiguity had never suited the city better than it did tonight. He'd just held one of its jewels . . . and now, with the others, he was about to cut out some of the rot.

Pulling on his jacket, he looked back down the alley toward the club, beyond it at the night sky visible through the storm wall at the alley's end. Even outside Carbuncle's artificial environment, night on this world was too bright—a glowing pyre of stars, the heart of a stellar cluster into which Tiamat's binary sun system had wandered eons ago. The magnificence of that sky always took his breath away, even as it reminded him of how very far from home he really was. . . .

"Come on, Nyx," Staun said. "Get your brain back in your pants. We all need you to be a hundred percent on this."

"Yeah." He nodded, shaking himself out. "I'm back. I'm ready." He checked the time, saw that it was midway through graveyard watch. He glanced at the others, noticed that MarDesta and SudHalek were having serious trouble walking. He wondered if they were really sober enough to be going anywhere, except home to sleep it off.

But hell, it wasn't like they were going into a high-risk situation—it was just another midnight hit-and-run, like last time, like the half dozen other raids they'd been on over the past year or so. He reached into his jacket pocket for his work gloves, put them on and pulled up his collar against the deepening chill.

At the alley's mouth they turned into the Street, heading downhill. The Closed Doors club lay on the perimeter of the Maze; now they were entering the Lower City, which housed most of the poorer and more provincial Tiamatans—the dockhands, fisherfolk, and laborers—as well as providing storage for all kinds of goods, both licit and illicit.

Under Hegemonic law, the Tiamatans' access to basic technology the rest of the Eight Worlds took for granted was strictly and severely limited, for reasons he had never particularly understood, or concerned himself about. It wasn't his world, the restrictions didn't affect him personally, and the people here in the city seemed content enough with what they were given.

But Arienrhod, Tiamat's ruler, wasn't content . . . and so she did everything in her power to get her hands on all the contraband that techrunners could smuggle in, while also doing her best to hamstring the Hegemonic Police stationed here to protect her people from the predators among their own. While the Snow Queen ruled, this bizarre relic of a city on a marginally habitable world became a haven for illegal activity on a scale that would be notable anywhere else in the Hegemony.

Technically, the Tiamatan government was autonomous, like the other world-governing bodies of the

Hedge. Any Tiamatans caught breaking the Hegemony's laws had to be turned over to the local constabulary, who generally released them the minute the arresting officers turned their backs. The Hegemonic Police were not even allowed to enter Tiamatan-owned property to search for suspects or illegal goods.

And so the Blues wasted their time putting away brawling burnouts and petty thieves, while some of the worst criminals in the Eight Worlds operated unmolested, abetted by the Queen and the locals she hired to front for them. And there was nothing the Police could do about it . . . at least not legally.

Staun turned in at the mouth of the next alley; the sign high on a wall read *Sienna*. Almost no one was awake in the Lower City at this time of night. It felt even colder down here, where the biting wind of Tiamat's interminable winter found its way inside from the sea. Shadows were deeper and more pernicious than in the Maze, with its gaudy festoons of colored lights; tonight darkness seemed to seep out of the walls like ink.

"We're there." Staun knocked on an unmarked warehouse door—a coded series of raps, muted but still loud enough to make the others flinch. The door opened a crack, then wider; a shadow gestured them inside. Tree entered, aware that he was sweating in the cold.

"Happy nameday, LaisTree." Dal KipuTytto, the sergeant who had set up tonight's action, grinned at him as they moved past. Tree counted nine Blues altogether in the cramped space of the receiving office, all dressed like he was in dark, nondescript clothing. KipuTytto's crew murmured greetings, their voices hushed but eager.

"Saint Ambiko's blessed us tonight," KipuTytto

said. "This party really could change something."

"What's our objective?" Tree asked. "Whose ass are we taking a bite out of this time?"

"The Source's," KipuTytto said, and smiled in satisfaction as Tree whistled. Thanin Jaakola, who called himself the Source, was the closest thing the Hegemony's criminal underworld had to a god. He manipulated the ebb and flow of his personal empire from here; his influence spread like a stain through the levels of the city itself, until sometimes it seemed as though he was the real reason for everything that was wrong with Carbuncle.

"Jaakola stores contraband in these warehouses between trade deals. They're off-limits to our inspections, of course, because as usual the actual real estate belongs to a local."

Somebody spat. "Gods, how many times have we risked our necks to save these fucking fisheaters from Jaakola's own thugs, or slavers, or—"

"—if one of us was lying bleeding in the street, they'd step over him like a pile of dung, those thankless shits."

"Hell, kick you in the face, more likely—"

"It's no wonder the Hedge won't make these illiterate bastards full citizens. . . ."

KipuTytto waved silent the curses of disgust. "Listen up. I got solid word that the Source had a transaction with the Motherlovers' Queen set for tonight—"

"The water of life?" Staun said. "You think Arienrhod's skimmed the take from another Hunt?"

"I'd bet my life on it. What else has this godforsaken planet got that's worth trading?"

"Besides a skirt to hide behind," Staun muttered.

"Yeah, well, not tonight," KipuTytto said grimly.

"All right, let's get to it. Who knows what we'll find? This could be our lucky night."

Tree followed the others to the waiting pile of pry bars and sledgehammers—anything that would smash delicate components easily and efficiently. Staun handed out EM-filtering goggles and Police-issue communicators.

"What about weapons?" SudHalek asked.

Staun shook his head, frowning.

"But it's the Source. If he's got something going on—"

"No," Staun said flatly. "We're the Police; we don't shit where we eat. We're not crossing that line."

"Anyway, we won't need guns. TeshRierden took care of the security systems." KipuTytto gestured at a mech from support services.

"Damn straight I did," TeshRierden said. "It wasn't just silent alarms, either. There are laser cross-beam arrays, heat and motion tagged every two meters, at every single point of access; can you believe that? This place is a fucking death trap." He lifted a hand in reassurance, answering their sudden frowns. "Not to worry. Anything they can do, we can do better. I blinkered their entire surveillance net, shunted the relays, and shut down their power grid for the duration."

SudHalek shrugged, mollified. "And you brought the pulse generators, right?"

KipuTytto grunted in amusement. "Does Tiamat have an ocean? Any stuff we can't fry with an EM pulse, we smash. There are two warehouses accessible from this point, and there's not a damn thing in either one of them that's not some kind of contraband. You all know why you're here: to hit that bloated shit peddler where it hurts—in the assets. Do I need to say more?"

Heads moved, answering in the negative; there were a few satisfied laughs. Tree picked up a pry bar.

"Right, then," Staun said. "Let's go do the job they really pay us for."

5

"Gods . . . is it actually halfway through graveyard watch already?" Gundhalinu smothered a yawn as he unsealed the doors of the waiting patrol-craft. He slid into the pilot's seat, peering at the displays.

Jerusha PalaThion settled into the hovercraft's shotgun seat, and sighed heavily. "I thought that damn ship would never get off the grid. Let's get back to the station."

Gundhalinu input the ignition code, glancing a last time at the two patrolmen on duty at the lift entrance, where they'd abandoned the patroller for the starport shuttle. The two Newhaveners looked on with obvious relief as the craft's doors sealed; as if guarding a Police vehicle while its occupants delivered deportees to the port had unreasonably compromised their evening of staring into space.

"Mouth-breathers. . . ." He nosed the hovercraft up and around, heading back toward the Police complex in the heart of the Maze.

PalaThion turned in her seat to give him a look.

He bit his tongue, and kept his eyes fixed on the way ahead. He had been her aide since shortly after he arrived on Tiamat, just over a standard year ago; as far as he could tell, he had been assigned to work with her because he was Kharemoughi, and therefore didn't share her own people's mindless prejudice against women serving on the force. She was currently the only woman officer in Carbuncle. He still found it incredible that there weren't others, considering that she was probably the most competent Newhavener he had ever met. From what he'd seen, the fact that she'd made inspector by the age of thirty only proved the truth of her own unamused observation that in the Hegemonic Police, a woman had to be twice as good as a man to get half the credit. But that didn't stop the Newhavenese street Blues from calling her a bitch, if she so much as made the same frank observations they'd slap each other's palm for.

And it only fed the jealousy that made them say, behind her back but in his plain hearing, that she'd made inspector only because Arienrhod was a woman . . . because LiouxSked, the Police Commander, had needed a female puppet he could use as his liaison to the Motherlovers' bitch queen.

That much probably was true. As her aide, he had been required until recently to accompany PalaThion on visits to the palace, there to endure the Snow Queen's infuriating petty harassment of Hegemonic representatives. He knew that PalaThion hated her job as liaison officer; he also knew that she resented wasting her time on tedious assignments like this one, just as much as he did. But because she was constantly on call to deal with the Queen's complaints and demands, the Chief Inspector rarely gave them work that would let her apply her intellect to real crimes.

He knew she resented the attitude of the other Newhaveners she served with, too. They belittled her ambition and denigrated her competence as an officer at every opportunity, or made brutal comments about her nonexistent social life, and even about her sexuality. He understood implicitly why she never let her guard down with anyone, even him, long enough for someone to catch a glimpse of vulnerability; but he had heard her curse them in blistering terms when she thought he wasn't listening.

Yet she still gave him that look whenever he expressed his own heartfelt opinions about their shortcomings.

PalaThion yawned, and took a pack of iestas from the supply box between the seats. "We have four hours left before morning watch. I say we use it to get some sleep. You can file the report tomorrow, BZ; it's not going anywhere." She shook out a small handful of pods and put them in her mouth.

He shook his head as, out of habit, she offered him the pack. The dried seed pods contained a harmless, mildly addictive substance that made the user both more relaxed and more alert—or so he'd heard. PalaThion spat a pod into the trash container. Any habit that required spitting into a trash receptacle was not one he wanted to acquire. "I can finish it tonight, ma'am. I don't want the Chief Inspector to think I'm slacking off on my record-keeping. Anyway, I'll sleep better if I know the files are up to date . . . I can do it in my sleep," he added as she looked at him again, and he realized she was checking to see if his comment was a veiled criticism. He met her gaze, and saw her relax imperceptibly.

"You should worry less about what other people think of you, and more about what you think of them," she murmured, looking away as she said it; so that for a moment he wasn't sure which of them she actually meant the advice for. "You'll be a better Blue for it." She shook her head. "Besides, I'd rather have you sharp in a crisis than up to date on your filework. It's still Saint Ambiko's Day, until dawn—"

"Saint Ambiko's Day?" Every day of the Newhavenese calendar was named after someone miraculous or martyred. He wondered what that said about Newhavenese history.

"Ambiko is the patron saint of unexpected change," she said, expressionless.

He grinned wryly. "The only real 'crisis' since I joined the force was that day the plumbing backed up at the station house, and nobody wanted to mop the floor."

"When you're a Blue, any day can turn into Ambiko's—"

"Inspector." He held up a hand. He had been monitoring the Police communications bandwidth with half an ear, and now he put it onto the speaker, upping the volume. A barely audible coherent signal emerged from static. "That's a shielded personal communicator." He felt adrenaline jolt his brain and body to vivid life. "On the Police band."

She listened for a moment, shook her head. "It's probably nothing."

"No. . . ." He looked over at her. "It's a vigilante action. It has to be. There was a nameday party tonight, wasn't there? For a patrolman named—"

"LaisTree. Yes." She half frowned. "What about it?"

"I ran a pattern search on the data about the raids—"

"Who ordered you to do that?"

"I took the initiative; all the information was right there in the files. I was surprised that nobody had done it before. I didn't think you'd mind. . . ." He looked down, as her frown suddenly deepened.

Forcing himself to meet her eyes again, he said, "Inspector, the results show an eighty-percent correlation between the vigilante raids and those nameday parties. And who the hell else would be out at this time of night, using shielded transmission, except—" He broke off as her expression registered. "You mean you don't even want to check this out?"

She hesitated, her hand covering the insignia on her collar. "BZ, as long as the vigilantes only destroy smuggled goods and contraband, they're just doing their job—the job Arienrhod does her best to keep them from doing." She looked back at him, her eyes shadowed. "Frankly, I don't see the problem there."

"They're *breaking the law*." He stared at her, incredulous. "It's as simple as that. Two wrongs don't make a right."

"It's not that simple, Gundhalinu—" she snapped. "In Carbuncle, two wrongs are only the beginning."

"We're Police officers! We uphold Hegemonic law. We don't take it into our own hands," he said angrily. "If we don't obey the law, who the hell will?"

"There's the letter of the law," she said, something hard and stubborn coming into her voice, "and there's justice. When you've been a Blue in this city as long as I have, you'll understand that sometimes they're not the same thing."

He looked away, his hands tightening over the controls. "So if you can't get justice, you'll settle for revenge?"

For an endless moment, her eyes were fixed on him

like searchlights. Then, finally, she said, "Track the transmission."

He activated a signal trace, waited. "It's Sienna Alley, Inspector. We're two minutes away—"

"All right then, Sergeant." She nodded. "Let's check it out."

KipuTytto led the way through the access into another, even darker space. Tree knew it for a storeroom by the sudden, distant echo of his footsteps. He pulled his lenses down into place, watched KipuTytto's wrecking crew fan out around him like eerily shining glowflies as they went to work. Staun gestured his own crew on across the room.

Another access opened on an intestine-like passageway, *that should have been a real alley, open to the sky; if this had been a real city, on a civilized world, like Miertoles lo Faux back on Newhaven.* . . . Tree felt a disorienting rush of homesickness hit him, a longing he hadn't felt in years for the parched heat and blazing white light of his remembered childhood. He followed Staun into the tunnel, swallowing the sudden tightness in his throat.

At the far end of the passage there was another access, closed. Its hatch resisted when Staun tried it. Tree watched him cancel the locks with a descrambler. Staun pushed the hatch open; stopped, staring. He said, "What the—"

Tree moved forward, peering past his shoulder into the space beyond.

"Nyx, no!" Staun flung out an arm, shoving Tree back.

And then he screamed, as a beam of superheated plasma punched his body backward into Tree's arms. Tree went down under the impact, stunned by blinding brilliance and blistering pain as the energy discharged kissed his exposed flesh.

He struggled out from under Staun's dead weight, barely aware that he was screaming . . . because now everyone everywhere was screaming, as their bodies were torn by strike after strike of laser crossfire from a security system that should have been without power and completely off-line, but had suddenly triggered along the entire length of the tunnel.

Tree doubled back like a mindless worm and took Staun's body into his arms, shielding it with his own. He went on screaming as knives of amplified light ripped open the black intestinal depths of Carbuncle, and its death cry was the sound of human agony. . . .

Gundhalinu stopped the patroller at the entrance to Sienna Alley. He studied the data coming up on his monitor, and frowned. "Inspector, all the security's out for this entire block. Somebody must've nailed it."

PalaThion glanced at the displays. "Shit . . ." she breathed. "Call for backup."

He called; nodded as he received confirmation. "ETA about three minutes, Inspector. Do we wait?"

She peered out through the windshield at the silent, time-eaten building walls. She turned back and pushed his hand aside to input another query on the CPU. He watched in disbelief as a sudden, massive energy spike gave the data displays a seizure. "No," she said grimly. "We don't wait—"

She unholstered her pistol, checked its charge and stuck it through her belt. She reached up to free the stun rifles racked behind them, pushed one at Gundhalinu, and hit the release stud for the doors.

Hastily checking his own weapons, Gundhalinu followed her down the deserted alleyway. He felt giddy, as if the strobing brilliance of the patrolcraft's flashers had affected his brain.

"Here." She stopped abruptly, midway down the alley's row of indistinguishable warehouses. "Ready?" she asked, looking back.

He nodded.

"Right. Let's go." She took a deep breath, adjusting her helmet as she started toward the nearest building entrance. He recited an adhani under his breath to calm himself as he followed.

PalaThion glanced back suddenly; his reflected image danced in the lowered flash shield of her helmet. "Face shield *down*, Sergeant." Her voice came at him through his helmet's headset, making him wince. "Use full-spectrum filters on your night eyes. No headlamp."

He obeyed, hiding his chagrin. Displays winked on at the limits of his vision as he activated the visual filters and the motion tracker.

PalaThion tried the ancient door. It swung inward, showing them an empty office. They entered, crossed cautiously to the access that stood open at the far side of the room. At her nod, they stepped through into a vast storage space.

His night vision showed him chaos, painted in the eerie glow of enhanced light: a floor littered with the remains of things he identified at a glance as tech items, all of them contraband. He swore under his breath as he shoved aside a charred crate.

And froze, staring. The dark stain on the wall of boxes beyond it pulled his gaze down, inexorably, to the body sprawled on the floor in front of him. He swept the room with his eyes, identifying another victim, and another, by their fading auras of heatglow— their bodies broken, burned, ruined, like the equipment they had been in the process of destroying when something—someone—had betrayed them. He suddenly identified the smell in the air.

He edged forward, reached down to turn over the body at his feet. A vacant face gaped up at him. He recognized the man: *a Blue, a support-systems mech named Tesh-something.* . . . He stood staring down into the empty eyes.

PalaThion's hand on his arm made him jump. He looked back; face-to-face with her, he could see her expression through the helmet's shield. She shook her head, gesturing: *All dead.*

She looked past him. He followed her glance, and saw the gleaming crescent of another half-open hatchway, offering them access to whatever lay beyond this stygian cave. PalaThion bent her head toward it; he nodded. Cautiously, they started across the room.

Tree stirred, rolling onto his side. As his arm slid down, light—real light—seeped through the lids of his eyes. Gently but insistently it reminded him that the flesh-searing agony-made-visible had ceased, he didn't know when; that the nightmare was over, and somehow he was still alive.

Slowly he raised his head, pushing his protective goggles up onto his forehead as he fell back against the wall's cold comfort. He sneezed and spat, clearing out his throat, rubbed his eyes until he made out the blurred motion of figures in the distance, beyond his brother's motionless body. He reached for Staun's shoulder, shook him. "Staun . . . wake up." Staun rolled onto his back. Tree stared, uncomprehending, at what had become of his chest. "Staun . . . ?"

"He's dead." Two men loomed over him, throwing

Staun's body into merciful shadow. He looked up at them, at the uniforms they wore, at the plasma rifles they carried. He looked down as a targeting beam fingered his heart. The bead of light slid upward, came to rest between his eyes. "Just like you're about to be." *Uniforms*—

". . . Police officer! Don't shoot—!" He lurched to his knees, hands high. Their faces were unshielded; he saw them look at each other, their expressions unreadable. Slowly, carefully, he lowered a hand to pull his badge from his coat pocket. He swore, almost dropped it . . . realized with dim surprise that his hand was badly burned.

One of the officers crouched down, peering at his ID, his face. "LaisTree?" the man murmured, his voice echoing and strangely distorted. "What are you doing here?"

"Captain . . . ?" The dark, aristocratic features of HN Cambrelle, the Kharemoughi who commanded his unit, swam and re-formed in his uncertain vision. A silver pendant with a shape he vaguely recognized dangled from a chain around Cambrelle's neck; it winked at him in the shifting light. Tree wiped his mouth, brought his hand away red with bloody spittle. "Doing our job . . ." he mumbled.

Cambrelle's mouth curved upward.

"What . . . what are you . . . ?" Tree watched the pendant spin and shine, hypnotized by its motion.

"It's really better if you don't know," Cambrelle said gently. He pushed the pendant back inside his clothing and stood up. "Better for all of us." The Blue standing beside him, another Kharemoughi, murmured something and pointed down the passage. Cambrelle looked away, frowning at something Tree couldn't make out.

Tree looked down at Staun's face, frozen in a rictus

of agonized disbelief. Gently he laid his hand over his partner's eyes, closing them for the final time, while the thought came to him that he had never expected to be making that gesture for his own brother. . . .

Cambrelle turned back, his face twitching as he looked down at them. And then, almost reluctantly, he raised his gun. The targeting beam toyed with Tree's heart again, like a betraying lover.

"Captain . . . ?" Tree whispered.

Sudden commotion at the far end of the passage made Cambrelle glance up; the plasma rifle's muzzle dropped.

Tree lunged forward. The other Blue's boot caught him square in the chin, slamming him back against the wall. Cambrelle swung the gun up; the beam retraced its path to a point above Tree's eyes. Cambrelle grimaced. "I'm sorry. . . ."

Gundhalinu was three meters from the access when its crescent of light burst open; the passageway lay before him like a glowing forge.

Something too small and fast for human eyes to track flew out, hit his shielded face, and dropped to the floor. He yelped in surprise, stumbling back . . . saw the oblate, nut-sized form of a fragmentation grenade pulsing redly on the floor in front of him. He felt the air in his lungs turn to stone.

"Move—!" PalaThion's shoulder collided with him, driving him into motion. "Go!" she shouted. He saw her kick the grenade, sending it back through the hatchway. "Go! Go!"

He ran as if his life depended on it.

*　　*　　*

"Oh, shit! *Incoming—*"

Something inscribed a glowing smear across Tree's vision; it struck a wall, then hit the floor, spinning like a top. Cambrelle made a strangled noise; the gun fell from his hands as the fragmentation grenade wobbled to a stop.

And detonated.

The shock wave exploded out of the tunnel, catching them from behind like a giant's fist before Gundhalinu had crossed half the warehouse. It picked him up off his feet and threw him into a wall of crates. He crashed to the floor and lay there gasping for breath, as if the explosion had driven all the air out of the room.

When his lungs began to function again, he struggled up onto his hands and knees, shaking his vision clear. He looked back toward the open access. The sight of PalaThion lying motionless between two already-dead bodies shocked his stupefied wits back into focus. "Inspector. . . . Inspector—?" He dragged himself up the wall of boxes until he was standing.

A wave of nausea hit him; he leaned against the crates until it passed, and then he crossed the storeroom to fall on his knees beside her. Rolling aside the body of a stranger, he checked her throat for a pulse; found it, strong and steady despite the blood blurring her face and soaking her uniform. Blood was dripping onto the floor—his own blood, he realized numbly, wondering why that did not seem to bother him more. PalaThion's left leg was broken; he could actually see bone jutting through her torn pants leg. Most of the blood was coming from there. He fumbled his belt off, cinched it tight around her leg above the wound. He sat back again, dazed and uncertain, afraid of doing more in case her injuries were worse than they looked. *Backup . . . call for backup, a med team. . . .*

He activated the radio function on his helmet's headset. "Officer down! Need help—" he said thickly. "All units . . . Code Red in Sienna Alley! Repeat, officer down—"

He broke off, as his own voice ricocheted inside the walls of his skull, the words echoing and re-echoing until his mind couldn't form a coherent thought.

But feedback triggered deja vu: *He had already called for backup. He had called it in. . . .* They were already on their way. They should have been here by now. *What the hell was taking them so long—?*

He got to his feet, goaded by a surge of sudden anger; shut off his headset as the voices responding to his call flooded his brain with more incoherent noise. He glanced toward the outer office doorway. *Still empty.* He looked back at the access the grenade had come through. Its hatch hung from one hinge, in a pall of languidly curling smoke.

He picked up a stun rifle, not even sure whose it was. His mind seemed to exist somewhere beyond the limits of his body as he checked the gun's function displays and thumbed the power to MAX.

He crossed the storeroom to the access. Bringing the rifle up with unsteady hands, he stepped through. He stopped, letting the gun fall to his side again.

The passageway beyond the access was a morgue . . . *no, a slaughterhouse:* bodies and parts of bodies everywhere, blood sprayed on the walls and ceiling, blood pooling on the floor. He leaned against the twisted doorframe and vomited.

When he could force himself to move again he started into the tunnel, setting his feet down with painful care, trying not to slip and fall on the red, slick floor as he searched the carnage for any survivors.

At the far end of the passageway there was another access, another hatch blown nearly off its hinges by the explosion. He went on until he reached it; peered through into another vast warehouse space. Movement registered on his helmet's sensors, pinpointing a figure in the indistinct terrain of boxes and equipment. He brought the gun up, shouting, "Freeze!"

A lightning strike answered him as someone fired a plasma rifle. The blast struck the hatchway, its backwash kicking him sideways out of the shooter's line of sight. He took cover against the wall, swearing as he looked down and saw the nearly indestructible monofiber of his uniform jacket smoking.

He ducked out again, fired at the shooter's remembered position, fell back to safety; his hands were shaking so badly now that he'd be lucky to hit a planet. *Gods, where was his backup . . . ?* He hugged the wall, shutting his eyes against the carnage around him as he waited for his attacker to return fire. And waited.

No blast. No sound at all. He swung around the hatchway again, bringing up the rifle—

Nothing. The sensors in his helmet confirmed what his eyes found: The shooter had gone; there was nothing moving, nothing alive, in that vast space now.

He stepped back, turning—jammed his gun into the chest of the startled patrolman half a meter behind him, caught in the act of reaching for his shoulder. The man's empty hands flew up in the air. *Backup had finally arrived.*

"Gods!" Gundhalinu gasped, letting the rifle drop at his feet. "Warn me next time . . . !" He sagged against the wall, pushing up his flash shield.

The patrolman's mouth moved as if he was speaking, but all Gundhalinu could make out was a dim buzzing.

"What—?" He shook his head. Beyond the patrolman other uniformed figures were making their way into the passage; he saw their stricken faces.

The patrolman gestured at Gundhalinu's head, and mouthed a word: *Ears.*

Gundhalinu slid a gauntleted hand under the flared rim of his helmet, touched his neck below his ear. His fingers came away red. He stared at the blood, realizing at last that the ringing inside his skull was not the sound of silence. As the others reached his side, he pointed to the blast mark on the door frame. They nodded, and went on through, carefully.

"Inspector—?" he asked, pointing, not sure if his speech was any clearer than his hearing. The Blue who'd found him nodded and gave a thumbs-up as they made their way back along the tunnel.

The warehouse was swarming with uniforms, men already tending to the bodies, or recording evidence. More Police came in from the street as he entered. Shrugging off everyone and everything, he went straight to the spot where the emergency medical team was working on PalaThion. She was still unconscious. He watched them put her on a floater and take her out; resisted when they tried to force him to go too. Finally one of the medics shrugged and treated him where he stood, wiping away blood, doing something to his ears that made him want to retch.

His head cleared as the transdermal painkillers and stimulant began to take effect. Slowly the vague, amorphous noises around him began to take on some kind of coherence.

"Sergeant—"

He turned, to see Chief Inspector Aranne ap-

proaching, grim-faced. He wondered how Aranne
had gotten here so fast . . . or whether his own time
sense had just been knocked sideways along with the
rest of his senses. He made a clumsy salute.

"You were investigating, with Inspector PalaThion?"
Aranne asked.

"Yes, sir." He glanced away, distracted, as another
body was carried past. "We were returning from—"

"Do you know what happened here?"

"I. . . ." He blinked, forcing his sluggish brain to
refocus. "Some off-duty Blues were engaging in vigilante activity, sir." He saw Aranne's expression hard-
en. "They must have walked in on something else.
They were dead when we got here. Gods, it's a nightmare in there . . . I don't know what . . . what kind
of . . ." He gestured at the passageway, and took a
deep breath. "Whoever did it was still here when we
arrived. They fired a fragmentation grenade through
the access. We'd be a null set if the Inspector hadn't
kicked it back." For the first time, he realized clearly
that PalaThion had saved his life. "Somebody with a
plasma rifle took a shot at me, inside the other warehouse."

"But you didn't get a look at them? Nothing at all
that could tell us who did this?"

"No, sir." His hands tightened into fists at his sides.

Aranne glanced away as another body bag was carried from the passage. "All right, Sergeant," he muttered. "Go with the med team. Get your injuries
properly taken care of."

"Sir, I'm fine. I want to stay and observe. I want in
on this investigation."

Aranne shook his head. "You're not in any—"

"Chief Inspector!" someone shouted from the passageway. "We've got a live one, sir!"

Aranne headed for the access without finishing his
sentence.

Gundhalinu hesitated, glancing toward the medics for less than a heartbeat before he followed Aranne back to the tunnel.

Bile rose in his throat as he remembered what he would find. He swallowed it down, moving stubbornly past the tight-lipped patrolmen who were collecting evidence and identifying body parts under the guidance of a forensics officer.

The Chief Inspector stood at the far end of the passageway, with the medics who were carefully lifting someone onto a floater. From what Gundhalinu could see, the lone survivor wouldn't be answering anyone's questions for a long time.

As the floater moved past him, he caught a glimpse of the survivor's face; recognized it, even swathed in bandages: *LaisTree. The nameday boy.* So this was how his celebration had ended, as Saint Ambiko's Day had drawn to its catastrophic close.

As they hurried LaisTree out, Gundhalinu watched someone else who hadn't been as lucky being lifted into a body bag. The mangled corpse wore the remains of a Police uniform; a captain's bars gleamed on the collar. He moved closer, half frowning. Something fell from the body into a puddle on the floor as the patrolmen sealed the bag, seemingly oblivious. Gundhalinu let them pass and then, pulling off his gloves, he leaned down to pick the object out of the pool of blood. He wiped the thing on his jacket front, turned it over. It was some kind of pendant or medallion. He put it in his pocket, and went on through the hatchway where the shooter had nearly added him to the fatalities.

There were still more victims in the warehouse beyond, more Blues dealing with their remains.

"What the hell is *this* thing—?" A patrolman swore in disgust, as if he had pulled up a fistful of entrails.

"I don't know. . . . Hey, I don't want it. Yo, Sergeant!" someone else called, spotting Gundhalinu.

Gundhalinu stopped as one of the patrolmen collecting evidence nearby came toward him. The man held up a piece of equipment. "Sergeant, do you know what the hell this is? They found it by one of the bodies over there." Surprised, Gundhalinu caught the fragile-looking mesh hemisphere as the patrolman shook it off his hands, grimacing.

The thing clung disconcertingly to his fingertips. It felt warm and supple, almost as if it were alive, although it appeared to be made of alloy. From its shape and size, he guessed it was some kind of headset. "I don't know," he murmured, shaking it from hand to hand. "I've never seen anything like this before." The patrolman shrugged, his disappointment obvious, as if he really believed all Kharemoughis instinctively recognized any piece of tech ever made.

Ever . . . ? Gundhalinu frowned and rubbed his aching head, struggling to make the connection. "You know, this almost reminds me of . . . of . . ."

"Sergeant!"

He looked up, saw the Chief Inspector coming toward him, accompanied by a medic. He sighed in resignation, and dropped the piece of mesh back into the patrolman's hands. "I don't know. Some kind of joy-job, probably. Bag it with the rest of the confiscated tech. At least then the wrong people won't get their hands on it."

The patrolman carried it away as Aranne reached his side. "Gundhalinu-*eshkrad*," Aranne said, putting a hand on his shoulder. "You should be at the hospital, not at a crime scene."

Gundhalinu looked up in surprise at the touch, at the concern in Aranne's eyes, and the unexpectedly personal form of address. "Sir. But I—"

"We lost over a dozen men tonight, Gundhalinu.

By my sainted ancestors, I don't want to lose another one. Go to the hospital. Now."

Gundhalinu nodded. Aranne started on across the storeroom, and Gundhalinu let the medic lead him away.

"And that was the last I heard that was of any interest, Your Majesty. Except—" Devony broke off, gazing at the nacreous wall of the meeting room. Its opalescent surface shimmered with the slight motion of her head as she tried to banish one final, persistent memory from her thoughts.

"What?" Arienrhod asked. "Tell me."

Devony made half a shrug. "Nothing, really. I danced with a Blue, at the club last night."

"What was his rank?"

"None," she said, surprised. "He was a patrolman. He came in with some others, off-duty. I've never seen a Newhavener Blue in there before; they're too conservative. The rest of them just sat at a table and drank like fish." She smiled wryly. "But just before he left, he told me that I should leave too, and go straight home . . . that 'something was going to happen' and it might affect my sensenet." She glanced up into the sudden, unnerving intentness of the Queen's gaze.

"And—?" Arienrhod fingered the single blood-red jewel that rested on the translucent skin of her throat.

"I went home. I asked him to come by later; he said that he would. But he never did . . ." Even now, she had no more idea of why she had invited him to than of why she had spent the rest of the night waiting for a visitor who never arrived.

"He wasn't a Kharemoughi—?" Arienrhod said. "What was his name?"

"LaisTree . . . Nyx LaisTree."

Arienrhod leaned back in her wingform chair. She stared at nothing for a space of heartbeats, her expression as shifting and elusive as the surfaces of the walls. "If he does come to see you," she said at last, "let me know."

Devony nodded. She looked down at her hands, seeing a stranger's flesh, as she usually did. Each time she came to the palace she came as someone different, to keep her frequent visits from being suspected by Berdaz or anyone else. Today she was Newhavenese. She glanced up again, along with the Queen, as a knock sounded on the closed door of the room.

Arienrhod's pale fingers rose to the jewel at her throat; she frowned faintly. Cupping the stone in her palm, she stared at it as though hypnotized for a long moment. Her frown deepened as she released it again.

Her gaze returned to Devony, although part of her mind was clearly somewhere else as she pulled open a drawer in the ornate desk. She took out a small box made of silverwood, simply but beautifully finished. Devony watched, perplexed, as the Queen removed the jewel she was wearing and placed it in the silk-lined box.

Arienrhod passed the box across the desk to her. "Have you ever seen anything like this?"

Devony took it, wonderingly. Studying the jewel up close, she saw that it was caged in a subtle mesh of almost invisible fineness . . . and that it was not a carbuncle, as she had thought. It was like no gem she had ever seen; something about its beauty was almost preternatural. "No, Your Majesty."

"Neither have I," Arienrhod said. "It's unique, and quite rare. And I want you to have it, with my gratitude, as a reward for all that you've done for your people, and for me."

Devony looked up, speechless with disbelief. Shaking her head she closed the box, and set it back on the desk with painful care. "Your Majesty, I can't . . . it's honor enough simply to be—"

Arienrhod held up a hand, smiling the smile that Devony had come to know so well, full of feeling and of meaning and yet completely unreadable. "Please take it, Devony. As a favor to me."

Devony picked up the box again with an unsteady hand. She slipped it into a pocket-fold of her caftan's sash.

"And now you must go."

Devony bowed deeply, and backed like a sleepwalker to the door. She took her eyes off Arienrhod only as she reached it, to let herself out, and let in whoever was waiting there.

As she left the room, Devony found an offworlder, a woman, standing outside—an Ondinean, from her night-black skin and indigo eyes. The woman wore a utilitarian coverall and heavy boots, and her shining hair was pinned haphazardly under a cap like a common dockhand's, although Devony doubted that small, fragile-looking body had ever done hard labor.

She met the blue-violet eyes; the other woman's piercing stare drove into her brain like a spike. She moved on past, the mask of her smile disguising her sudden need to be far away when Arienrhod's agate gaze met the Ondinean's.

She had shaken off her unease by the time she found the Winter courtier who was to escort her out of the palace. But the Ondinean's face haunted her thoughts until, with a subvocalized command, she added the woman's image to her sensenet's permanent file. She didn't know when or why she would summon up that presence again; only knowing, somehow, that she would.

6

Tree opened his eyes, and his nightmare changed again: The dream of endless darkness filled with blood and screaming, where he huddled beside his brother's lifeless, gutted corpse, became the dream where he opened his eyes on a world of pain, unable to beg or weep or even remember how he had come to be a torture victim, with tubes violating every orifice of his helpless, suffering body. . . .

"Hey, Tree," a familiar voice said. "Welcome back. You ready to stick around a while, this time?"

"Staun—?" he whispered, as the blur of blue-gray above him slowly congealed into figures . . . into two of the men from his unit, wearing their duty uniforms. The calm, deeply lined face of Sergeant Haig Krai-Vieux and the pinched features of Ailm TessraBarde smiled at him uncertainly; they shook their heads.

He took a deep breath of disbelief, and realized that he could breathe on his own. He said, "Shit. . . ." faintly, and discovered that he could speak. *All a nightmare . . . all of it . . . ?* He tried to sit up; floundered, as his strengthless body lost its struggle with restraining straps.

"Easy . . . easy, boy. . . ." KraiVieux laid a large, weathered hand on his forehead, gentling him, although Tree couldn't feel the touch through the layers of bandage. "Don't pull your sutures, or they'll make us leave. . . . You're gonna be here for a while yet." TessraBarde passed over a cup of water, and KraiVieux helped him drink.

"Gods . . . *hospital* . . . ?" Tree gazed up at the ancient ceiling with its webwork of paint cracks, and down at the foot of the unfamiliar bed. He looked over at the two men again as KraiVieux helped him lie back on the pillow.

"Yeah," TessraBarde said, as if it was perfectly logical. "For about a week now."

"*Why?*"

He saw them look at each other. KraiVieux asked, "What's the last thing you remember?"

"Dancing. . . ." Tree turned his head from side to side; the motion felt surreal. He gazed in astonishment at what appeared to be his own arms. One was coated with a shining haze of bandage from fingertips to shoulder; the other one still sprouted tubes and sensors hooked up to the life-support system at his bedside. The faces of the two men strobed as he looked back at them, and reality began to slide in his grasp. . . .

KraiVieux caught his flailing hand. Tree hung on to the solid strength of the other man's grip until the room stabilized again. "Sarge," he whispered, "where's Staun?"

"He's d—" TessraBarde began.

"He's on duty right now," KraiVieux said. "He'll be by later."

Tree nodded, or thought he did. "What . . . happened . . . to me?"

"Long story." KraiVieux shook his head. "We better save it for another time; right now, you need your rest. We're gonna go tell the others we've got you back."

"Yeah," TessraBarde grinned. "You take it easy. Don't be giving the meds any of your lip." His grin fell away as someone dressed in Judiciate black entered the room. "Special Investigator Jashari, sir!"

The two Police officers stiffened to attention. Jashari barely acknowledged their salutes before he gestured them out of the room. TessraBarde headed for the door.

"Sir—" KraiVieux hesitated, murmuring something that Tree couldn't hear.

"I'll be the judge of that," Jashari said.

"Yes, sir." KraiVieux's lips thinned. He glanced toward Tree a last time, lifting his hand in farewell, before he followed TessraBarde out.

The living shadow in a Judiciate uniform replaced the field of blue in Tree's vision. "Do you know who I am, Patrolman?"

"Later. . . ." Tree mumbled, still answering the others' goodbyes, as the slick slope of consciousness tilted further out from under him.

"No." Jashari's hand moved to the touchboard of the monitor at his bedside. "We've waited too long already."

Tree gasped as liquid fire seared his veins, shocking every synapse of his neural net to screaming life, jolting his consciousness fully awake. He looked up into the eyes of the shadow, seeing Jashari clearly for the first time. "Hurts—" he whispered.

"I regret that. But I need you alert." Jashari gestured at the monitor. "It will stop hurting as soon as you've told me about the raid."

"Raid . . . ?"

"The raid the Nameday Vigilantes made on a warehouse in Sienna Alley seven nights ago, where everyone died but you."

"What . . . ?" Tree moved his head from side to side. "Last raid was . . . months ago. Nobody gets hurt—"

Jashari laughed, incredulous. " 'Nobody gets hurt'—? Your partner is dead, LaisTree! Blown to pieces, along with a dozen other men. You're the only one who survived."

"What're you . . . talking about?" Tree's body spasmed; he bit his tongue. "My partner's on duty! Ask KraiVieux!"

"KraiVieux didn't believe you were strong enough yet to face the truth." Jashari held a holographic imager in front of Tree's eyes. "This is the truth. Take a look at it."

Tree stared at the incomprehensible smear in shades of red, as it slowly began to resolve into recognizable forms. *Forming an image of . . . of. . . .*

Tree turned his face away, crushing his eyes shut; tears spilled down his cheeks. "You fucking liar!"

"Look at where you are! They had to restart your own heart three times!"

"No . . ." he moaned. "Staun!"

"What happened to the artifact?"

"Staun! *Staun*—!"

"What in Fah's name is going on in here?" A blur in medical pastels swept past Jashari to the bedside monitor. "Did you reset these feeds?" a woman's angry voice demanded. Her night-black hands made a swift pass over the touchboard; the sensation that molten lead was flowing through Tree's veins began to fade. The doctor turned back, glaring at Jashari. "Who the hell are you, and what the *hell* do you think you're doing?"

"Special Investigator Jashari, authorized by the Judiciate and the Police to question this man about the warehouse massacre," Jashari snapped.

"In other words," she said, "you are not a medical practitioner." Arms folded, she blocked his access to the bed.

"He has vital information—" Jashari's tone was murderous; he took a step toward her.

"Which you will never get, Special Investigator, if you kill him." The woman stood her ground, unfazed by the implied threat as he moved in on her. At her nod, two more figures entered the room, wearing Police blue.

"Staun . . . ?" Tree mumbled.

"I'm reporting this," the doctor said. Her unflinching indigo gaze never left Jashari's face. "If you touch so much as a bedpan in this hospital room again, I'll have you banned from the complex." She indicated the two uniformed officers waiting behind him. "Sergeant KraiVieux and Officer TessraBarde will escort you out, Special Investigator—"

Jashari looked toward them, his mouth like a laser cut. He looked back at Tree.

Tree watched as the features of his face, the shadow-black of his uniform, the midnight blackness of the doctor's face all began to blur and run and flow together . . . until the shadows bled away from his bedside and were absorbed into the waiting field of blue.

"Staun . . . don't go—" He struggled against the restraints and his own dissolving consciousness as the men in blue began to disappear. "Staun!"

But it was only the doctor who returned, to lay a reassuring hand on his arm. Her fingers seemed to pass through his flesh, as if one or the other of them had become the insubstantial figment of a dream.

"Don't go away yet, Officer LaisTree," the doctor murmured.

But it was too late.

"Sir." Gundhalinu entered the office of Chief Inspector Aranne and came to attention, managing a salute that was considerably more regulation than the last one he had made, on the night of the massacre. "Reporting as requested."

He had been inside the Chief Inspector's office exactly once before, shortly after his arrival on Tiamat. He had been surprised then by how small and cramped it was, barely large enough to hold two native-made chairs and a potted plant, plus Aranne's desk/terminal, which he would have considered an antique, back home. But he was not back home anymore . . . and after a year in the living tesseract that was Carbuncle, he found himself surprised by how spacious Aranne's office seemed to have become.

Aranne looked up from his monitor screen and motioned Gundhalinu toward a seat. "Welcome back, Gundhalinu. How are you feeling?"

"Fine, sir." Gundhalinu sat down gingerly in the hard wooden chair, hiding his grimace at the discomfort every wrenched muscle in his body still caused him each time he moved. Compared to Jerusha PalaThion and the one other survivor of the massacre, he had no excuse to complain. "It's good to be back."

Aranne nodded, but his attention was on his monitor again. He stared at it for a long moment. "Gods, all those senseless deaths. . . . Such a waste. Vigilantism was bound to spill over into killing. That's what comes of having disdain for the law."

"Yes, sir." Gundhalinu shifted uncomfortably. "Chief Inspector, about the vigilante massacre—why wasn't I assigned to the investigation?"

Aranne glanced up at him. "Sergeant, I already have every man I can spare working on the case." He gestured at the screen. "The Judiciate has even sent us a special investigator, from Internal Affairs." His voice soured ever so slightly.

"Yes, I know, sir. But Inspector PalaThion and I were first on the scene. It's our call—"

Aranne frowned briefly. "You and PalaThion deserve the credit you'll be given for discovering the crime while it was still in progress. You probably saved the life of the only witness—I've put each of you in for a commendation. But the Inspector isn't even out of the hospital yet; she'll be on medical leave for weeks. And you don't have the street experience or the background for a homicide investigation." He shook his head. "You'll do more good by continuing in your present duties."

"Until the Inspector returns, I have no duties to speak of," Gundhalinu said stubbornly. "I'm university certified in biopsychiatric pathologies, and in data interpolation. I was top of my class at the academy. I am an excellent shot. And with all due respect, sir, how the hell will I ever *get* any street experience, if I spend my entire career behind a desk?" He leaned forward in his seat, his hands tightening on the chair arms. "I have a personal stake in this—"

"Enough!" Aranne's gesture cut him short. "That is exactly why I don't want you involved, Gundhalinu."

His frown deepened. "You're too close to the situation to keep a clear head."

"Yes, sir. I'm sorry, sir." Gundhalinu looked down, shamefaced, forced to admit even to himself that Aranne had a point. "I'll get back to my . . . duties." He pushed his fists deep into the pockets of his freshly cleaned uniform jacket.

Aranne's expression eased. "Gundhalinu-*eshkrad,* you come from one of the most respected Technician families on Kharemough. You are clearly intelligent, capable, and ambitious—you are virtually assured of a successful career in the Hegemonic Police. But you're young. Learn patience. Only time can teach you the rest. . . ." A pained grimace took the place of his smile as he leaned back in his seat. "Now, about the reason I called you in—"

Gundhalinu froze, midway through the motion of getting up, and sat back down.

"Special Investigator Jashari has your report. But he wanted to know if you have anything further to add, any details you might have remembered since that night."

Gundhalinu forced his clenched fists open; his fingers touched something small and cold, deep in his right-hand pocket. He pulled it out, pulling loose a raveled thread of memory as he saw what lay in his palm. "Survey . . ." he murmured.

Aranne leaned forward. "What?"

Gundhalinu held out the silver pendant.

Aranne took it from his hand, turning it over and over. "Where did you get this?"

"At the crime scene, sir. It fell from one of the bodies they were carrying away. I should have given it to someone then. I wasn't thinking very clearly. . . ." He rubbed his face. "It looks like a Survey symbol." Survey was an old and respected social organization, to which most Kharemoughis of Technician rank belonged. It had members from all of the Eight Worlds except this one. Back on Kharemough, he had found its meeting halls to be stodgy and somewhat dull places; but here on Tiamat, far from everything he knew, he actually enjoyed the familiar surroundings of the local Hall. The star-and-compass pendant matched the symbol over the entrance to every Survey Hall, although he had never seen it worn as an ornament before. "I suppose he must have been a member."

"Yes . . . yes, I suppose so." Aranne laid the pendant on his desk; his expression turned distant and unreadable. "Do you know which body it fell from?"

"The victim was wearing a Police uniform. I think he was a captain. . . . It must have been Cabrelle."

"All right. I'll see that it's put with his personal effects." Aranne nodded. "Thank you, Sergeant. That's all."

Gundhalinu got to his feet, hesitated, as a half-formed thought brushed the back of his eyes like moth wings.

"Was there something else?" Aranne asked.

He shook his head, feeling suddenly, unspeakably, tired. "No, sir," he said. "Nothing else." He saluted, and left the office.

7

"What the hell do you mean, it's over!" Tree demanded. "They didn't *wait*? I needed . . . needed to *see* him, before . . . Sarge, you know I had to be there! He's got nobody else to say the Words for him! For gods' sakes—!" He pushed to his feet; fell back into the padded convolutions of the seat, as pain split his skull like an ax. "He was my—"

"I know, boy. . . ." KraiVieux glanced away at the others, out at the view of ocean and sky that lay beyond the sunroom's window-wall. The lines in his face deepened as he turned back. "I know it's hard. But tradition says the dead should be cremated within a day. Commander LiouxSked insisted—"

"LiouxSked?" Tree said fiercely. "Since when did he give a rat's ass about tradition! If you skinned him, you'd find a Kharemoughi—" He broke off, as another spasm stopped his voice in his throat.

KraiVieux's hands rested on his shoulders, supporting him, gently but firmly, until it passed. "I know the Commander's more Tech than the Techs, most times . . . And I do know what Staun meant to you. But the Chief Inspector said it was LiouxSked's order."

Tree bit his lips, shaking his head.

"We brought you the reliquary, Tree." Ness Tier-Pardée came forward hesitantly, holding out the small inlaid box.

Tree took it, nodding his gratitude; his hands trembled so much that he was afraid he might drop it.

"There'll be a memorial service for the force," KraiVieux murmured. "I know, I *know* it's not the same—" he paused, as Tree looked up at him with red-rimmed eyes, "—but it's something, a place to speak the Words. . . ."

Tree nodded again, his throat working. "You got . . . any new leads, on the killers?"

"Nobody's cracked yet," KraiVieux said, frowning. "The Source must have sewed shut every mouth in town. But the entire force is busting ass on this; you know we'll get them."

"You still don't remember anything?" TessraBarde asked.

Tree shook his head, looking away. A phantom haunted the room, always just beyond the limits of his sight; as if his brother would be standing there, if he could only turn his head quickly enough—

"Listen, Nisha said you should come stay with us for awhile, when you get out of the hospital," KraiVieux said. "She needs somebody to fuss over, since our boy went back home to school."

Tree smiled; it bled into a grimace. "Thanks . . . tell her thanks. But I think my next stop's going to be a cell down at the lockup. That's what Jashari says, anyway, every time he comes to interrogate me." His hands tightened over the reliquary until his fingers turned white. Pain forced him to let it go, and he set the box on the low table beside his seat.

"That bastard . . ." TessraBarde muttered. The others exchanged glances, and looked down at the floor.

"It'll work out," KraiVieux said at last. "It'll all work out."

"I wouldn't count on that."

Tree looked up with the others. His heart missed a beat as he saw a uniform . . . *a uniformed Kharemoughi* . . . standing in the doorway of the sunroom. But it was only PalaThion's aide, Gundhalinu. He vaguely recalled being told that Gundhalinu had been first to the scene at the warehouse, along with Jerusha PalaThion, and had almost gotten killed for it.

KraiVieux and the others exchanged glances again. Gundhalinu started toward them, stopped; he looked as though he was trying to find the courage to enter a minefield. Finally he came on across the lounge and stood in front of Tree, frowning.

"You want to go back to your room now, Tree?" TessraBarde asked pointedly, offering him a hand.

"Not yet," Gundhalinu said, glaring at TessraBarde. "I have some questions to ask him first."

Tree shrugged wearily, in answer to the others' dubious stares. "At least the view's not four walls and a ceiling." The Med Center took up most of an alley, abutting the storm wall; the lounge had a rare view of the city's shell-form exterior falling away toward the sea, the sea merging imperceptibly into the fog-bounded sky.

The others murmured their farewells and started out of the room, forcing Gundhalinu to move aside as they passed. He watched them go, his dark eyes wary, his expression grim.

"LaisTree. . . ." Gundhalinu turned back again. His bitter gaze looked Tree up and down as if he was tallying a damage report.

Tree returned the stare, his eyes empty. There was no mark on Gundhalinu that he could see, no proof that the sergeant had narrowly avoided his own unticketed passage with the Boatman. He was still the perfect Tech recruiting-poster-boy: slender, medium height, his brown fine-boned face salted with pale freckles, his uniform impeccably neat—an arrogant, over-educated spoiled brat playacting the role of a Police officer. He'd never have what it took to be a real Blue, even if he rose to the rank of Commander, which he probably would. He'd never be anything but a bureaucrat with a stick up his ass.

"Have a seat," Tree said, resigned. He gestured at the couches and chairs around him, glad that there was no one else in the room just then.

"I'll stand." Gundhalinu folded his arms.

"Then could you stand where you're not blocking my view?"

Gundhalinu looked over his shoulder at the window and back again. He didn't move.

Tree grunted. "What do you want, Sergeant?"

Gundhalinu glanced toward the doorway, almost as if he was afraid of being seen, before he said, "I want you to tell me about the warehouse massacre."

Tree shifted position, grimacing as a suture pulled in his side. The deep foam of the seat reshaped itself to his body, making him feel trapped. "I already did that today, for Special Investigator Jashari." Jashari had come to see him every day, as persistent as his pain; another soulless Technician bastard, asking him questions he couldn't answer, over and over and over, until he felt like screaming. "Like I've done it every single day since I woke up here. Watch the damn tapes, why don't you?"

Jashari had forced him to watch the tapes. Jashari had forced him to do much worse . . . His brainwave profile was synched to a full-sensory feed of the virtual record from the crime scene, via a consensus loop he had never consented to. Whenever Jashari decided it was "necessary", his still-fragile consciousness was dropped through a trapdoor in reality, into the massacre's aftermath.

Reborn among the dead, he was forced to wander the reeking, ghastly landscape of shattered bones and charred unrecognizable flesh, enduring the silent accusations of smoking sightless eyes, tongueless mouths . . . until he waded once again into a river of blood, to stand gazing down at his brother's mutilated body, tangled with his own like a lover's.

Every time, no matter where in Interface Hell he started from, he knew the journey would end that way: that he would find himself once again staring down at his brother's face, distorted by a death-scream for all eternity.

It was the only way out. The program's key would disengage a codestring lock only when he surrendered his last illusory shred of free will . . . when he kneeled down beside his brother's corpse and felt his mind go fetal, as his soul bled out of him into the empty husk of his own broken body. . . .

And when he opened his eyes again, he would be back in his hospital room, and Jashari would be waiting for him . . . and still he could only answer questions about the massacre with "I don't know."

His memory of that night was gone forever, and his career as a Hegemonic Police officer was gone with it; nothing would bring either one back, now.

And just ten minutes ago, he had learned that he'd lost his final chance to see Staun's face at peace, one last time. Now the tortured vision Jashari had seared into his brain would be his final memory of Staun forever, because he would never see his brother, alive or dead, ever again. . . .

"What—?" he said thickly, as he realized that Gundhalinu was still speaking to him. "What?"

"I said I've seen all the tapes," Gundhalinu repeated impatiently. "You just keep saying you don't know anything. I think you're a liar. I can't believe you really don't remember *any*thing—"

Tree looked up at him with burning eyes. "I *don't— remember—anything*," he said, dropping each word on Gundhalinu like a stone.

"Maybe you don't want to. Who are you protecting? Your partner? He's dead; they're all dead, for gods' sakes! More than a dozen officers are dead. You're the only witness. If you don't cooperate, if you don't help us, we'll never get the ones who—"

"*I can't remember*, damn you!" Tree shouted. He pushed to his feet; fell back as the pain blindsided him. "I nearly got my fucking head blown off—" *by a uniform, a Kharemoughi, with a gun targeting his face*—He sucked in a ragged breath. *No* . . . He hunched over, hugging his chest. *No. . . . he couldn't, not ever. . . .*

"LaisTree?" Gundhalinu murmured uncertainly.

No. . . .

"No, damn it!" he said hoarsely, struggling back into the light. "You caught that blast too, Gundhalinu. How the hell much do you remember?"

Gundhalinu made a sound too painful to be a laugh. "I remember everything," he said bleakly. "I don't want to. But I can't stop seeing it. . . . "

Tree stared at him.

Gundhalinu looked away, down at the reliquary

box on the table. He reached out to pick it up.

Tree caught his hand, bent it back hard. *"Don't touch that,"* he said, his voice raw. "Get the hell away from me, you fucking prick!"

Gundhalinu backed up, blinking too much, as Tree let him go. He looked toward the window, out at the sky, his stunned expression hardening into spite. "Enjoy the view," he said at last, rubbing his hand as he started out of the room. "You won't have one much longer."

Gundhalinu forced himself to slow down, to take shorter strides, longer breaths; getting his emotions under control before he finished walking the distance down the hall to Jerusha PalaThion's hospital room. His heartbeat had almost dropped back to normal by the time he knocked on the frame of her open door.

"By the Boatman, Gundhalinu, you're late!" PalaThion was fully dressed and pacing the floor—a feat she did with considerable difficulty, because of the cast still encasing her left leg nearly to the hip. "Where the hell have you been?"

Gundhalinu hid his guilty start by looking down at his watch. "I'm here exactly when you told me to be, Inspector."

She stopped pacing to look at him. "You're always early, BZ. *Always.* Do you have any idea of how much I want to get out of this place?"

"Yes, Inspector. Believe me—" He nodded with heartfelt empathy. "I already have you signed out and the patroller waiting. I can take you straight home from here." He offered his arm for support.

She shook her head, and he knew better than to insist. "You can carry those." She gestured at a headset, a tape reader and an assortment of documents on the bedside table. "At least I got caught up on my backlog."

He gathered them together and dropped them into a carryall. When he looked up again, she had already left the room, and was making her way down the hall toward the lift. He hurried to catch up with her, then slowed his pace to match hers.

"So why were you late?" PalaThion asked.

He took a deep breath. "I saw LaisTree." He pointed ahead toward the sunroom, directly across from the lift at the hall's end. "I stopped to ask him about the . . . the massacre."

She glanced at him. "I thought you told me the Chief Inspector—"

"I know. I know. . . ." Gundhalinu looked down. "But I can't believe LaisTree hasn't remembered something, with all the memory drugs, and the interrogation he's been through."

"He probably has, on some level. But I've seen the tapes. He's not faking." PalaThion's face pinched, and she shook her head.

"How can you be so sure?"

"Because I've seen a lot of trauma victims," she said sharply. She looked away. "That Internal Affairs investigator the Judiciate assigned to the case has his head so far up his own ass he could kiss himself goodnight."

Gundhalinu stared at her. "Did you say that simply because he's from Internal Affairs?"

"No, I didn't." She met his stare, expressionless. "Assumption is the mother of screwups, Gundhalinu; stereotyping is bad procedure, and also damned dangerous. But Jashari uses his IA privilege like a blunt instrument. His interrogation methods are inappropriate to LaisTree's condition—he's only reinforcing the trauma. It doesn't matter whether LaisTree's one of us or not, or even if he's guilty of breaking the law or not. Jashari needs to back off and give him room to breathe. Then I think his memories would start to surface."

Gundhalinu frowned. "I got the feeling that LaisTree might not admit he remembered, even if he did."

"Why not?" PalaThion looked back at him. "What possible motive could he have for not wanting us to catch the killers?"

Gundhalinu hesitated. "When I spoke with him, there was a point when I could almost have sworn he was . . . afraid."

Her eyebrows rose. "Of what?"

"I don't know . . . That doesn't really make sense, does it?" Gundhalinu sighed. "Unless maybe it's the vigilantism charges."

"He confessed to those the first time Jashari questioned him. I don't see how admitting the details could get him in any deeper trouble."

"Maybe he doesn't want to further dishonor the reputation of his partner and his friends."

She was silent for a few steps. "You could have a point."

"Damn it!" Gundhalinu said angrily. "If he'd cooperate, he'd probably get off with just a reprimand. If he helped to break the case, he'd restore the dead men's honor, as well as get back on the force. He's ruining his own life, and for what?" They reached the lift; he hit the call plate with his fist. "Can he really be that blind?"

"No, he's not." PalaThion leaned against the wall. "That kind of loyalty's not logical, or even rational." She glanced away into the sunroom. "But it's human. . . ."

He followed her glance. LaisTree was still in the

same spot, sitting with his head in his hands. He didn't seem to be enjoying the view. Gundhalinu turned back to the blank face of the lift doors. PalaThion went on looking into the sunroom, until a chime announced the lift's arrival.

They descended to the main floor. "By the way," PalaThion said as they crossed the lobby, "LaisNion wasn't just LaisTree's partner, BZ. He was also his brother."

Gundhalinu looked over at her in disbelief. "What? He couldn't have been."

"It's against regs . . . I know," she said. "They shouldn't have been stationed together. I guess they got away with it because they're half-brothers—that's why their last names aren't identical. But any New-havener could have told you they were related."

"So everyone knew it. And no one reported them." *Not even you.*

She looked at him.

"Loyalty," he muttered.

"Gundhalinu, plug 'honor' and 'Technician' into the same equation, and see what answer you come up with."

"It's not the same! If you knew anyth—" He broke off, barely remembering in time that he was speaking to his superior officer. "It's not the same."

"So you're saying that if you suspected another Kharemoughi Tech was corrupt, or even just guilty of some infraction, you wouldn't hesitate to report him?"

"Of course I'd report him," he said shortly. "If I ever meet one who is."

She arched an eyebrow. "Sergeant, I hate to be the one to break it to you, but a clear conscience is generally the result of a faulty memory, not a faultless life."

Gundhalinu glared at her.

"Does that mean I've given you the same look, too many times?" She laughed unexpectedly, and shook her head. "We grow up on the day we have our first real laugh, at ourselves," she said. "And we grow—or we die, BZ."

His frown only deepened.

". . . 'And tomorrow's not looking so good, either'. . . ." she muttered under her breath. Her mouth formed something that only faintly resembled a smile. "Sorry if I've offended you, Sergeant," she said. She didn't say anything more, as they went out of the Medical Center and into the street.

"Yes," Mundilfoere repeated, to the amorphous mass of deeper blackness she could just make out, within the darkness of the hidden room. "I am certain that Arienrhod still holds some part of the artifact. But she has hidden it—quite effectively, I might add." The words carried the ironic weight of her smile, even though she was equally certain that her companion could see her face clearly. "The warehouse debacle has made her doubt us in more ways than one."

"The Queen is a provincial, superstitious woman," the Source muttered. "Even after a century and a half of experience in dealing with offworlders."

"You continue to underestimate her—which explains why she has never trusted you," Mundilfoere said acidly. "I will see to it that she regains her full trust in me, at least. But it will take time."

"What about the rest of it?"

"There are no new leads on the whereabouts of the missing piece. One would almost think that Vanamoinen is avoiding us—"

The Source made a gutteral noise of disgust. She saw his dim, misshapen bulk change position. "The dead do not walk of their own free will, Black Rose." His voice was like a dead man's, if the dead could be forced to speak. "Not even if they live on in their creations. . . ."

Vanamoinen, like his collaborator Ilmarinen, had been dead for millennia. Those legendary geniuses of the Pangalactic Interface's final days had created the sibyl net—a galaxy-spanning artificial intelligence network with living human beings as its ports, meant to preserve the collected knowledge of humankind for future generations.

Their selfless work had helped the former worlds of the Interface survive and rebuild, in the millennia since its collapse severed the lifelines of interstellar trade and communication. The Founders had also bioengineered the virus that the so-called sibyls passed blood to blood, which allowed them to access the AI's hidden databank.

Vanamoinen and Ilmarinen were the Founders of Survey, as well: Not simply the tedious social club known to most of the Hegemony's citizens, but the secret network of influence its star-and-compass facade disguised.

Originally its members had been responsible only for preserving the databank and protecting the sibyls. But knowledge—especially secret knowledge—was power; and the nature of power being what it was, by now Survey's reach extended much further, and their influence ran much deeper, than the Founders had originally intended. All of Survey's members still followed the same road—but often to very different ends.

The Brotherhood, the cabal that Mundilfoere and the Source both served, was just one of the many splinter groups within Survey, all of them vying to influence the future of the Hegemony, or some other isolated remnant of the Old Empire. Kharemoughis dominated the other faction operating on Tiamat—called, with typical hubris, the Golden Mean.

The fact that the prize they competed for, here in Carbuncle's convoluted heart, still existed and was viable after so long could only be due to its having been left on Tiamat, a world nobody but the Tiamatans really wanted. Such an occurrence must have been intentional, and it only fed Mundilfoere's hunger to know what other secrets Carbuncle, the city where time stood still, was keeping to itself.

If she had been on any other world, she might have asked a sibyl—although whether even a sibyl could answer that question was anyone's guess.

Here in Carbuncle, the question was simply moot. The only sibyls on Tiamat lived virtually at the other end of the world, far out among the scattered islands inhabited by the primitive Summer clans, who still believed that sibyls spoke with the voice of the Sea, the Goddess Mother for whom this world was named.

Not even the Hegemony would dare to eliminate sibyls from an inhabited world. But with relentless propaganda and subtler, more ruthless forms of suppression, it kept the technology-hungry Winters of Carbuncle convinced that sibyls were lunatics, victims of an infectious, incurable disease; thereby guaranteeing the Tiamatans' ignorance of their true value, generation after generation.

Even Arienrhod did not suspect the truth—and she could never be permitted to learn it. The cultural chaos such a discovery would bring about would have repercussions throughout the Hegemony. Even the Brotherhood, which thrived on chaos, was not prepared to deal with that . . . at least, not yet.

Not until the prize was safely in their possession. The faction that got its hands on the artifact might be able to discover why, more and more often, the sibyl network's answers to their questions were hopelessly cryptic, or almost willfully incomplete.

Perhaps they still had not learned how to ask the right questions in the right way. But the sibyl net was also completely, maddeningly, silent on certain vital subjects: there were no star maps of the former Galactic Interface's member worlds; there was no data at all describing the production of smartmatter, the nanotechnology that had underlain the Interface's greatest achievements.

Not even Survey knew why those omissions, which could not possibly be oversights, existed. But if the artifact was all that Mundilfoere believed it to be, they might finally have the key to unlock all those answers. And if she had her way, it would soon be firmly in the closed fist of the Brotherhood. . . .

She had come here for one reason, to obtain that seed of the Interface's potential rebirth for the Brotherhood—at any cost. But after all these ages, and all of Survey's best-laid plans, it seemed that whether anyone ever saw the artifact complete again came down to whether one ordinary, all-too-human street Blue regained his memory of a single hour on a single night. . . . "LaisTree still doesn't remember what happened at the warehouse," she said. "I'm absolutely certain of it."

"One can never be 'absolutely certain' of . . . anything." The Source's corroded murmur ran an insinuating finger down her spine.

She frowned. Even wearing vision-enhancing eye membranes, which allowed her to access a range of the EM spectrum far wider than the purely visible, she could tell nothing more about him than that someone—something—alive shared this black box of a room with her. She functioned within the Brotherhood's inner circles at a level at least equal to his own, but she had never been able to get closer than this to the truth about the man who had once been Thanin Jaakola, but who now had no true identity other than his chosen one.

It was rumored that the Source had a wasting, incurable disease that forced him to live in darkness. But she was all too aware that darkness could be one more form of disguise, allowing him the freedom to be anyone, or no one. And she knew that he knew it, which gave her less than no tolerance for his insipid mind games.

"Speak for yourself, Jaakola." She addressed him by his name, which she knew annoyed him, rather than by the title he demanded of his underlings: *Master.* "The Police—"

"—are as much in the dark as you are at present, my dear Mundilfoere."

She fingered the star-and-compass pendant she wore, touching the gem called a solii, the symbol of enlightenment, set at its heart. "Speak for yourself. LaisTree is about to be released from the hospital. My Judiciate and Police contacts have been . . . persuaded to let him go, instead of locking him up. His memories will begin to surface once he's left alone. We must leave him alone, as well. Give him time."

"Time. . . ." The word was a groan of anticipation. The Source laughed unexpectedly, a sound like flesh tearing. "In time, I'll get everything I desire, Mundilfoere."

She only smiled as she turned away, starting for the door; refusing to respond to his laughter. *Let him wonder what she was smiling about, instead.* He would never come close to imagining the truth.

8

They had let him go. Tree dressed himself, slowly and painfully, in the plain, dark clothing that someone—he had no idea who, or when—had supplied to replace the blood-soaked rags he had been wearing when he was brought in. Yesterday he had been told that he'd be leaving the hospital to-day . . . under arrest.

But today Jashari, as pitiless and inhuman as ever, had come to his room to tell him they weren't going to hang him with the weight of all the dead around his neck, after all. Internal Affairs had changed its mind. Jashari hadn't bothered to tell him why.

Tree fastened his Police-issue belt, the only part of his uniform he had been wearing on the night of the massacre, and the only thing that had survived it. He looked down at the Hegemonic seal on its buckle, rubbed the metal clean of a brownish-red stain, rubbed it until it shone. *They'd let him go.* But he was still a vigilante, and still tangled up in Blue: They'd suspended him from duty pending further action, taken away his right to wear even this much of his uniform.

His hands tightened over the worn leather. *Fuck it*— If they didn't want him wearing the belt, they could come and take it off him.

He stared at his reflection in the mirror above the sink, facing the stranger he had become: his black hair shorn, his dark eyes haunted, half his face still pied with fading bruises where it wasn't covered with bandages. A synthetic matrix supported the shattered bone in his leg; he could feel it shift, maddeningly, inside him every time he took a step. He had stopped listening when the medical staff discussed the salvage job they'd done on him the night he'd been brought in, how many of his internal organs they'd had to clone. . . . Even with his pain receptors clogged by massive doses of analgesics, he felt as if his guts were held together with spit and razorwire.

Resisting the urge to lie back down on the bed, he picked up the reliquary from his bedside table and put the box carefully into his jacket. Less than an hour had passed since Jashari had given him the news. He hadn't called anyone; hadn't had the strength—emotional or physical—to deal with their response, even to good news. He left the Medical Center alone, unnoticed, and managed to walk the mercifully short distance home to Celadon Alley, and the rooms that he'd shared with Staun.

He climbed the narrow stairs to their apartment above the Newhavenese grocery, one halting, painful step at a time, sinking more deeply into the past with every step . . . *reliving the first time he had climbed these stairs with Staun, their entire lives crammed into the duffel bags slung on their backs, and the dizzying pressure of an alien world underneath their feet . . . the grin on the face of their Tiamatan landlord as they struggled to communicate in a newly learned language. How Staun had sweet-talked the Newhavenese grocer's wife into giving them dinner and three bottles of imported madreus,* oh, you poor boys, so far from home. . . .

He pressed his thumb to the lock. Swallowing the urge to shout a greeting, or call out Staun's name, he opened the door and went inside. He pushed the door shut behind him, resting his back against it until he could find the strength to go on. *Remembering how the two of them had drunk and talked their way through that first interminable night, both of them sleepless in unsleeping Carbuncle. . . .*

At last he started on down the hall toward his bedroom, glancing in as he passed the doorway of the single large room where they had cooked and eaten and passed the time with friends. He stopped, staring.

Somebody had been here. They'd been robbed—

No . . . somebody had been here, searching for something. The common room had been ransacked. The heavy native furniture lay overturned, and dried seahair from its cushions littered the floor. Electronic equipment was smashed open; every storage cubby in the kitchen alcove had been emptied out, food and utensils were strewn everywhere.

He moved numbly down the hall to Staun's bedroom, to his own . . . seeing clothes and bedding piled ankle-deep on the floor around ruined mattresses. Even the bathroom was a reeking disaster of spilled medicine and smashed containers.

He made his way back to the common room and stood in its entrance, clutching a crushed tin of bitterroot chews that Staun had bought at the botanery down the alley on the day that they'd . . . that they'd. . . .

The tin dropped from his nerveless fingers as he raised his hands to his face. Shaking with helpless sobs, he slid down the wall to the floor.

Gundhalinu entered the Chief Inspector's office, stopped short as he found Special Investigator Jashari already there. He took a deep breath and saluted both men stiffly, refusing to let even the unexpected presence of IA distract him from his purpose. "Chief Inspector, I want to know why Nyx LaisTree isn't under arrest."

"I know, Sergeant," Aranne said irritably. "You have been making that quite clear to the entire station house."

Gundhalinu held his gaze, tight-lipped.

"Do you know Special Investigator Jashari, from the Internal Affairs Division at the Judiciate?" Aranne's voice was utterly toneless as he made the introduction.

"We haven't met, sir." Gundhalinu kept his expression guarded as he glanced at the IA investigator. Jashari's patrician features were honed blade-sharp, as if the man led a personal life so ascetic he barely even ate. The starkness of his face gave him an almost predatory aspect; or maybe it was just the adamantine stare that met Gundhalinu's gaze and passed habitual, unspoken judgment on him. Gundhalinu couldn't help thinking how well the severe lines of a black Judiciate uniform suited the man. "I have seen the tapes of LaisTree's questioning, however."

"I take it you found my interrogation unsatisfactory," Jashari said bluntly; and, when Gundhalinu stood speechless, "Well—?"

Gundhalinu rubbed his neck; realized that he was making a reflexive threat gesture, and hastily lowered his hand. "I found it . . . frustrating, sir."

"So you went to the Medical Center, and interrogated LaisTree yourself." The resentment smoldering in Jashari's voice made the act a personal affront. "Did you honestly think a naive, untrained boy who sits behind a desk all day, doing nothing of any importance, could get an amnesiac to give him answers that a veteran special investigator could not?"

"No, sir!" Gundhalinu shook his head vehemently. "It wasn't like that at all. I . . . I encountered LaisTree by chance at the Med Center. I was there to take Inspector PalaThion home—" Dumbfounded by Jashari's attack, he suddenly remembered PalaThion's remark about clear consciences . . . and recognized Jashari's hostility as a calculated preemptive strike.

He wondered what he had said or done to make the man so defensive. *Because he* had *made the man defensive.* . . . Perhaps Jashari simply regarded anyone who even spoke to LaisTree as invading his turf. Gundhalinu forced himself to remember that Jashari was only human, just like any other man, even if he did work for IA. . . .

He wasn't sure whether realizing that left him feeling relieved, or simply worse. PalaThion's vivid, anatomically impossible description of the Special Investigator flashed into his mind then, and forced him to bite his tongue so hard that his eyes teared.

"But still, you questioned LaisTree, without authorization," Aranne said, his voice heavy with disapproval. Mercifully his real attention remained on Jashari: a visit from Internal Affairs could make anyone, even the Commander of Police, start counting his sins. "I understand you've been to the forensics lab, too," Aranne went on. "And also asking to see the contraband seized as evidence from the warehouse—"

"Yes, sir." Gundhalinu looked down.

"Are you assigned to this case, Sergeant?"

"No, Chief Inspector." He felt himself flush, making his humiliation completely obvious to both of his superiors.

"Then explain yourself, before I put you on suspension."

Gundhalinu raised his head. "After studying the reports on the . . . the massacre," he swallowed painfully, "I found I still had . . . questions, about some of the details. I needed them answered, sir."

"And also you've barely slept since that night, after what you saw at the warehouse." Jashari's gaze suddenly put him in stasis. "Am I right?"

Reluctantly Gundhalinu nodded, and rubbed his bloodshot, fatigue-bruised eyes. "Yes, sir."

"You should be seeing a counselor—" Aranne began.

But Jashari held up his hand. "What are your questions, Sergeant? Tell me."

Gundhalinu met Jashari's stare again, feeling only relief this time, as he realized there was no longer any rebuke in the man's voice. "Well . . . for one thing, why does the coroner's report say that all the victims had on street clothing? No uniforms were mentioned. But I saw at least one uniformed body, Captain Cabrelle's—" He turned back to Aranne. "Sir, you remember the pendant I picked up, after it fell from the body? The Survey symbol?"

Aranne nodded.

"Go on, Sergeant," Jashari said, his expression unreadable.

"Captain Cabrelle's very presence there doesn't make sense to me." Gundhalinu shook his head.

"Why would Cabrelle be engaging in vigilante activity? He was a captain, a Kharemoughi, for gods' sakes!" He looked up again. "It doesn't fit. Something's wrong with that picture."

Aranne exchanged glances with Jashari. Jashari raised his eyebrows, and nodded.

"Sergeant, I'm afraid you put us in a difficult position. . . ." With a look of resignation, Aranne gestured him toward a seat. "You're right. There is more to the warehouse massacre than what you saw in the official report. The vigilantes did not simply encounter unexpected criminal activity. They disrupted a Police action authorized by the Chief Justice, and executed by one of our own Special Ops teams."

Gundhalinu sat down, not taking his eyes off the two men.

"We know that the Snow Queen skims some of the take from every mer hunt," Jashari said. "She uses the water of life to acquire proscribed technology from the onworld criminal element. In the past we've let her get away with it, in part because we have the means to ensure that any equipment left behind at the Departure is nonfunctional . . . in part because she could, with very little effort, make obtaining the water of life virtually impossible for us."

"Yes, sir, I understand." Gundhalinu nodded. "But—"

"But," Aranne said, "this time she was attempting to exchange the water of life for an experimental AI prototype stolen from a research center on Kharemough. It became a matter of Hegemonic security, so we intervened. The vigilantes disrupted an elite Special Operations team—you saw the results. Besides the terrible loss of life, we failed to recover the prototype. What makes the situation even more critical is that no one seems to know what became of the stolen tech. It's missing."

"Missing?" Gundhalinu said. "How is that possible?"

Jashari gave an unamused laugh. "I wish you could tell me that, Sergeant. We have convincing evidence that it wasn't destroyed during the firefight. But what actually became of it seems to be a mystery, even to the criminals involved. It isn't with the contraband we seized at the site. So where is it?"

"You think the vigilantes were after the stolen tech," Gundhalinu murmured. "That their interference wasn't accidental; this time they were planning a real crime?" He took a deep breath. "LaisTree . . ." At last he had an explanation for LaisTree's behavior that actually made sense.

"Exactly," Jashari said. "We let him go because we believe he'll lead us to the missing prototype—one way or another."

"And that will draw the criminals responsible for the massacre out into the open." Gundhalinu leaned forward in his seat.

For a split second, Jashari's face went as blank as if catching the killers had been the last thing on his mind. But then he nodded, murmuring, "Yes. Exactly. Now you're seeing the big picture."

"And since there seems to be no way to keep you out of this investigation, Gundhalinu," Aranne said with a tight smile, "we have decided to add you to it. I want you to track LaisTree's movements: who he sees, where he goes, what he does. Do not discuss your assignment with anyone on the force."

Gundhalinu hesitated. "Does that include Inspector PalaThion, sir?"

"Yes, it does."

He half frowned. "May I ask why, Chief Inspector? Inspector PalaThion is—"

"Newhavenese. So were all of the vigilantes," Aranne said, glancing again at Jashari, "and you know how those people are about their own."

" 'Loyal,' sir?"

Jashari looked sharply at him. "Loyal, yes . . . to a fault. Confide in no one, and report only to Aranne, or to me. Is that clear?"

"Yes, sir." Gundhalinu rose from his chair, feeling completely alert and alive again for the first time since the night of the massacre.

"I hope you'll answer your own questions, along with ours," Aranne said. "Good hunting, Sergeant."

"Thank you, sir. Special Investigator—" He saluted, and left the office.

"Well, what do you think?" Jashari turned to Aranne as the door of the office closed. "Will the patch hold?"

"I hope so. Gundhalinu could be very useful to us." Aranne went on staring at the door as though he could see through walls. "You saw how quickly he catches on. He has a lot of potential—his record shows that he excelled at everything from deductive reasoning to marksmanship. He's smart, resourceful, determined; he comes from the right background. . . ." He broke off, wary of pressing the point too hard.

"And he's hardly more than a boy, Aranne," Jashari said. "He may have simmed his way through a hundred virtual crime scenarios, but he's never had to kill a flesh-and-blood human being. Look at how the massacre has affected him. In every way that matters, he's a virgin . . . and completely moral." Jashari grimaced. "He's too rigid to understand the kinds of choices we may be forced into here. If he learns too much—"

"We attempted to exclude him," Aranne said, with a flash of impatience. "We failed. Gundhalinu is involved in this, whether we like it or not."

"Then that leaves us with only two options, doesn't it?" Jashari sat back, mating his hands fingertip to fingertip, a habit that Aranne found increasingly annoying. "Use him as you suggest . . . or remove him from play."

"Sainted ancestors, this isn't a game!" Aranne snapped.

A mirthless smile pulled at Jashari's lips. "Of course it is; it's the Great Game. The future of the Hegemony, and perhaps of Survey itself, depends on our securing that Old Empire artifact—and on making absolutely certain that the Brotherhood never lays hands on it."

"How many more lies, how many more deaths in our own ranks, can we justify in Survey's name, for gods' sakes?" Aranne said angrily. "Where exactly *does* the line fall that separates Order from Chaos, and keeps us from becoming the enemy, all for the greater good?"

"I presume those are rhetorical questions," Jashari said, his voice like acid. Seeing Aranne's face freeze, he looked away abruptly. Aranne couldn't tell what thoughts Jashari kept to himself, but the other man's tone sounded grudgingly apologetic as he said, "Aranne, the gods know I'd rather use the boy than sacrifice him, too. . . . But I'll still pay whatever it costs, to ensure that we win. And so will you."

"This game has cost us a ransom in blood already." Aranne pulled the chain bearing a silver star-and-compass out of the collar of his uniform. His fist tightened around the Survey symbol as he muttered, "It will be a bloody shame if it costs us any more. . . ."

9

In the dream he was always running ... running away, fists clenched around a rock, or something he'd stolen, or nothing at all ... *frominthothrough a bewilderness of ragelosspain* ... always running in circles back to the same inevitable, inescapable end—

But always, just as he flung himself headlong over the brink of disaster, somehow Staun would be there, to catch his straining, outstretched hand, to save him before he could self-destruct ... Never letting go, no matter how Tree cursed and fought to get free. Holding him the way Ma had held him, when she was alive ... holding him for as long as it took, until the nightmares faded, and he had cried himself to sleep. ...

Staun had never broken his promise. In the filthy coveralls of a day laborer or in Hegemonic blue—with his own fists, or laying his badge on the line, Staun LaisNion had protected his younger brother like an avenging saint. He had never given up on the worthless, thankless little bastard who was only half his kin: *Always forgiving him . . . always loving him*, even when Staun's slap knocked Tree across the room as they got home, and his voice broke as he shouted, "Goddamn it, I can't take any more of this shit! If you don't kill yourself, you're gonna end up killing me!"

And there in the bowels of hell, his hand had shoved Tree out of Death's sight-line one last time, as his own body took the full force of the burn that should have killed them both. . . .

"No, *Staun*—!"

Tree woke, sitting bolt upright, his brother's name still ringing in the stagnant air of their apartment. *Staun . . .*

He fell back on the ruined mattress, drew up his knees and sank his teeth into the wad of blankets half-covering his naked body; lay still while the agony of his sudden motion ebbed slowly, slowly back into the range of the bearable.

He levered himself up again, shifted a centimeter at a time until he could reach his clothes, and the pain medication he had brought with him from the hospital. He took a dose of the inhalant, then lay back, letting it begin to work before he even tried to get out of bed.

Staun's notebook lay beside him. He remembered falling asleep with it clutched in his hand; remembered fever dreams shot through with fragments of his brother's past that bled into his own the way their life's blood had pooled on that cold metal floor.

The notebook held everything from lessons Staun had learned during academy days to last week's shopping list: the database was peppered with vivid descriptions of each new experience they had had since arriving in the strange, hermetically sealed world of

Carbuncle, and sharp-edged insights about people they knew . . . the good, the bad, and the ugly.

There were also stomach-knotting glimpses into the depths of loss, fear, and despair that his brother had tried to keep from him all those years: the pain that life had force-fed them both like fistfuls of broken glass, that Staun had somehow been strong enough to carry until at last he'd reached a place where he felt safe enough to call them by name, and purge them one by one.

And always there was the wellspring of hope and resolve that had never run dry for Staun the way it had for him, no matter how often or how deeply his brother drank from it. . . .

There was also a large file on Tree.

Tree had opened the file with the same commingled grief and revulsion that he felt now every time he faced a mirror. He had read the file from beginning to end, like a voyeur; watching his life strobe by: *a portrait of Nyx LaisTree, as a work-in-progress.* . . .

But his brother's memories of too many things in his past hardly resembled his own. Time and again he saw the truth he knew distorted by the lens of Staun's sometimes grudging, yet always unyielding, belief in him.

Staun had never lost faith in the grieving, guilt-ridden boy trapped inside the hellion who punished them both with his suicidal self-destructiveness . . . who had survived, in spite of himself, to become the man Staun had always known he could be—streetwise and stubborn, but also smart, honest, fair. Someone who had every right to wear the uniform of a Hegemonic Police officer with pride. . . .

Tree's final waking thought, already dissolving into dream, had been of searching for Nyx LaisTree in the mirror of his dead brother's eyes, and finding a complete stranger. . . .

Tree closed his eyes, and chose a random file; hit AUDIO PLAYBACK, choking down his grief as the notebook began to recite in a haunting imitation of his brother's voice.

Registering the date, Tree realized that the entry was one from the day they'd first seen the shapeshifter in Blue Alley. *"Why is experience something you never get until after you need it?"* Staun had written. Tree wondered whether he'd meant life in general, or simply his damnfool kid brother. . . .

He fast-forwarded for the length of an indrawn breath. *". . . in her eyes, never seen anything like it. She's so fucking good, too. Why can't anybody else see that? The guys are assholes, the way they treat her . . . and I'm a coward not to say anything.*

"She knows I stare at her; I just wish she knew why, I just want to talk to her! I want to—Hell, even without the name thing, is a patrolman allowed to ask an inspector to go on a date? Is that fraternization? Do you have to salute? 'Beg pardon, ma'am, you wanna have a couple beers with me, after work?' . . . Shit, it's Gundhalinu—"

Tree sat up on the ruins of his mattress, replayed the final words in disbelief. *PalaThion?* Staun had had a secret crush on the Warrior Nun? For how long—?

Gods . . . had he and Staun ever really know each other at all?

He dropped the notebook, suddenly unable even to form a coherent thought. He sat, head bowed, while grief leaked through his fingers and dripped from his chin, soaking the mattress like tears.

After a time either as brief or as endless as eternity, he raised his head again, and saw his reflection in the skewed, shattered mirror on the wall across the room.

He touched his face as he stared at the fractured image—at what had become of his possessions, of his life, of him. The sense that he had only wakened out of one nightmare into another still haunted him, as it had in the hospital. As if it was still happening to him. . . .

It was still happening to him. His physical pain had ebbed until it was no more than the dull ache of despair; finally he was able to get up, and get dressed. Stumbling through the mess on his floor he reached the doorway, and went down the hall. *His brother was dead. His best friends were dead. Everyone, dead—*

"They had to restart your own heart three times, Lais-Tree." Jashari's voice still haunted him, like the truth: like the holos of the crime scene still burning holes in his vision . . . surreal, indelible images of his own bloody, broken body lying among the mutilated corpses.

Maybe he was *dead. Maybe this was hell.* He had no idea anymore even of how to tell the difference. All he knew for certain was that the world he had accepted as reality his whole life was gone; all that was left where it had once been was a gaping hole, like the gaping hole the plasma beam had left where his brother's heart and lungs should have been. He knew how his brother had died—how they had all died—because Jashari had made him look at the pictures, again and again, always claiming that he was the only one who knew *why* it had happened.

But he didn't know why—any more than he knew why fate had stripped him of even the memory, left his mind as sterile as the Police had left the bloodstained murder scene in their search for clues.

All he knew was that the murderers were still out there, free and alive and breathing—like every fucking dog and rat and maggot in the festering sore that was Carbuncle—while his brother, the best human being he had ever known, would never draw another breath. And it was his fault—because he couldn't remember. And that was the real hell of it.

There was only one genuine memory he still possessed from that night . . . one person who might be able to answer his questions about what he had done, or why this had happened to him. Who could tell him whether he really was in hell, or only deserved to be.

And at least he knew who he had been, once: Hegemonic Police Officer Nyx Ambiko LaisTree. Which meant that there was one thing he still knew how to do . . . and that was find her.

Tree entered the club called Behind Closed Doors and limped across its empty dance floor to the bar. There was no one in front of the bar, or behind it.

"We're not open." A pale Tiamatan dressed in off-worlder clothing emerged from a shadowed recess along the wall; his annoyance was obvious, even from across the room.

Tree's breath caught as the room and the voice and the face suddenly catalyzed a memory: *he was dancing . . . dancing with her . . . and the Tiamatan had cut in, telling him to go*— "Hegemonic Police," he said. "I'm looking for a woman."

"Aren't we all?" The Tiamatan smiled sardonically as he leaned against the bar. "Well, some of us, at least. . . ."

Tree took a step forward, his jaw tightening.

The Tiamatan's smirk fell away. "What's her name?" he asked.

"I don't know."

The Tiamatan gave a soft snort of laughter. "Then I don't see how I can help you."

"She's a 'shifter. . . . she wears a sensenet." Tree controlled his sudden urge to throttle an answer out of the man. "She comes in here all the time, to pick up paying customers. That means you probably both work for a Samathan named Berdaz, who really owns this place. Now, who is she and where does she live?"

The Tiamatan looked him up and down, taking in his bandages, his rumpled street clothes. "You know, you haven't even shown me a badge . . . Officer LaisTree." He met Tree's gaze with a measuring stare. "Would that be because you no longer have one—?"

Tree looked down; his hand covered the Hegemonic seal on his belt buckle.

"That's what I thought. Now, why don't you go away and leave me alone, like a good boy?"

Tree closed the space between them with one stride, catching the Tiamatan by the front of his expensive tunic. He jerked the man forward until they were face to face. "You're right, Motherlover, I don't have a badge anymore. That means there's nothing to keep me from beating the shit out of you, if you don't tell me what I want to know—" He twisted the knot of clothing, gritting his teeth against the pain it caused him. The Tiamatan began to make inarticulate choking sounds. "I'll report you!" he gasped.

"You want to bet that any Blue on the Street will take your word over mine, even without a badge?" The Tiamatan's pale skin had turned deep red. Tree let him go, shoving him back, and watched him wheeze. "Who is she? Where is she?"

"She . . . she lives in Azure Alley. Up by the palace."

"What's her name?"

"I don't know."

Tree's hand caught the front of his tunic again.

"Gods and Goddess, I don't know! That's all I know—"

Tree released him, and left the club.

He made his way up the Street on foot all the way to Azure Alley, cursing the slowness of his stumbling, crippled body, and the tricks his eyes played on him every time he caught sight of a blue uniform; cursing this miserable backwater planet that didn't even have a decent public transit system in its only major city. At last he reached Azure Alley, and turned into it.

The Upper City was a part of town he rarely saw. Most of the crime, and most of the Police, stayed in the Maze, or down by the warehouses and docks in the Lower City. The Upper City held the exclusive townhouses of wealthy Winters and offworlders, the kind of people who settled their problems privately, through networks of influence and means of coercion to which no ordinary Blue had access. He realized belatedly that Azure Alley was not the sort of neighborhood where he could go up to strangers' doors, bandaged, bruised and unshaven, and expect people to answer his questions about a woman who—

"Are you looking for the Changing Lady?"

He turned, startled. A group of native and offworlder children sat together in the middle of the alley, drawing a mural of colorful scrawls on the impervious, immaculately clean pavement. The small girl who had called to him got up and started forward, looking at him in wide-eyed fascination.

"The Changing Lady?" He hesitated. "You mean, a woman who always looks different . . . ?"

The girl nodded, her red curls bobbing. "And she always has guests. My Da says she's a *who*-er."

"Kefty!" A bigger girl came up to the child and took her hand impatiently. "No talking to strangers!" The older girl glared at Tree as she dragged her sister away.

"Wait!" he called. "Please . . . where does she live, the Changing Lady?"

"In Number Twenty-three, with the red flowers!" the smaller girl cried, before her sister pushed her firmly back down into the circle of artists.

Tree sighed, relieved; his relief faded as he made his way down the alley to Number 23, which had a window box of red flowers below its diamond-paned windows. Its entrance was discreetly set in shadows beneath a second-story balcony. He banged the door knocker, not giving himself time to think about what he was doing.

The sound echoed loudly in his ears before the Upper City's proprietary silence could smother it. Quiet returned; even the voices of the children seemed muted and distant.

He waited, twitching with fatigue and indecision, shifting from foot to foot to ease the pain in his side and back and leg. He raised his hand to knock on the door again, then lowered it and began to turn away.

The door opened behind him. He turned toward the sound.

The woman he remembered from the club—Newhavenese, stunningly beautiful—was standing in the doorway, gazing at him with an expression he couldn't name. He stared at her, struck dumb by a sudden, powerful emotion he couldn't name either.

"Come in," she murmured.

He went inside, and she closed the door. He stood in the softly lit elegance of her living room, abruptly feeling self-conscious as he observed his surroundings. All the furnishings were from offworld, but from no world in particular, as if the room was meant to suggest whatever setting a person's expectations brought to it.

He realized that the room reminded him of New-haven, even though he had never lived in a place remotely like this. He turned again, looking back at the woman.

"Officer LaisTree," she said, and smiled. Her smile was so warm and welcoming that he could almost believe she was glad to see him. "You've come at last, to see if I got safely home."

"Tree," he said, looking down. "It's . . . just Tree, now."

"Tree." Her eyes flickered over his face, down his body, taking in the bandages and street clothes. Her expression shifted, deepening and softening as she met his eyes again; he looked away from it. "I'm so sorry," she whispered.

He looked back. Her face, her body, were everything he remembered, everything he'd ever wanted in a woman. . . . "About what?" he said flatly.

"About what happened. That night. . . ."

He forced his gaze to let her go. He stared at the furniture, at the floor with its subtly patterned carpet. "I guess you know more about that than I do."

Her expression turned puzzled.

His hand rose to the bandages on his face, fell away. "I don't remember anything, after you . . . after us—" He shook his head. "I don't remember any illegal raid on a warehouse full of contraband; I don't remember walking into an ambush, or how they died—" His voice roughened. "They all died, except me. On my nameday, on Saint Ambiko's Day. We were the Nameday Vigilantes. But I guess you know that."

Her eyes were fathomless pools. She neither nodded nor shook her head; she seemed barely to be breathing.

"The last thing . . . the last thing that I really remember . . . is being with you." He moved toward her; his hand rose on its own to caress her cheek. "I wanted you to be safe."

She nodded, unblinking, trapped in the spotlight of his gaze.

His hands closed over her arms as his pain and grief suddenly catalyzed into fury. "You told someone, goddamn you! *Who did you tell*—?"

She made a small, startled noise as his grip bruised her flesh, but she didn't struggle or try to pull away.

He let her go, backing off, looking anywhere but at her as the soul-killing pain inside him slashed his resolve to ribbons. He wiped tears from his face; furious at himself now. "I'm waiting," he said hoarsely.

A tremor ran through her, as if she was fighting the urge to put more space between them. She stayed where she was, rubbing her arms while she gazed back at him in clear-eyed reproval. "I went *home*. I didn't speak to anyone else that night! I went directly home. . . ." This time she put a hand on him; her touch was as soft as a drawn breath. He flinched as if she'd struck him. "I waited for you. I thought you'd come. I was sure you'd come."

He looked at her hand on him, up at her face again. "Why?"

She blinked. "Because . . . because you said that you would. Because I wanted you to."

"Don't lie to me!" He stepped back out of reach, shaking her off.

"I'm not," she said, still holding his gaze.

"Everything *about* you is a lie—"

She stood motionless in front of him, refusing to look angry, to look ashamed, to look away. "Not everything," she said.

He suddenly realized that she wasn't lying . . . *that he knew she wasn't lying*. He reached blindly for something to hang on to, and found her outstretched hand.

She led him to the couch; he sank onto it gratefully. She left him there, coming back with a drink in a fluted, ruby-red goblet. He took it from her and swallowed its contents.

"Gods . . ." he gasped, as the liquor slid down his throat. "What—?"

"The water of life," she said, smiling. "Just the drink. But it should clear your head." She sat on the couch an arm's length from him.

He took a deep breath, somehow experiencing every cell and nerve ending in his body at once with ecstatic clarity. He looked down into the empty goblet, before he passed it back to her.

She took it from him; sat turning it pensively by its fragile stem. "So," she murmured, looking up at him at last, "you came here because dancing with me is the last thing that you remember . . . ?"

He nodded, letting the couch support his dazzled body. "I thought—" He broke off, remembering what had come next in the only way he could, from the official report. "That night . . . there was a laser crossbeam security system, with a failsafe so sophisticated our equipment couldn't even sense it. And the weapons . . . they used plasma rifles, not stunners. Somebody set off a frag grenade—! Gods, what the hell was going on in there? And who was doing it? Nobody knows, except me. And I can't remember. . . ." He slumped forward, propping his head in his hands. "I thought if you'd . . . told somebody, it might give me a lead." He looked up at her again.

"Why didn't you tell the Police about me?" she asked softly.

He shook his head. "I didn't even know your name."

"But you found me."

He stared at her for a long moment, then finally looked away. "The Special Investigator, Jashari—"

Her breath caught.

"You know him?"

"Yes," she said faintly. Her hands twisted in her lap. "He questioned you?"

Tree nodded, taking a breath that made his chest hurt. "That bastard questioned me every day, every fucking day! He made me look at pictures of body parts, lying in pools of blood—" his voice began to tremble, "and he said—he said those were my *friends*. What was . . . left of them." He clenched his teeth, and tasted his own blood.

"Oh, gods." Her words were like a whispered prayer in the silence.

"Jashari—" the name forced its way past his lips as if he were possessed, spitting out demons, "he said that I had no right to be alive, when the rest were dead. He told me their deaths would be on my head, if I didn't tell him everything I knew . . . when he *knew* I couldn't tell him anything! He made me want to rip out all the tubes and wires and just stop breathing—"

He shut his eyes, as pain and remembered pain closed their hands around his throat. "Dancing with you . . . that was the only thing I had left that didn't make me wish I was dead. I wouldn't have given him that, even if . . . even if . . ." He pushed to his feet. "Forget it. I'm sorry. I have to go." He started unsteadily for the door.

"Go where?" she asked.

He stopped, speechless.

She rose and came to his side, drawing him gently around. He followed her, unresisting, back to the couch. "Thank you," she whispered, "for protecting me." She sat down again, closer this time. "He had no right."

He looked at her. "How do you know?"

She touched his bandage-covered cheek, brought her hand away with fingertips that were wet and glistening.

He reached up, and discovered that tears were running down his face again, he had no idea for how long. He wiped them on his sleeve. "Somebody... somebody searched my place while I was in the hospital. They tore it apart, and I don't even know why. What the hell did they *want* from us?"

"Us?"

"Me and Staun. We had a place together."

"He was your friend?"

Tree nodded; shook his head. "He was my brother."

Her face pinched. "And he was with you, that night...?"

He nodded again, looking at his hands.

"What can I do?" she murmured at last. "Is there anything I can do, to help you...?"

"You speak Klostan, don't you?" It was the language he and Staun had grown up speaking, on Newhaven.

"A little."

"Do you ever... can the sensenet... image a man?"

She looked startled. "That's not a request I've had before. Why?"

Tree pulled Staun's ID from his pocket, stared at the holographic image of his brother's face before he held out the card. "This is my brother."

She averted her face as if he had set off a flare. "No," she whispered. "Oh, no—" Fumbling blindly, she closed his fingers over the image and pushed his hands away. "I can't. Please, don't ask me that. I can't—"

He put the ID away, blinking too much.

She looked back at him again, finally. "Would you . . . like another drink?"

He shook his head.

She glanced down at herself. "This isn't . . . it's not what you want, either, is it?"

He stared at her, the beauty of her face, her perfect body. He shook his head again and looked away.

"What, then . . . ?" she asked softly, touching his shoulder.

He shut his eyes, thinking that there was no answer he could possibly imagine making to that question. *But there was.* "I want you to be real with me . . . I want to see who you really are."

Her touch disappeared. "No," she said, folding her fingers into a knot. "No . . . I don't do that."

"Why?" he asked, sitting up, leaning forward. "Why not?"

She moved her head from side to side. "That's not playing by the rules."

He opened his mouth, closed it over a noise of pain as the gutworm of loss twisted inside him. Finally he said, "I don't want a drink. And I don't want sex. I want . . . I *need* . . . somebody I can just . . . *talk* to. Please."

As he looked into her eyes, he realized suddenly that she was afraid of him—of what he wanted—in a way that she hadn't been afraid of his anger, or his physical strength. "You're never just . . . yourself . . . with anybody?" He read the answer in her silent stare. "Never . . . ?" he whispered. "Don't you have any friends?"

Her expression was a void, but her eyes were suddenly too full.

Hating his weakness, afraid of her pity, he blurted, "Don't you ever need to just . . . be *real* . . . with someone?"

Her hands rose to her mouth. She sat motionless, staring at him.

He looked on, bewildered, as the color of her brimming eyes began to change.

And then her skin began to change, and her hair, and the shape of her face . . . until she sat before him as nakedly vulnerable, as real, as he was.

"You're Tiamatan . . ." he murmured, not sure why that surprised him. He reached out tentatively to touch her arm. The gray sleeveless tunic and pants she had been wearing were still the same, like the blood-red jewel at her throat. But her eyes were gray-blue, sea-colored. Her hair—still long, falling in waves—was the color of sand, with a hint of copper. Her skin, paler now than his, bore a tracery of synthetic filaments so fine that they were almost invisible, except where they caught the light, shimmering like an aura.

Aside from that, her face reminded him of faces he passed every day in Carbuncle without really seeing them; her features were no longer so perfect that they took his breath away. He realized that he was actually relieved.

"Is that . . . all right?" she murmured. Her hands moved restlessly, as if she were weightless, and unsure of what to do with her body. "Am I . . ."

He nodded, still looking deeply into her eyes; left without words by the unexpected gift of her trust.

She relaxed visibly as he went on gazing at her, smiling at her; until he felt as if he was in the presence of a different mind and soul, as well. The inscrutable mistress of a game he would never know how to play had vanished. The relief that filled her

face made the fact that it was a Tiamatan's, and not
Newhavenese, meaningless. Relief eased his own expression, eased his entire body, until he felt as if he
had come to be sitting next to someone he had
known forever.

"Tell me about you, and your brother," she said,
resting her arm on the back of the couch, beginning
to smile again at last. "Tell me about your life, when
you were boys back on Newhaven."

He pulled Staun's ID from his pocket again, and
sat looking at the picture. "He was my half-brother.
Our mother died when I was twelve. Staun took care
of me after that; he was just fifteen. He used to say,
it was 'us against the world'." Tree laughed softly, biting his lip.

"What about your father?"

"Ma never talked about him." He shook his head.
"Once I overheard her say he was a bastard. . . . I
don't know what he did, to make her hate him that
much. Staun said his old man abandoned them, just
got on a ship and never came back. Ma had lousy
luck with men—'except for us', she used to say. She
had lousy luck, period. . . ."

"How did your mother die?" she murmured.

"Freak accident. She worked at the starport. One
day a . . . a . . ." He shook his head. "Doesn't matter.
She died." He gazed up at the ceiling, finding a white
and empty vision of eternity.

Her hand extended further, just far enough to
close over his unbandaged one. His fingers twined
with hers, tightened; he looked at their joined hands,
and away again. "Staun had to work two, three jobs
sometimes, just so we could eat . . . and still try to
keep me out of trouble, besides. Gods, I had a real
mad-on at the universe, back then. We lived in Mier-

toles Porttown; they called it the Hellhole, and I raised a lot of hell—" He grimaced.

"Then how did you ever end up in the Hegemonic Police?" She looked incredulous.

Tree's mouth twitched. "When I was fifteen, the Police arrested me. For vandalism, at the starport. Staun thought he'd lost me for good that time. But when he came down to the lockup and begged them to spare my miserable ass—not to press charges, not to let Social Reform take me away from him—somebody actually listened to what he said." He shook his head. "Some Blue officer I never saw again took great pains to scare the hell out of me about what they'd do if they ever caught me again . . . and then he let me go. He said . . . he said it was because my brother needed *me* so much. . . ."

Tree made a sound that wasn't really a laugh. " 'He needs you,' he said. 'Don't let him down.' I couldn't imagine why he'd even say something like that. Like I didn't need Staun ten *times* as much—" He broke off. "But somehow after that, everything I did began to feel different to me. Not like I became a candidate for sainthood or anything, but. . . ."

"But you became a Blue."

"Staun did." Tree shrugged. "He was smarter than anyone I knew. He could have done anything, if someone had given him a chance. Or if I hadn't always been. . . ." He looked down. "Anyway, the Blues were the only ones who ever did give us a break, and believe me, that was the last place either of us expected it to come from. That was what made him decide to join up. By the time I was old enough to join the force, all I really wanted was to be like Staun. . . ."

Memory's half smile faded as he traced the Hegemonic seal on his belt buckle, realizing that he had

never really understood how much he had wanted it—
any of it—until now, when it was too late. "Now he's
gone. And my badge is gone. My whole goddamn *life*,
gone with the Boatman. Only, I'm still breathing. . . ."
He stared at the layers of synthetic skingraft and bandage that hid the half-healed burn on his hand. They
had told him there wouldn't be many scars—

He made a fist, brought it down on the arm of the
sofa. "I don't want it to stop hurting!" he said fiercely,
as her hands rose in protest. "The less my body hurts,
the more losing him hurts! I mean, I don't even hurt
for him; he doesn't feel anything, anymore." He
stared at his bandaged fist. "But I feel like . . . like he
was ripped out of me whole," his voice faded to a
whisper, "and that he was the only part of me that
was real." His throbbing hand loosened, as he covered his eyes. "Everything I see, everyone I know, reminds me . . . I don't know what to do, without him.
What the fuck am I going to do? *Goddamn it! It's not
fair—!*"

He looked up again, into the blurring watercolor
of her gaze. "That's all I can think about. Is that selfish? Am I a selfish bastard?"

"No," she whispered, shaking her head. "I think . . .
I think that's grief. The sorrow you feel because you're
left behind. The sorrow you feel because you're all
alone. Life is all about loss . . ." she glanced away suddenly, "loss . . . and pain. Pain tells us to *do* something,
when sometimes it's all we can do, just to remember
we're alive—"

He held his breath. She looked back at him, and
he saw in her eyes that she knew.

"Sometimes it's all you can do," she said softly. "But
that's all right."

He nodded, taking a deep breath as the pain inside
him finally began to ease.

"Do you . . . have family here?" he asked then, wondering what her words had just told him about her own life. He knew almost nothing about Tiamatans, beyond how to speak their language. He had been force-fed an indoctrination tape when he arrived, like all the other Blues assigned to Carbuncle; it had left him with no interest whatsoever in learning more about the natives' traditions, customs, or behavior—except when their behavior kept him from doing his job.

He waited for her to tell him that her personal life was none of his business. But she nodded, surprising him again. "They live in the outback, on a plantation. We don't have much in common anymore. Maybe we never did. . . ." She glanced down. "I don't see them a lot. I suppose we take each other for granted."

"Maybe we all do." He sighed. "Does it bother them, what you do for a living?"

"They don't care. . . ." She hesitated. "As long as I'm happy."

He realized that she wasn't meeting his gaze. "No. That's too easy. I don't buy it." He shook his head.

She did look at him then, and raised her eyebrows. "What do *you* think about what I do?"

"Me?" he said, blinking. He shrugged. "I don't have any problem with it, if that's what you mean."

She gave him a skeptical look.

"As long as it's really your choice," he said. "As long as you really have a choice. . . ." He saw the question lingering in her eyes. "I've been a Blue for a while; it kind of changes your perspective on some things."

"So does Carbuncle." Slowly her smile came out of hiding. "Because everything happens here. I love this city! I like meeting people from other worlds, hearing about their lives. I like having a beautiful home, and the money to buy anything I want. And I like sex; I like having it often, with new people, and in new ways. We're a lot more comfortable here with what human beings naturally need than you offworlders seem to be. Sex is like air: it's only important when you aren't getting any."

His mouth quirked; he felt his face redden unexpectedly. "How long have you had the sensenet?"

"For about five years." She ran her hand along her arm. "I also like being inside someone else's skin . . . trying on how it feels to be somebody new."

"What are you going to do after the Departure? You'll have to give it—all of this—up."

"Oh, maybe by then, I'll miss the outback. . . ." She glanced away as if she was considering the room around them; he realized that she was just avoiding his eyes again. "Or maybe I'll marry and go offworld with someone. I've had a few proposals. What about you?"

He felt all the expression drain from his face. He forced himself to acknowledge her question, and answer it. "If they let me back on the force, I guess I'll be here till the Departure. Then, I'll be sent somewhere else. If they don't . . . If they don't, I don't know." He shook his head; his hands tightened into fists. "Either way, I have to get the bastards who killed Staun. If I can't do that, if I can't even pay the Boatman's Due, then it doesn't matter what happens to me because my being alive is meaningless." He stared at the ceiling again. "Goddamn it, I just want to *remember*—!"

His hands unclenched. "Oh, gods . . ." he whispered, looking down at the floor, "I just want to forget. . . ."

"I can help you," she murmured, caressing his face, "for a little while, at least. If you let me."

He raised his hand, covering hers; his newly healed

skin tingled with real or imagined sensation as he traced the delicate web of the sensenet. Her fingers gently brushed his lips. He kissed her fingertips, sliding his arm behind her, drawing her closer. "Tell me who you are—?"

She closed her eyes. "Devony," she murmured, her hands tightening over the cloth of his shirt as she pressed up against him, "Devony Seaward . . ." Her hands slid down his body, beginning to loosen his clothes.

Sudden, breathtaking arousal relieved him of all pain. He put his arms around her and began to kiss her. She drew him back and down, and her body was like a warm sea. . . .

─── 10 ───

Gundhalinu started awake from a doze. He glanced at his watch, yawning, and up at the sign that marked the entrance to Azure Alley. Looking down again, he realized that the well-dressed citizens passing on the Street were beginning to stare at him, even though he was in uniform. He pushed away from the building wall, shaking his head; admitting to himself that his body had finally won its unrelenting war with his brain. *He had to rest. . . .*

Earlier today he had followed LaisTree to the Closed Doors club, and then to the Upper City. LaisTree had entered Number 23 Azure Alley exactly forty-seven minutes ago. Gundhalinu had checked the time every few minutes since then, with growing impatience.

He knew that the tracer they had planted in LaisTree's bandages at the hospital was working; he could follow LaisTree's movements no matter where in the city either of them were. He didn't have to stand in the Street for hours on end. His remote would notify him when LaisTree's location changed.

He sighed and started back downhill into the Maze, almost turning in at Blue Alley . . . except that he had no real reason to go to the station house, or any duties to attend to there. He almost stopped by Jerusha PalaThion's apartment, which he did daily to fetch her things she needed from the market . . . except that she would want to talk about how the investigation was going, and he couldn't talk to her about that, because until he got some sleep he didn't trust himself not to say too much. . . .

If he could only get some sleep. He arrived at the alley and finally the building where he lived. Resigned to facing his room, his own bed, he opened the front door and went inside. Making his way along the hall as quietly as possible to avoid his oversolicitous Tiamatan landlady, he let himself into his flat.

He crossed the ordered space of his bed/sitting room, listlessly shedding his helmet and jacket as he went, and collapsed onto the daybed. His limbs twitched and quivered as he tried to settle into the quiet rhythms of adhani breathing. At last he felt his exhausted body growing dim and heavy; his fatigue-deadened mind began to let go of consciousness one reluctant finger at a time, slipping over the brink into the peaceful depths of sleep. . . .

  . . . *Slipping, as his mother's hand released him, and she faded into the rose-colored dawn of his childhood with a murmured,* "Be a good boy. . . ." *Slipping further, as his father's aged hand let him go in despair, when he could not bring himself to be anything more than his mother had asked of him. . . . As his brothers' pitiless hands pried loose his last fingerhold and sent him spiraling down the red-walled tun-*

*nel where the hands he seized in desperation were not at-
tached to anything, because no body was left whole . . . and
he plunged into the blood-red drowning pool from which no
one escaped alive—*

He jerked awake, his heart pounding as if he had
almost fallen off a cliff. Mumbling curses, he rolled
onto his side. His fingers pitted the mattress foam as
he stared out across the silent, indifferent space of
his room, proving to himself once again that its walls
were not running with blood.

He rolled onto his back and shut his eyes, muttering another curse and then an adhani, beginning the
process all over. . . .

He woke up an hour later, feeling more exhausted
than before. Checking his remote, he saw that
LaisTree's location still hadn't changed. He got up
from the bed and stood for a long moment staring
vacantly toward the door. Then, rubbing his eyes, he
crossed the room to his desk.

As he sat down at his terminal he paused, frowning.
He reached for the holostill of his family that he had
buried deep inside a cubby, on the day he had
learned of his father's death . . . *gods, was it really four
months ago?*

He pulled the holo toward him and slowly removed
the cloth he had draped over the frame. He gazed
down into the past, studying the faces in the picture.
All of them were male; there had not been a woman's
face, a woman's constant presence, in their lives since
. . . since. . . .

What was beyond fixing should be beyond grief.

He forced his mind away from what might have
been, to confront what was: the image of a white-
haired man with stern, patrician features, wearing the
traditional uniform of a Technician head-of-family
. . . a face that might be his own someday, although

the uniform never would. Beside the white-haired man stood a youth with a face as insipid as pudding— whose unquestioned right it was, under the laws of primogeniture, to inherit the uniform and everything it represented. Beside him stood a second youth, his face frozen in a perpetual smirk of bitter contempt. Last in line, literally and figuratively, was a half-grown boy who stared straight ahead, his face so doggedly expressionless that he might as well have been screaming. That had been his face, half a lifetime ago.

The eyes of the figures followed him as he moved his head from side to side. None of them smiled. None of them had ever smiled; not when they were all together.

He thought of LaisTree and his brother . . . only his half-brother really. Yet the bond between them had been so strong they'd flouted Police regulations long before they ever thought of turning vigilante, just so they wouldn't be separated for their entire careers.

Loyalty over honor.

And look where that had gotten them.

He dropped the cloth over the portrait again and began to rewrap it. The cloth seemed to defy his fumbling hands, slipping sideways, refusing to shroud the memories of his own past.

In sudden, blind fury, he struck the picture with the flat of his hand, knocking it off the desk.

It hit the floor with a *crunch*, like the sound of hope being broken under a boot heel.

Slowly he leaned down, forced himself to pick up the frame. *It was broken. He had broken it.* He stared at his father, his brothers, himself . . . the ruins of memory. He touched the scrambled holographic image, the faces blurred to unrecognizability like a violently shaken sand painting in a jar.

No, dammit . . . it had always been broken. He wrapped the cloth around the frame and crammed the picture back into its hole.

His father's final words on the day he left home, bound for Tiamat, came to him suddenly, as he rose from his seat: *"Remember this—when everything seems to be coming your way, the odds are that you're traveling in the wrong direction."*

He sat down again, stunned, as he suddenly realized the words had not been a curse, but rather an odd sort of benediction.

"Trust your gut," he'd heard the street Blues say. He brought the Police data files up on his screen. Finding the place in the complete records of the warehouse massacre where he had stopped reading last night, he continued his restless search.

"You don't have to go," Devony said; Tree hesitated in the doorway. "Stay longer . . . stay the night."

"I can't." He shook his head. Slowly, reluctantly, he closed the lower half of the split door between them. She laid a caressing hand on his arm; he took her hand in his. "I've got to go . . . got to research some things in the official report that don't make sense to me." He looked up at her, hoping his eyes were saying all the things he didn't have words for.

She smiled after a moment. "Well, you know where to find me. If you need a friend. . . ."

He grinned fleetingly. "Count on that." He touched her faintly shimmering face; his smile fell away. "Thank you." He turned and stepped out into the alley, before he could lose his resolve in the depths of her eyes.

He made his way back downtown to Police headquarters. He went inside, exchanging as few words as
possible with the men coming on duty for the evening shift. Moving through the station house in his
street clothes, surrounded by a sea of uniform blue,
he felt as if he had walked into headquarters naked.
His eyes kept searching the crowd, his heart lurching
every time he caught sight of a familiar face, always
the wrong one. . . .

"LaisTree!" Haig KraiVieux called from the dispatch desk. "How you doin', boy? They put you back
on the roster already?"

Tree smiled wanly as he reached the counter. "Not
exactly. . . . Look, Sarge, I need to ask you a favor.
Can I access the datafiles for a couple of hours?
There're still things about the . . . the warehouse massacre I just can't understand. If I could get a real look
at the full record, I thought . . ." he shrugged, "you
know, maybe it'd help me remember something."

KraiVieux's forehead furrowed. "Well, if you're not
cleared for duty, it's against regs. I'm not supposed
to—"

"Come on, Sarge, help me out or I'll never get back
in uniform! Staun's dead, for gods' sakes! Let me do
something about it or I'm gonna go crazy—"

KraiVieux grimaced, and nodded. "Okay, boy. . . .
The Chief Inspector isn't here to bust my ass about
it, so I guess I can let you into the system with my
passcode. Just this once." He stepped out from behind the counter, gesturing Tree after him.

"Thanks, Sarge." Tree followed him to an empty
office and settled into the chair behind the terminal.

KraiVieux opened the port and brought up the files
on the warehouse massacre. As the data flashed on the
screen, Tree felt the restlessness that had drawn him
here transformed into something stronger, deeper,

more relentless. *What was it . . . the thing he knew? He knew—if he could only find the key, lost somewhere in a million bytes of data, that could open the right lock. . . .* His hands closed over empty air, tightening into fists. He forced them open again, flexed his fingers, and began to input his first query.

KraiVieux stood staring down at him for a long moment; then, with a sigh and a murmured, "Good luck," left him in peace to run his searches and compares.

Gundhalinu stepped up to the door of Number 23 Azure Alley, knocked, and waited. LaisTree had finally left this address, after being inside for hours; he had gone back downtown to the station house like an insect drawn to a flame. The Newhavenese Blues on duty there had welcomed him as if he were a long-lost friend, and not a walking disgrace to the uniform they wore. He wasn't likely to be going anywhere else for a while.

The top half of the split door opened, and Gundhalinu started in surprise. A striking, elegantly dressed Kharemoughi woman, clearly of Technician rank, stood gazing back at him.

"Yes, Sergeant . . . ?" she prompted, when he didn't speak.

". . . Gundhalinu, ma'am." He touched the rim of his helmet, nodded politely.

"What can I do for you, Sergeant Gundhalinu?" There was something almost insinuating, and not quite innocent, about the question.

He cleared his throat, suddenly trying to remember what it was he'd come here to ask. "Uh . . . Nyx LaisTree visited this residence earlier today. I'd like to ask you some questions about him."

She bent her head at him. "Nyx LaisTree. And if I said I know nothing about him—?"

"I'd still like to ask you some questions."

She made a small shrug of acquiescence and opened the bottom half of the door. She wore the simple robe and trousers that were casual dress for most Kharemoughis of Technician rank; her dark, shining hair lay in a neat plait down her back. She smoothed it absently as she stepped aside, allowing him to enter.

He glanced around her living room, taking in its expensive, elusive decor; trying to get a sense of its owner, and failing. The pure, limpid notes of an artsong by Zaille suffused the quiet space. He looked back as the woman moved on into the room, gesturing at him to join her. In spite of himself he found that his eyes followed her every motion, perhaps because her sensuality was so at odds with who she was, or seemed to be.

"Would you like something to drink, Sergeant? Or something else—?"

"No," he said, "thank you."

She looked back at him. "Is that against regulations? Or just personal preference?"

"Both," he said, a little abruptly.

Amused, she gestured him toward a seat.

Annoyed, he sat on the couch.

She sat down across from him, in a chair wide enough for two, and set an oval cup made of violet glass on the low table between them. He couldn't tell what the cup held. She drew her feet in their soft city shoes up under the hem of her robe.

Her fingers played absently with the blood-red jewel she wore on a silken cord around her neck as she sat gazing back at him. The gem did not look like any stone he had ever seen, and yet an odd sense of déjà vu filled him, as if it was something he ought to recognize. . . .

He forced his eyes away from it. The chair the woman was sitting in had Old Empire lines. He thought suddenly of the novel he carried in a pocket of his uniform jacket, with its haunting images of that lost world and the somehow more-than-human ancestors who inhabited it. The world of Ilmarinen and Vanamoinen . . . the vanished world he had hoped to catch a glimpse of by coming to Carbuncle, only to be so profoundly disappointed by the city's reality.

He realized suddenly that the tension he had sensed in the room existed entirely inside his own mind: that it was a kind of surface tension, and that he was attempting to walk on water. . . .

"What was it you wanted to ask me about, Sergeant?" the woman said, reminding him that his silence had gone on for too long.

He looked away from her unnerving golden eyes. "This townhouse is leased to a Gestin Berdaz?"

"Yes." She nodded.

"And you live here?"

"Yes."

"With him?"

"No." She smiled. "Alone."

"And you are—?"

"His tenant. And his employee." She leaned forward. The jewel dangled between her breasts; he realized that her robe was open almost to her waist. "But I thought you wanted to ask me about Nyx LaisTree."

"Uh," he said, forcing himself to meet her eyes again, "I know that LaisTree came here today. I want to know why."

"He came to see me."

"For what reason?" He realized suddenly, with a

pang of disbelief, that he knew what she did here for Berdaz.

"He needed someone to talk to."

"Really," Gundhalinu said skeptically. "LaisTree has plenty of people he can talk to."

She picked up the violet cup and took a sip from it; held it in both hands as she leaned back in her seat again. "Do you mean the kind of people who would hound a man who nearly died until he wished that he was dead? Or the kind who tell a man who has amnesia that if he can't remember what happened to him, the deaths of his brother and a dozen other men are on his conscience? The kind who vandalize the apartment he'd shared with his brother while he's recovering in the hospital? The people who spy on him, and invade the privacy of anyone he even speaks to?" As she spoke her gold-flecked eyes, which seemed to miss nothing, passed judgment on him and found him wanting. "Are those the people you mean? People like you?"

"I assume LaisTree told you that." Gundhalinu let his mouth twist, trying to keep his tone cynical and not sullen as he added, "He probably neglected to mention that he and his brother, and the others with them, were all Police officers engaged in vandalizing private property when they were attacked."

She hesitated. "Are you saying two wrongs make a right, Gundhalinu-*eshkrad?*"

He felt himself flush. "No, *eshkrad*—" he said, habitually responding as one Technician to another; realizing as he did how skillfully she had avoided telling him even her name. "Those men didn't deserve to die. I didn't mean—" He looked down, trying to refocus his thoughts. "You said that someone vandalized his apartment?"

She nodded. "They tore it apart . . . as if they were

looking for something, he said. But surely you knew that."

"It wasn't the Police." He shook his head. *But could he really be sure of that?* "All the Police want," he said stubbornly, "is to catch the murderers. He must want that too. If someone searched his apartment, he should have reported it. There may be more to this crime, and the criminals, than he realizes. We want him to remember what happened that night because it could give us some new leads. We want the murderers brought to justice, that's all."

She looked searchingly into his eyes, but this time she didn't respond. She took another sip from the violet cup.

Gundhalinu got to his feet. "Is there anything else LaisTree said that might be of help with the case?"

"Only that he wanted to be able to remember. And that he wanted to be able to forget. . . ."

"What did he mean by that?"

"I would think you'd understand that better than most people, Sergeant," she said. "Weren't you also a survivor of the massacre?" She rose from her seat. "Don't look so surprised. It was in the news for days."

He nodded, looking away, all his momentum suddenly lost.

She came around the table, put a hand lightly on his arm. "And now I really must ask you to leave. I am expecting a guest." The scent of her perfume reminded him suddenly of a warm afternoon in the garden at the family's. . . . *No. It was his brother's estate now. He no longer had a family, or a home.*

He looked back at her, not really registering her presence, any more than he registered her words. When he didn't move or respond, she took his hand and attempted to lead him toward the door, as if he were a recalcitrant little boy.

He resisted, turning toward her as the jewel she wore caught the light. He reached out impulsively to lift it from the folds of her robe, felt her start as his fingers brushed her half-exposed flesh. "I'm sorry. I only meant—" But she moved forward before he could let it go again. She stood perfectly still and dangerously close to him, gazing back at him with eyes that still seemed to find his own brown eyes transparent.

"Where . . . where did you get this?" He forced himself to concentrate on the jewel, realizing as he did that it was not a gemstone at all, that it was not really any substance he could identify. *Except.* . . . "Is this an Old Empire artifact?"

Her hand rose as if she was going to take the jewel back from him; it dropped to her side again. "I don't know."

"I think it may be," he murmured, more to himself than to her.

"How can you tell?" She looked at it where it lay in his palm.

"Because it's not like anything else." He glanced up at her. "You get a feel for these things. . . . My mother excavates Old Empire ruins." He let it go, gently, his fingers barely contacting her skin, and watched it slide back into the hollow between her breasts. He breathed deeply, controlling a sudden, dizzying sense of arousal as he inhaled her perfume. "Where did you get it?"

"It was a gift."

"From whom?"

"From the Snow Queen."

Surprise caught him. "Where would she get a thing like that?"

"I have no idea."

"Why did she give it to you?" His gaze left her face

again for the spot where the jewel rested on her radiant skin.

"Use your imagination. . . ." He looked up, startled, and she smiled. "I see the Old Empire has you under its spell, Gundhalinu-*eshkrad*. You read about it—" Her hand touched his hip, the pocket of his coat, as if somehow her eyes could penetrate his clothing. "Do you dream about it . . . ?"

And before his eyes she began to change, her coolly perfect Technician features transforming until she was a woman from his even deeper fantasies, clad in stranger garments than he had ever seen, and the past enveloped her like perfume. . . .

"What—?" he whispered, before he lost his voice altogether, as the succubus of a long-vanished age pressed her ghostly lips to his, and took his breath away.

"No one is ever quite what they seem in Carbuncle, Sergeant Gundhalinu," she murmured, drawing back again. "Including you. Why are you following Nyx LaisTree? What do the Police really want from him?"

"I. . . ." He shook his head. "I can't tell you that. I don't know—" He pulled away from her and strode to the door. He opened it and went out, almost letting it close behind him without looking back—

He looked back. The woman stood motionless, watching him go . . . but she was Kharemoughi again, not a vision out of his dreams. Only the necklace remained unchanged.

He shut the door, and went on down the alley as quickly as he could without running. He had nearly reached the Street, and the waiting patrolcraft, before he let himself realize that she had been wearing a sensenet; that she was completely human, and perfectly ordinary, after all. . . .

* * *

Devony entered the Snow Queen's nacre-walled conference room and bowed. For once the room did not distract her, because Arienrhod was already there . . . and she was not alone.

The Ondinean woman who had been waiting before to see the Queen stood beside her now, like night beside day, dressed in the same pragmatic style that Devony remembered. Both the Ondinean's blue-violet gaze and the agate-eyed gaze of the Queen were fixed on her, measuring and more than a little curious.

She had come to the palace this time wearing the persona of a Winter clanswoman; she had not let herself think too much about why she had chosen a face so close to her own, even though the sensenet was not imaging her own face. She saw the Ondinean's glance catch on the Queen's necklace, which she was wearing too, as she had worn it every waking moment since Arienrhod had given it to her. "Your Majesty."

"Devony . . . you have more news." Arienrhod smiled her approval, and gestured at the woman beside her. "This is Mundilfoere; what you have to say may concern certain interests that we share. In any case, speak freely."

Devony glanced again at the Ondinean, made unexpectedly self-conscious by the other woman's silent appraisal. She looked back at Arienrhod. "Nyx LaisTree came to see me this afternoon."

"Did he?" Arienrhod's smile widened. "What did he want?"

"He wanted . . . someone to talk to."

Arienrhod exchanged a look with the Ondinean. "What did he want to talk to you about?"

Devony accessed her memory files and repeated

the conversation. The two women listened intently, neither smiling nor interrupting. And yet for the first time since she had begun to give information to the Queen, the words left a bitter taste in her mouth. She told herself it was the presence of a stranger that bothered her; that nothing she repeated here would harm Nyx LaisTree; that he would never even know how she had used his vulnerability, or violated his trust.

"And then he said . . . he said, 'I just want to remember. I just want to forget. . . .' " She touched the jewel in its cage of filament, suddenly too aware of its pressure against her throat.

The Queen and Mundilfoere exchanged glances again. "And . . . ?" Arienrhod murmured.

Devony felt herself flush, glad that her reaction was hidden from their sight.

"And that was the end of our conversation." Keeping the emotion out of her voice took more effort. She pressed on, before either woman could ask her anything further. "After he left, a Kharemoughi Police sergeant named Gundhalinu came and questioned me. The Police are watching LaisTree, following him . . . but I don't think he knows that." She realized what that implied only now, as she spoke the words.

"Sergeant Gundhalinu?" the Queen said. She made a small, amused noise. Devony looked at her in curiosity.

"He used to accompany Inspector PalaThion when she made her monthly reports to me. I know him." Arienrhod made a dismissive gesture, but Mundilfoere fixed Devony with a pensive stare that only worsened her discomfort.

"What kind of questions did he ask?" Arienrhod said.

Devony repeated their conversation. The tendrils of her unease grew as she saw the change that came over each woman's face when she said, "And then he asked me about the necklace—the one you gave me."

Mundilfoere leaned forward. "What did he say about it?"

"That it looked like Old Empire technology. He asked who gave it to me."

"Did you tell him?"

"Yes. Was that wrong—?" she asked, suddenly doubting her judgment about everything she had said and done since she entered the room.

"No," Mundilfoere said. "No, that was exactly the right thing to say." She leaned over and murmured something to the Queen.

Arienrhod smiled faintly. "Devony, I want you to let me know as soon as LaisTree regains his memory. I want to know everything he says."

"Why?" Devony asked. Her voice echoed in the sudden silence. She looked down in confusion and embarrassment. "I mean . . . I'm sorry, Your Majesty—"

"He may have information about something that belongs to me." The Queen waved aside Devony's stumbling apology. "Something that disappeared on the night of the warehouse massacre."

Devony looked up in surprise. She swallowed the question already forming on her lips. *If Arienrhod wanted her to know more about it, Arienrhod would have told her.* "But I'm not even certain that he's coming back, Your Majesty."

The Queen smiled. "He'll come back. If you want them to badly enough, they always do."

Devony glanced down again, not sure of whom the Queen was speaking, or if she was simply speaking in generalities.

"Thank you, Devony." Arienrhod nodded in dismissal.

As she began to turn away, Mundilfoere said, "Wait."

Devony turned back.

"Change," Mundilfoere said. "I want to see you change, before you go."

Surprised again, Devony subvocalized instructions to her sensenet's CPU. She watched as the change spread up her hands and arms in a rippling wave, until her skin was the exact shade of the Ondinean's—knowing, without needing to see it, that her face had transformed into the perfect image of Mundilfoere's.

Mundilfoere stared at her with amused fascination. "Very impressive. . . ." she said. "Thank you."

Devony bowed, already becoming an anonymous Winter clanswoman again. She left the room, and the palace, as quickly as she dared.

11

Tree shut down the port and rubbed his eyes, fighting the urge to rip the layer of bandageskin from his itching face.

If only he knew half what Staun had known—about data searches, or about human nature—he would have found his key by now. But he didn't even know what he was looking at, any more, let alone what he was looking for. . . .

He got up slowly, stretched tentatively, trying to ease the tightness of his muscles—gasped and doubled over as the movement impaled him on a red-hot spear of agony. He leaned on the desktop, swearing helplessly until the worst of it passed.

Pressing his arm against his side, he shuffled out of the office and back down the hall. He stopped at the dispatch desk, where KraiVieux was still on duty.

"How did it go?" KraiVieux glanced up from the

report he was inputting on his terminal. "Did you find anything that helped you?"

"I don't know." Tree shook his head. The more he studied the data, the less sense it seemed to make . . . the less he understood why Jashari had put him through an emotional hell to match his physical one. The circumstantial evidence said he'd never even seen what hit them; and that none of them had been guilty of anything more than common vandalism. "I can't . . ."

"Go home. Sleep on it," KraiVieux said gently. "Ye gods, Tree, I don't know what the hell you're doing out of bed at all."

"I'm fine."

"You're a walking wound. I took the liberty of checking your medical records—" KraiVieux gestured at the screen as Tree frowned. "Nisha's cooked up a pot of tapola for you; it'll do you good. I'll send somebody over with it tomorrow. Meanwhile, for the love of All Saints, just get some rest."

Tree looked down, nodding. "Thanks, Sarge." He left the dispatch desk, heading for the exit; he tried not to limp too badly where the others could see him.

"Take it easy, boy," KraiVieux called after him. "It'll all come out in the wash."

Tree looked back over his shoulder. *Unless it's a whitewash—*

He staggered as a chink in the wall of his inner vision suddenly opened on the monstrous, bloody-eyed face of Truth, and it struck him blind.

A cold flood of panic swept through him, sweeping his vision clear. Shaken, dazed, he reached for the double doors, for the way out—

"Hey, LaisTree." Someone caught his arm, pulling him back around. "Congratulations!"

He found himself staring at TierPardée. "What—?" he said stupidly. "For what?"

"Getting that bloodsucker Jashari off your back. Getting out of the hospital. How come you didn't call anybody?"

"Sorry," he muttered. "I just . . . couldn't. I—" He looked down at TierPardée's uniform, waved a hand at his own clothes.

"Look, that's okay," TierPardée said, easing off. "We're just glad you're out . . . you know. Come on down to the rec room. We got some major new entertainment that'll cheer you up."

Tree shook his head, groping for an excuse that would let him refuse; he was too stupefied even to think about a drunken evening of playing interactives in the rec room. But all his burned-out brain would give him was the memory of his apartment: empty, wreckage-strewn, haunted by his brother's unshriven ghost. "Sure," he mumbled. "Sounds good."

He let TierPardée lead him down the hall to the room set aside for social gatherings, and endured the noisy welcome of the off-duty Blues already there. He was relieved to see that they were all Newhaveners. The Kharemoughis tended to go to the Survey Hall further down the Street. There was something about Kharemoughis and Survey: they acted as if they'd invented it, and maybe they had—it was dull enough, from what he'd seen.

From what he'd seen . . . he'd seen something . . . he knew something, about Survey, and Kharemoughis. . . .

"Shit!" He pressed the heels of his hands against his eyes, as memories flickered like heat lightning at the borders of his consciousness.

"Tree, you all right—?"

"—you okay?"

"You need something—?"

He blinked the room and its occupants back into focus, shaking his head. "Just need to sit down. . . ."

Abruptly he found himself in a chair, and somebody was passing him a bowl of fried rinds. He stuffed a handful into his mouth, chewing, swallowing. He couldn't remember the last time he'd eaten anything.

He sat eating rinds and drinking hot, overbrewed tea, watching from a distance that had nothing to do with the size of the room as the others unloaded a crate of new interactive gear.

He felt his curiosity stir as he satisfied his hunger, and saw them unpacking headsets, gloves . . . other equipment a lot more expensive and sophisticated than anything he was used to seeing, or using.

And yet he *had* seen gear like that somewhere, recently. Not here, and not at someone else's place . . . not even at a gaming hell in the Maze, because he never went into those places off-duty anymore; it had always cost him too much of his pay—

"What the hell is this thing?" someone asked, holding up a cobweb of filament. "Some kind of jerkoff device?" Laughter.

"That is a piece of shit," TierPardée announced. "Doesn't interface with any system I've *ever* seen. RigaNaren, you never took that back to the storeroom, like I told you?"

"No. You just said to forget about it."

"Pardée?" Tree pushed up out of his seat. "Where did you get this stuff? You got this from the storeroom? Is this evidence from the warehouse massacre—?" The others turned to look at him as he crossed the room toward them. He saw them glance at each other, heard somebody mutter "Fuck. . . ."

"Tree—" TierPardée intersected his trajectory, slowing him down. "Ye gods, I didn't realize . . . it was just seized contraband; you know we borrow that stuff from the storeroom all the time. We never stopped to think that maybe it was—"

"—from the massacre?" Tree felt his disbelief curdle into fury. "You sons of bitches!" he shouted, shoving his way forward. TierPardée caught him again, keeping him away from the crate of equipment. "What the hell do you think you're doing with that? Did you remember to wipe off the blood before you used it? Was the blood still *wet?*"

"Tree, take it easy, for gods' sakes," TierPardée said desperately, as two other men grabbed Tree's arms, trying to hold him back.

Tree wrenched free, driven by the goad of his pain. He elbowed his way through the men who were hastily throwing contraband gear back into the crate. "Get your fucking hands off that." He picked up the unidentifiable piece of mesh from the tabletop, and tried to toss it into the box. It clung to his hand like cobweb, until finally he stuffed it into his pocket. Clutching the fabric of his jacket he pulled his hand free, swearing. He picked up the box, shoved his way back through the ring of embarrassed and guilt-stricken faces, and left the room.

He took the crate through the halls directly to the storage annex. As he entered the check-in area he saw someone already waiting there, a Kharemoughi sergeant.

The other man glanced up as he dropped the crate heavily on the counter.

"Gundhalinu—?" Tree felt the resentment and unforgiving grief inside him harden into a knot of hatred. "What are you doing here?"

Gundhalinu looked at the box on the counter, and back at him. "I could ask you the same thing, Lais-Tree," he said, his eyes filling with suspicion. "And with a lot more reason." He reached for the crate.

Tree blocked his motion, shoving the crate out of Gundhalinu's reach. "KindaSul!" he shouted. The property clerk's name echoed and reechoed through the high-ceilinged storeroom.

"Keep your shirt on!" an aggrieved voice bellowed, from somewhere deep in the interior.

"Move aside," Gundhalinu said, his eyes cold. "I want to look at what's in that crate." He stepped forward.

"Get out of my face, Tech." Tree shoved him back.

"Hey! Hey—" KindaSul emerged from the storage area and laid claim to the crate. "What do you think you're doing? You damage any evidence, I'll throw you both in a cell. Together!" He leaned across the counter, glaring at them.

Gundhalinu subsided and backed off; he looked relieved.

Tree shook out his fists, propped his shaking body against the edge of the counter. "Try keeping this locked up, instead." He jerked his head at the crate of equipment.

"What is this?" KindaSul asked, frowning.

"And what are *you* doing with it?" Gundhalinu added sourly.

"It's part of the contraband seized at the warehouse massacre." Tree kept his voice steady and his gaze fixed on KindaSul. "It was in the rec room."

"The rec room?" Gundhalinu repeated, in disbelief. "For how long?"

KindaSul took in Gundhalinu's expression, and turned back to Tree. His annoyance was visible. "Didn't happen while I was on duty," he said.

"Give me that container." Gundhalinu reached for the crate.

KindaSul shoved it at him without comment. Gundhalinu tipped it on its side and began to empty it out like a man digging for treasure.

"You lose something?" KindaSul asked.

"Yes," Gundhalinu murmured. "Something I saw at the warehouse that night. I know it went in with the rest of the evidence, but it wasn't catalogued in the files." He dumped out the last of the interactive gear, swearing under his breath. He hit the empty crate with his hand. "This is everything?"

Tree nodded, meeting his stare. "What was it you saw?"

Gundhalinu hesitated, looked back at KindaSul. "A piece of meshwork. It looked like it could be a head-set, but nothing like these—" He waved at the equipment strewn across the counter.

Tree slid his hand into his pocket, touched the alien texture of the mesh he had picked up from the rec-room table. "What's so important about it?"

Gundhalinu's mouth thinned. "Whether it's important or not, it's no business of yours, LaisTree. You're off the force."

"Suspended. It's temporary—"

"Don't bet on that." Gundhalinu turned back to the property clerk.

Tree listened as Gundhalinu began to question KindaSul about missing equipment. Then, pushing the mesh deeper into his pocket, he left the room.

Devony entered her townhouse, struggling with the armload of bundles she carried as she made her way through the living room and into the first bedroom off the hall. She dropped the half-dozen packages onto the bed, with a sigh that was more weary than satisfied.

Hearing the sigh, she forced herself to smile, out

of habit; her hand moved unthinkingly toward the
drawer of the bedside table. Rummaging through its
assortment of drugs, she found a mood-enhancing
neurotransmitter and inhaled a dose.

She tore open the wrappings of her parcels with
more force than necessary, spreading out her purchases on the satin bedcovering: the stunning vase
that had caught her eye in the window of an expensive import shop . . . the rainbow array of clothes with
their sensual textures and sophisticated design . . . all
the things that she could never get enough of, and
that the offworlders seemed to have in endless supply.

A trip through the Maze always made her senses
sing, always distracted her from her moods, no matter
how difficult or unnerving the day had been. An armload of offworld treasures could fill the empty places
inside her just as easily as they had filled the empty
spaces of this townhouse. . . .

She imagined the faces of the family she had left
behind when she had run away to Carbuncle, tried
to picture their expressions if she were to bundle up
these purchases and ship them to the outback. She
wondered fleetingly whether a single person in her
family—in their entire community—would feel his or
her imagination begin to stir. Whether anyone might
question, for even a moment, the way they had always
lived . . . the traditions that had denied her every
yearning, and punished her every dream.

But, no. Any reminder that a Hegemonic presence
even existed on their world would be met with viru-
lent hatred of the Other—fear of the alien, even in
human form. Generation after generation they had
followed the same bitter, self-defeating way of life,
clinging to traditions that were old when the Snow
Queen had been young. Because to do anything
else—to accept the Change—was to admit that all the

hardship and the suffering they had endured, generation upon generation, had been pointless. . . .

Arienrhod had embraced the Change, instead; had made herself its Queen. Her love affair with the technology the offworlders brought back with them had only grown stronger over time . . . while time stood still in the outback.

No one there would even think of changing now; because they believed that within their lifetime, it would all change back. Already the even more ignorant and superstitious Summer clans were beginning to arrive in the north, ready to take the place of the offworlders who would abandon the city, and their world, at the Departure. High Summer would prove to her people that they had been right all along; prove the futility of everything Devony had ever believed, or tried to make of her life.

Except that this time, the Snow Queen was going to prove them wrong.

The Queen had chosen to remake her own future, just as Devony had. And Devony would do anything in her power to help the Queen ensure that their chosen vision remained intact. Arienrhod was changing the rules, by changing the Change. And Devony refused to regret anything she had done to help make that vision a reality. . . .

She opened the doors of the wardrobe beside the bed, exposing its mirrors; stood in front of them, trying on one piece of clothing after another . . . a bare slip of a dress, a clinging wrapshirt, flowing silken pants. . . .

Wearing each of them, she changed the shade of her skin, the style and color of her hair, sometimes even the details of the clothes themselves, until she had chosen which of her faces suited each outfit the best.

And then, one after another, she tossed the pieces of clothing aside onto the bed, feeling the excitement of the new pall more rapidly with each outfit she tried on.

Because what difference did it really make what she wore—? She could shave her head and go naked: the sensenet would still transform her into whatever object of fantasy a would-be lover desired.

She put on a shapeless robe and stood before the mirror again, letting her image morph at random, watching her features dissolve and re-form endlessly into the face of one stranger after another.

With an unspoken word, she canceled the program; the illusion faded. She stared at her own face as if it were a stranger's. . . . *Because it was a stranger's.*

Abruptly she turned away. Lifting the vase from the yielding surface of the bed, she ran her hands over it, experiencing the fluid texture of a material she had never even heard of until today.

And then, with another, smaller sigh, she carried the vase back into the living room. The bouquet she had found on her doorstep earlier, along with an invitation to late dinner, still lay on the empty side table where she had abandoned it. With painstaking care, she arranged the fresh flowers and exotic rill feathers in the newly purchased vase. The bouquet was from a successful Newhavenese trade broker who had called on her several times in the past. She knew it would flatter his considerable ego to see his gift so prominently displayed.

The broker was full of amusing tales about bizarre cargo mixups and cultural miscommunications, once she distracted him from his obsession with interstellar shipping schedules. And he always showed plenty of enthusiasm in the bedroom. At least seeing him would take her mind off the unexpected events of this odd day: her unsettling encounter with the Queen and Mundilfoere . . . and with Nyx LaisTree.

Where was LaisTree now . . . what was he doing? Was he all right? What if something she said—

She set the vase down abruptly on the side table, not even sparing a backward glance to check its placement. With sudden impatience, she ordered the house system to change the music that was playing. She frowned and changed the music again, then canceled it entirely.

She poured the false water of life into a ruby goblet; left a ring of silver fluid on the surface of the table as she heedlessly filled the cup to overflowing, and then half-emptied it with one draught. She took a spicestick out of the jeweled box that reeked of the herb's exotic scent, lit it and inhaled the drugged fumes deeply.

She carried the goblet and incense across the room, set them on the table next to her before she curled up, alone, on the couch that she had shared with Nyx LaisTree earlier in the day . . . where, as she had carefully removed his clothing, she had witnessed the full extent of his ordeal: all the colors of pain made visible on his bruised flesh; the coolly deceptive expanses of bandage that had replaced the human warmth of his skin.

He had seemed as surprised as she was by the unexpected passion of the lovemaking that followed— as if, after his narrow escape from the embrace of Death, his body had rediscovered the sheer joy of being alive. . . .

She took another long drink from the goblet and ran her hand over her arm, its tracery of embedded filaments—the armor of illusion she had taken on so eagerly when Berdaz had offered it to her, to replace her own feeble defenses of sheer attitude.

Her clients came to her now like tourists, strangers who paid to explore their most intimate erotic landscapes projected on the screen of her living body. And like tourists, they went away still strangers, taking with them whatever memories fulfilled their voyeuristic desires; rarely leaving a trace even of regret when they were gone.

She could not remember ever looking into another human being's eyes without experiencing a head-on collision, a dead end, a wall. The sensenet had given her a far more effective way to protect the naked, defenseless creature she had been when she first came to the city—that she had always been, she realized, from the day she was born. But it had not, could not ever change what she found in another person's eyes.

She wondered why it had never occurred to her before how much a fortress was like a prison.

She set the goblet back on the table, watched its viscous, silver contents settle: an intimation of mortality, an imitation of life. She remembered gazing unseen into Nyx LaisTree's eyes as he stood on her doorstep today, seeing his expression unwittingly laid bare on the screen of her townhouse's security system. She retraced in her mind the random acts of compassion and violence that had brought him to her door.

He had come here out of simple human need, nothing more. And she had let him in, because for once she had looked into a stranger's eyes, and seen. . . .

No. Stop it! She picked up the ruby goblet, swallowed what remained of the false water of life as if it were a dose of poison. Its deceptive rush swept through her body like a purifying wind. Nyx LaisTree was only one more stranger: a charity case, a favor repaid at best. No more. *She would be like Arienrhod. She would regret nothing—*

The fingers of her empty hands twined together, like lovers in an embrace, as she sat gazing out into the empty silence of the room.

12

Gundhalinu entered the familiar surroundings of the Survey Hall and paused, searching the room with a long glance. At the station house they had told him he would find the Chief Inspector here. He spotted Aranne beside the food-and-drink dispensers on the far side of the hall, along with the Police Commander and two Judiciate officers, one of whom was Jashari. Other Police and government officials, most of them Kharemoughis, were scattered throughout the room, along with a few offworlders— presumably legitimate traders, if they didn't mind sharing space with so many representatives of Hegemonic law.

He made his way through the obstacle course of settees, padded benches, and game tables; saw the officials around Aranne look up as he approached.

"Gundhalinu-*eshkrad*," Aranne said, addressing him

simply as a Technician, because Survey tradition required that its members maintain a semblance of equality within its halls.

"Aranne-*eshkrad*." Gundhalinu nodded, and acknowledged the other men in turn.

"It's good to see that you've made a full recovery, Gundhalinu-*eshkrad*," LiouxSked said. The Police Commander did everything possible, short of having himself wired into a sensenet, to act and speak like a born Kharemoughi; it was probably why he had achieved the rank he had. But Gundhalinu still found it disconcerting when a Newhavener addressed him as a fellow Technician.

"Thank you, LiouxSked-*eshkrad*." He managed to answer with proper courtesy, not bothering to add that he doubted he would ever have a night's sleep again when he didn't wake in a cold sweat out of a nightmare more vivid than life. "Aranne-*eshkrad*, I need to speak with you."

"Excuse us for a moment, if you will." Aranne left the others and led him to a corner of the hall occupied only by curio cabinets and shelves. Gundhalinu's eyes scanned the beautiful, odd, and uncategorizable souvenirs that had been deposited there by visitors from all over the Hegemony, throughout the nearly one hundred and fifty years of the Hegemonic occupation. At this point, there were similar displays all around the hall.

"Is this about LaisTree?" Aranne asked. "Where is he now?"

"He's gone to see a woman," Gundhalinu said, "who may have ties to the Source."

"Who is she?"

Gundhalinu glanced down, remembering her face ... *her faces.* "I—I'm not sure. But I know she works for a Samathan vicemonger named Berdaz, as a shapeshifter, and I know that she lives in Azure Alley. Berdaz gets his operating money, and anything else he needs, through the Source. LaisTree spent several hours at her place earlier today; he just went there again. I doubt he'll leave before morning." He felt an unexpected twinge of envy, and blamed it on fatigue.

Aranne nodded. "All right. Anything else?"

"Yes, sir. I questioned the woman this afternoon. I didn't learn much, but I did notice one thing that was unusual: she was wearing a necklace that looked like an Old Empire artifact. She said the Queen had given it to her—"

"The Queen?" Aranne said, frowning. "Why?"

"She wouldn't tell me." Gundhalinu looked away. "But that made me remember something else, something from the warehouse crime scene. One of the men collecting evidence that night asked me about a piece of gear they'd found; they didn't know what it was. I didn't even make the connection until I saw the necklace, and then having it linked to Arienrhod reminded me. . . ." He stared at the mute, fantastic forms trapped behind glass within a curio case. "The object I saw at the crime scene was either Old Empire technology, or based on it. Could that have been part of the missing tech?"

"The missing prototype is not with the evidence," Aranne said flatly. "We checked everything thoroughly."

"Yes, sir—everything that was in the storage annex. But there were other things from the crime scene that never even got entered in the system."

"What?" Aranne said, incredulous.

"I went down to the annex tonight to take another look, and LaisTree walked in with a crateful of contraband interactive gear that had been diverted to the rec room—"

"LaisTree?"

"Yes, sir."

"Father of all my grandfathers!" Aranne glanced toward the other officers still conversing across the hall. "How the hell did that happen?"

"Apparently it's ... quite common, sir." Gundhalinu felt his mouth pull down. "According to Sergeant KindaSul, who was on duty tonight, the men—Newhaveners, I'm sure, not Kharemoughis—frequently 'borrow' confiscated goods for recreational use. He says they get bored. . . ." He shook his head.

"Gods!" Aranne muttered. "You searched the crate of evidence LaisTree brought in, I assume."

"I did. The headset that I remember seeing wasn't in it."

"Headset?" Aranne looked back at him. "How did you know it was a headset?"

"Well, I didn't, exactly, sir." He looked down, made abruptly uncomfortable by Aranne's stare. "That was just what it looked like: a kind of mesh alloy that seemed almost ... alive, somehow." He shook his hand, shaking off the memory of how it had clung to his fingers.

Aranne was still looking at him with an expression he couldn't really be certain was disbelief.

"I thought, since the missing tech was related to artificial-intelligence research—" He shrugged. "It was only an educated guess, sir."

"A very perceptive one nonetheless, Sergeant," Aranne murmured, looking toward Jashari again. "You said it wasn't with the equipment LaisTree brought back?"

"No. But it made me wonder whether there might be other 'misplaced' evidence out there somewhere."

"Or perhaps LaisTree took it out of the box before he turned the rest in." Aranne's expression darkened.

"How did he seem? Is it possible that he did find the object and it triggered his memory?"

Gundhalinu swore under his breath, wondering why that had not occurred to him immediately. But nothing had struck him as evasive, or even particularly unusual, about LaisTree's behavior. He looked up again, shaking his head. "No, sir. If he had found the thing, he'd never have brought the rest of the equipment back himself. He's not smart enough to be that devious. In any case, the other men should be questioned about it—and reprimanded."

"Obviously," Aranne said. "So that brings us back to this mystery woman, whom LaisTree has already visited twice, you said?"

Gundhalinu nodded.

"I'll have her picked up. Jashari will want her for questioning."

Gundhalinu looked toward Jashari. The Special Investigator's gunmetal gaze shifted abruptly, and caught him staring. Gundhalinu looked down. "Sir," he murmured, turning back to Aranne, "I strongly urge you to reconsider."

Aranne looked at him in surprise. "Why?"

Gundhalinu kept his face expressionless for a long moment, as he struggled to find an acceptable alternative to the truth. "Because . . . I think we'll learn more if we leave her alone. She's obviously someone significant to LaisTree; simply letting them interact could be productive in helping him regain his memory. And her sensenet will be easy to trace. If I keep a record of her movements, as I'm doing with LaisTree's, we'll know who her other contacts are."

"Hm." Aranne nodded. "That's a good point, Gundhalinu. All right. . . . We'll leave her where she is for now."

"Thank you, sir." Gundhalinu smiled briefly.

"LaisTree went to his apartment before he headed back to her place tonight. Maybe I should check it out again, while he's not there."

"Again?" Aranne said.

"Then the Police did not search his apartment, while he was in the hospital?"

"No." Aranne looked hard at him. "He had no opportunity to hide anything from the warehouse there."

"I was told someone searched the place. . . . It must have been the Source's people."

"Then I suppose it's our turn." Aranne nodded. "Give it your best effort, Gundhalinu."

"Yes, sir," he said. "I will."

Jashari came to join Aranne where he stood watching Gundhalinu exit the hall. "What news did he have? Was that about LaisTree?"

Aranne nodded. "LaisTree's involved with a woman, a shapeshifter, which ties him to the Source, at least indirectly."

"Are you familiar with the so-called 'six degrees of separation,' milords . . . ?" A female voice reached them seemingly out of the air, along with the faint sound of chiming bells, and the exotic, erotic perfume of scented oils. "Each one of us is no more than six steps removed, in some way, from any other human being . . . or so they say. What sort of random conclusions may be drawn from such incidental proximities, do you suppose?"

The two men turned to face the veiled woman emerging like a whisper from a shadowed doorway.

"What are you suggesting—" Jashari's expression darkened, "Mundilfoere? That LaisTree's visiting this woman today was a coincidence?"

"No, Special Investigator. Only that a room awaits us, like our destinies, in which we may discuss these matters more . . . intimately." She gestured down the hallway from which she had emerged, toward meeting rooms whose actual degree of privacy depended entirely on the level of hidden influence possessed by their occupants.

"You have a hell of a nerve," Aranne muttered, when they were safely within the confines of the chamber she had chosen, and all sitting cross-legged around a low table. The table's surface was inscribed with the pattern of a *tan* board, set up for the seemingly innocuous game that was not simply a game, any more than Survey was simply Survey: *Tan* was as much a key to, and a reminder of, the Great Game in which they had previously been opposing players and were now, unexpectedly, allies.

Aranne scooped up the gaming pieces, scattered them across the board. "And who has called this fellowship into being," he recited, observing the pattern made by the fall of stones, "and given us our duty, and shown us the power of knowledge?"

"Mede." Mundilfoere answered with the name of the third secret Founder of Survey, the only woman. She studied the game pieces, gathered them in and tossed them out again.

Jashari swept up the stones before she could speak the next question; before the game pieces had even finished forming their final pattern. "In the name of Mede, Ilmarinen, and Vanamoinen," he said impatiently, "I say we dispense with the ritual pleasantries. We all know why we're here." Ignoring Aranne's annoyed frown and Mundilfoere's sharp, indrawn breath, he said, "What about LaisTree, and this woman . . . a shapeshifter, you said?"

Aranne nodded. "The only unexpected thing

LaisTree did today was go to see this woman—twice. I doubt he's seeing her professionally, on a patrolman's salary. She works for Berdaz, out of the Closed Doors Club, which ties her indirectly to the Source. And the club *was* the last place LaisTree was seen on the night of the warehouse raid."

"He never mentioned any woman to me." Jashari looked up, his gaze glacial. "Who is she?"

"You know how 'shifters are about their names. Gundhalinu couldn't get it out of her. But he said she lives in Azure Alley."

Jashari froze; Aranne saw something come into the other man's raptor eyes that made him want to look away.

"I know this woman you speak of," Mundilfoere murmured. The words were casual, dismissive, but the faint sound of bells marked her own speculative glance at Jashari. "Her ties to the Source are incidental, and extremely inconsequential. You should know, however, that she repeats everything she learns about her clients to the Snow Queen."

"Everything?" Jashari said. This time Aranne saw a subtle, telltale flush burn the Special Investigator's face.

"Everything," Mundilfoere repeated, and Aranne heard her smile. "The Queen's interests are quite eclectic. . . ." She shrugged, her bells singing. "At least that has been my experience of her."

Aranne stared at her, wishing fervently, not for the first time, that he could see her face clearly. He looked away again, with a sigh of resignation. "Well, that explains the jewelry, I suppose."

Looking back, he found them both staring at him. "Gundhalinu said the Queen had given the woman a necklace; but the woman wouldn't tell him why. He thought it might be—"

"Have her arrested." Jashari's fist tightened around the gaming pieces as though he wanted to crush them. "Arrest LaisTree, too. I want to question him again."

"No." Aranne shook his head. "I don't think that's a good idea." He felt a perverse satisfaction at the sight of Jashari's sudden frown. "Gundhalinu suggests that we simply leave them alone, and see where it leads."

"Gundhalinu?" Jashari's frown deepened. "Now you're taking orders from that boy—"

" 'That boy,' " Aranne cut him off, "may actually have seen the missing reader device, among evidence being gathered at the warehouse on the night of the massacre. He even recognized that it was some kind of headset."

"What?" Jashari said, incredulous. "They why don't we have it?"

"I'll explain later," Aranne muttered, acutely aware of Mundilfoere's all-too-attentive silence. "In any case, given your previous failure to get the answers we need from LaisTree, I think Gundhalinu has a point about leaving him and the woman alone. LaisTree's been through enough; I don't see how rearresting him and subjecting him to more interrogation will improve his memory."

"I agree with Aranne," Mundilfoere murmured. "They say the winding path is often the shortest route to a goal. . . . I will make certain that the Source does nothing to interfere with them."

Jashari nodded, with a grunt of acquiescence. "I can wait," he muttered. "Where is Gundhalinu now?"

"On a fool's errand," Aranne said sourly. "I sent him to search LaisTree's apartment; although according to him, someone else has already been there and taken it apart." He watched Jashari's face for a reaction, not seeing one this time. He looked again, with growing annoyance, at the woman who had thrown the fragile balance of the Golden Mean's power struggle with the Brotherhood into calculated chaos. He could tell nothing at all from observing Mundilfoere, who kept her real motives as veiled as her face.

It was Jashari who had first introduced Mundilfoere to him, and he knew Jashari's thoughts all too well by now. He didn't like the Special Investigator personally any more than he liked the work Jashari did for Internal Affairs—but they shared an allegience to Survey, which carried an authority even higher than the Hegemony's. He would do whatever was necessary to further Survey's goals, including cooperate with both Jashari and Mundilfoere. But when that higher authority forced him into situations like this one, the potential consequences did not weigh easily on him.

As Chief Inspector, he was responsible for the welfare of the men under his command. Every day he was reminded all too keenly that those men were human beings, forced to put their trust in him—even as he was forced to violate it. To Jashari, they meant less than the game pieces on a *tan* board: their flesh-and-blood bodies were merely the tools of Survey's elite, to be utilized as Survey saw fit in maintaining the ever-precarious balance of power in the Golden Mean's favor, in the Great Game. . . .

Survey was a single entity, and at the same time, a singular one. Like the hidden AI that controlled the sibyl network, Survey seemed to be everywhere at once, overseeing the work of countless hidden hands. But the hands more often than not appeared to be functioning in opposition to each other, rather than in accord—each splinter group drawing on Survey's far-flung resources, following the same secret path, but to their own selfish ends.

He had risen to a high enough level within Survey

that he was now at least aware that there were count-less levels still above him, mysteries within enigmas inside of conundrums that he would never live long enough to fully comprehend. But he had come to believe—perhaps out of his own personal need for meaning and order—that each splinter faction was manipulated by a higher Order in ways it never imag-ined, all of them subtly guided along their disparate paths toward a destiny that none of them were far-seeing enough ever to understand.

And he believed that ultimate goal involved knowl-edge that would be reinserted into the equation of Survey's existence once the missing artifact was re-covered . . . because the prize they sought to reclaim was nothing less than the brainscan of one of the long-dead Founders: Vanamoinen himself.

That an artificial-intelligence construct of someone who had lived so long ago still existed—was still viable, and complete with the reader device necessary to imprint it on the mind of a living human—was astonishing in itself. That the functional seed of Sur-vey's genius had reappeared, here, now—in Carbun-cle, of all places—only proved to him that the sibyl net's own artificial intelligence had chosen to reveal that crucial key specifically to the Golden Mean.

Among all Survey's multitudes, theirs was the fac-tion that had been chosen to replant the seed of the Old Empire's greatness, here and now. And whoever possessed Vanamoinen's brain would control an ava-tar of the greatest genius in recorded history . . . the one man who could help them re-create smartmatter, the nanotechnology on which the Old Empire's greatest technological advances had been based. Van-amoinen's knowledge could make real-time contact between the Pangalactic Interface's former member worlds more than a matter of random chance.

"Come the millennium" was a saying repeated end-lessly throughout the Hegemony—by which its citizens meant the return of the day when they would again have a viable faster-than-light stardrive and the freedom to explore the galaxy. Vanamoinen's consciousness, imprinted on the brain of the proper living human, could make that dream reality.

Aranne knew Mundilfoere was as aware of that fact as the Golden Mean was. She had admitted that she belonged to the Brotherhood—that she was here on Tiamat working with the Source to obtain Vanamoinen's brainscan, which the Golden Mean was equally committed to keeping out of their hands. The Brotherhood embraced Chaos—creating it, profiting from it. They were anathema to stability and progress, to everything the Golden Mean stood for. And right here, right now, the Golden Mean was the only group that could ensure the resurrected Vanamoinen was allowed to continue doing his work for the side of Order, as well as for the greater good of the Hegemony. . . . They had to succeed, no matter what the cost.

Mundilfoere had come to them, she claimed, because the cancerous spread of the Source's influence within the Brotherhood had become too much of a threat for her to tolerate. That she had turned against the Source, and also claimed to know enough about him to eventually deliver him into their hands, only proved she was as treacherous, and at least as dangerous, as the Source himself.

But they had reason to believe she might actually make good on that promise: it suited her needs to rid herself of the Source as competition. Beyond that, there was no more chance that she planned to let the Golden Mean have Vanamoinen's brainscan than that she might actually believe they trusted her.

But they had plans of their own, to match their suspicions. They were fully prepared to take her down, as ruthlessly and completely as they would destroy the Source himself once they were finally able to get at him . . . once she was no longer of use to them.

She was the one who had given them precise, detailed information about the clandestine meeting in which the Source's representatives were to acquire the missing artifact . . . because she herself had arranged the time and place. Her information had enabled the Golden Mean's core within the elite Police Special Operations unit to infiltrate the warehouse without detection, that fateful night—

—only to have LaisTree and the other vigilantes burst in on them, and turn a certain victory into a bloodbath.

The plan had seemed foolproof. But nothing was foolproof to a truly gifted bunch of fools.

And now, if Mundilfoere was to be believed, even she did not know what had become of the brainscan, or of the reader device—the headset Gundhalinu might actually have seen that night in the warehouse. And lacking either piece of the irreplaceable technology rendered the other part useless. Vanamoinen would be lost to them forever.

Which brought everything back, ultimately, to LaisTree. LaisTree was the answer. *He had to be,* even though the most sophisticated memory-retrieval therapy, and days of grueling interrogation, had failed to extract the truth from him. The promise of a grand future for the Hegemony, at the center of a renewed galaxy-wide empire, could not possibly be thwarted by one renegade patrolman, an ordinary street Blue who had turned vigilante, and then forgotten he had ever done it. . . .

*   *   *

Tree waited on the doorstep of Devony Seaward's apartment, his arms hugging his sides, no longer even trying to find a way of standing that would ease his pain. He had gone back to his apartment from the station house, just needing somewhere to lie down; sure that his exhaustion would let him sleep, even among the ruins of his life. . . .

He had been wrong.

The top half of the door opened. The Newhavenese beauty he had asked to dance on the night they met gazed out at him.

"Devony—?" He looked down, away from the eyes of the total stranger he unexpectedly confronted. "Did you mean it . . . ?" he mumbled, his own gaze fixed on the pavement. "You said that I could come back. If . . . if I needed . . ."

"Yes," she whispered.

He looked up. Devony the woman, not some skin-deep fantasy, was resting her head against the painted door frame; her face looked as soul-weary as his own. But as she opened the bottom half of the door, she leaned up to kiss him, and what he saw then in her eyes caught at his heart.

"I thought you might . . . have to work." He stumbled over the words as he entered, made awkward again by his surprise.

"I canceled my plans." She looked away this time. "I had things I needed to . . . think about." She put her arms around his hunched body, carefully supporting his weight; surprising him with her strength as she guided him across the room, past the couch they had shared this afternoon. She led him slowly up the stairs to a second-story bedroom.

Music filled the quiet space: it was a song he knew,

he realized, one he'd heard all over the city lately; he barely recognized it, played on native instruments. The bedding on the plain wooden bed was rumpled. He could see from the way the covers lay that she had been sleeping—or trying to sleep—alone. He glanced again at her fatigue-shadowed eyes as she shrugged off her robe and slipped under the blankets. He barely had the strength to pull his own clothes off before he lay down beside her.

She moved closer to him, until their bodies felt like one. He put his arms around her, comforted. "What were you thinking about?" he murmured.

"You," she said; he raised his head. "My life. My family." Her lips found the hollow of his temple in a kiss, as she avoided his eyes. "You were right. . . ."

Suddenly their bodies were no longer even touching.

She lay on her back, staring at the empty plane of the ceiling. Her voice when she spoke again was like the crying of sea birds, desolate and lost. "I hated my life, when I was a child . . . Everything about it was hard, and mean, and cold. The people were. The land sucked all the life out of them. That was what it cost, to keep a plantation alive in the outback. . . ."

She sat up abruptly, hugging her knees; the muscles in her arms knotted. "They treated me like I'd fallen out of the sky . . . like a freak. Like I was crazy. I *felt* like I was crazy. . . ." Her voice began to tremble. "And I was so *angry*, always, all the time—"

He stroked her hair, not speaking, only listening as her wounded words bled into the air: "They threw mud on me, for seeing shapes in the clouds. They locked me in the shed for days. They beat me, for pretending I was a mer, or an offworlder—or just for dancing by myself. . . . They kept trying to make me be like *them!* No one ever understood. No one ever wanted who *I* was—"

She held up her hand; its long, graceful fingers tightened into a fist. "Then, one day, I realized that Tiamat's seasons really were changing. Nothing my family did could stop them. The world didn't end at our fence. . . . So I ran away, to Carbuncle, where I could be anyone I wanted to be." Her fingers loosened again, and fell from the air. "Only, here no one cares. . . ."

"I do." He reached out, catching her hand as it fell. "I care who you are."

"I know," she whispered. She looked at him, and for a moment her expression was utterly lost. Then, at last, she lay down again, and turned her face to his. A single tear slid down her cheek as she moved into his arms. She kissed him on the mouth, tenderly and deeply.

"I do love this city," she murmured, as she drew away again. "It showed me that I *wasn't* wrong. It *was* them, all along. Carbuncle is so alive, so full of wonders—of minds that change and people who really are from beyond the sky. And I enjoy what I do." She bit her lip. "But I'd never go home again; not even if the Change meant I had to lose everything I have. I'd rather die. That place, that life, was like a wasting disease—"

"I know," Tree said.

She looked back at him again.

"My brother . . . my brother taught me about that. Staun hated how we lived, in Porttown. He joined the Police because he thought he'd found a way that he could really make things better—not just for us, for everybody. That was all he wanted: Not to look back and feel like he'd wasted his whole life. Not to . . .

not to live and die for . . . for no reason. . . ." He shut
his eyes.

Her arms went around him; he drew her closer.
They lay quietly, with no need for anything more, as
her heartbeat slowed and his thoughts grew formless.
As he drifted off to sleep, he was dimly aware of her
touching his bandaged face, his hair. . . .

Gundhalinu pressed the canceler to the lock of
LaisTree's apartment door and went inside. The
apartment's interior was dim, as if someone had
drawn most of the shades; he closed the door and
leaned against it, waiting while his eyes adjusted. The
smell of rotting food mingled with a miasma of unidentifiable odors, as if every container in the place
had been left open, or spilled.

Every possible container had. He went from room
to room, stunned by the thoroughness—the utter
ruthlessness—of whoever had searched the apartment before. Even the furniture had been torn open.
He stood in the hallway staring at the ruins of what
had been a common room . . . realizing that if he
were LaisTree, the last thing he would have done tonight would be to leave something important here. A
search this thorough was not a random incident; whoever had done it once would do it again, given the
slightest excuse.

Even LaisTree must suspect by now that there was
more than one faction involved in this conspiracy;
and that all of them knew where he lived.

Gundhalinu thought suddenly of his own apartment. He could barely stand to be there alone
now, and no one had raped his life while he was ab-
sent, the way some nameless thugs had done to

LaisTree. Small wonder LaisTree hadn't stayed here long tonight.

Gundhalinu looked down at his uniform, and wondered all at once why he was here, about to do the same thing. *Because you're a Police officer, damn it. It's your duty.* He sighed as he entered the common room, remembering that he had asked for this.

He began his search in the kitchen area, cleaning up spills and disposing of rotten food as he went along, to ease his conscience.

He had picked through barely half the mess in the common room when he heard the apartment door open. He straightened up and turned around, groping for an excuse even as his hand reached for his stunner. "LaisTree—" He started toward the entrance hall.

It was not LaisTree in the hall. An Ondinean woman stood there, dressed in dark coveralls, flanked by four armed men.

In the fractured moment of surprise before Gundhalinu raised his gun, one of the men fired. Gundhalinu collapsed in a heap on the floor, as his voluntary nervous system abruptly ceased to function. The Ondinean stood over him, smiling. "Hello, Sergeant," she said. "You're very young to be a stranger far from home. . . . I have some questions for you. I hope for your sake that you know the answers."

13

Tree woke to an empty bed in an unfamiliar room, and the smell of food cooking. He sat up, shaking his head clear as he looked toward the artificial morning of drawn-back drapes, and met Carbuncle's unsleeping eye. Reaching down for his pants, he inhaled the last dose of painkiller he found in a pocket, then began the slow painful process of facing another day. *Reality*, he thought, *was only the dream that let you take a piss when you really needed to.* . . .

He used the bathroom, then pulled on his pants and crossed stiffly to the window. He stood for a long time gazing down at the quiet alley, struggling to make sense out of yesterday, and last night, and the simple aroma of home-cooked food.

He turned away at last to finish dressing. Then he went downstairs, one step at a time, following the smell of food almost reluctantly—almost afraid to believe that the familiar routines of everyday life could still exist in his own permanently altered reality.

Devony sat in a small, plain kitchen at a small, plain table covered with platters of fried fish and steaming bowls of native foods. She looked up at him as he stood in the doorway. "No," she said, to his look. "I don't cook for them. And I didn't cook for you. . . . This is my breakfast." She ate another mouthful of gravy-soaked bread. "But sit down and don't act like a *shevatch*, and you can have some."

He laughed in disbelief as he squeezed into the cramped space across from her. *"Shevatch?* Me?" It was Klostan slang for an oversized male body part; in Miertoles Porttown it was either a compliment or an insult, depending on the context. He didn't need to ask which she meant.

There was enough food on the table for four people. He heaped some of everything into an empty bowl and began to eat. He had no idea what most of the foods were, but for once in his life that didn't bother him. Neither of them spoke again until all the platters and dishes were empty.

"You always eat like this?" he asked finally, propping the back of his chair against the wall.

She shook her head, with an amused smile. "No— almost never, anymore. I just missed it. . . ."

He grinned. "Glad I didn't miss it. It's *good!*"

She began to pile bowls onto platters. "Did you learn anything more yesterday? Did it help you to remember?"

His smile fell away. "Nothing there but more questions." He leaned forward again, trying to focus his thoughts. "The reports from the crime scene just don't add up, Dev. Damn it, there *has* to be something about what went down that night that I'm just not getting. And it's not locked in here. . . ." He touched his head, feeling his thoughts spiral down-ward like Carbuncle's Street. "But gods, I don't even know where to look, who to question. At Blue Alley, they're saying the streets are a dry well—"

Her expression changed. "Tree . . . did you know the Police are having you followed?"

"What?" He frowned.

She glanced down. "A sergeant named Gundhalinu came here yesterday, after you'd gone, to ask me questions about you."

"Gundhalinu?" He pushed to his feet. "That son of a bitch came here?"

She nodded.

"Did he threaten you, or hurt you? If he—"

"No." She smiled, shaking her head. "He was per-fectly *eshkrad*; he was almost sweet in a way. . . . But when I tried to find out who sent him, he said he couldn't tell me—"

Tree's frown faded. "Couldn't . . . not wouldn't?"

She nodded again.

"What did he ask you?"

"Why you'd come here. He also asked about my necklace. He said it looked like an Old Empire arti-fact." She fingered the jewel she was wearing even now. "But maybe that was an innocent question."

"Not with him." Tree rubbed his arms, scratched irritably at the bandages, and winced. "I ran into him last night, at the station house. Maybe that wasn't a coincidence either; he was asking about something that looked like Old Empire tech then, too."

"What was it?"

"I don't know." He shrugged. "Gundhalinu called it some kind of headset. And he *wants* it . . . gods, I saw it in his eyes." Suddenly seeing their encounter in parallax view, he realized that its true form might have been far different than he had imagined. "That brass-kissing prick knows something I don't . . . but at least now I know who to question next." He leaned across the table impulsively and kissed her on the mouth.

"Be careful," she murmured. Her fingers rose to her lips, lingered there, as if she were touching him.

"Count on it," he said.

Hours later, deep in heart of the Maze, Tree reached Citron Alley and started down it. He looked left and right, his sense of futility growing stronger as he searched the haphazard building fronts for any sign of an address. Unlike the Upper City, the Maze cared nothing about appearances; but in its own perverse way, it was just as indifferent to whether or not anyone found what they were looking for.

He had already been to Blue Alley, and to Gundhalinu's apartment building. No one at either place had seen Gundhalinu since yesterday. Coming here was a long shot, but KraiVieux had told him that Gundhalinu looked in on Jerusha PalaThion every day, to see if she needed anything while she convalesced.

If his luck continued to run like it had, he'd never even find her apartment. And even if he did, it would be a miracle if she didn't throw him down the stairs—

Gods, what was he doing here? His footsteps slowed. *How could he even face her, now that she knew everything . . . and probably blamed him for all of it?* He stopped, suddenly unable to force his spent, aching body to do anything but turn around in its tracks.

He stumbled as something gray and sinuous slipped between his ankles; it squalled as he stepped on it. Swearing furiously, he saw the gray cat bolt back onto a nearby doorstep.

"Goddamn it—!" He broke off as he saw the middle-aged Tiamatan woman sitting on the stoop among trays of bright-colored beads and trims.

"Malkin!" she cried, trying to catch the aggrieved cat, which was now making chaos out of her assorted decorations. "Are you all right?"

Tree started back down the alley toward the Street, his fists clenched, cursing under his breath with pain and disgust.

"Are you all right—?" the woman called out again, more loudly.

He stopped, and looked back. "You mean me?" he asked.

"Well, yes, of course I did." The woman was trying to clear off her spread skirts, which were covered with whatever she had been making, or selling. Her face was filled with concern as she began to get up, but the gaze she fixed on him was oddly lifeless.

Blind. He realized the obvious belatedly, as he spotted the imported vision sensor she wore like a headband. "Don't get up." He waved his hand, coming back to her doorstep.

"I'm so sorry," the woman said, holding onto the cat; he saw how she clung to the animal, stroking its fur, more to reassure herself than her pet. "He's such a nuisance; he assumes that everyone who passes is coming to see us." She smiled apologetically. "I am Fate, after all."

"I should've watched where I was going," Tree muttered. ". . . Did you say, you're *Fate?*" His fingers made an unconscious warding sign, even as he glanced up and saw the sign on the wall beside her door: FATE RAVENGLASS, MASKMAKER. "Oh. You mean, that's your name."

"A blessing, and a curse. . . ." She laughed. "I was

born in a Festival year; we're always given 'meaning-ful' names, you know."

He didn't, but he nodded to be polite. "It's no worse than being called 'Tree,' I guess."

"You're limping, Tree . . . did you hurt your leg?"

"Yeah." He grimaced, hoping it would pass for a smile, at least to a woman who was half-blind. "But that's not your cat's fault." He leaned down to scratch the cat under its chin in apology, and saw the mask the woman had been working on. Half of the face was patterned with textures and colors as vibrant as the Maze itself; the other half was blank, empty, a void. . . .

"By the Boatman—!" He swore by the older, darker Newhavenese god who still ruled the lives of the street Blues, as he jerked back from the mask's vacant stare.

"It isn't finished yet," Fate said, peering up at him with her own dim, vacant eyes. "It will look so differ-ent then. If you could only see the whole pattern. . . ." She gestured helplessly.

"I *know*, damn it, I—" He broke off, forcing himself to remember that she was a complete stranger, and that she had no more idea of all he had been through than she did of why he was standing here. "I'm sorry, I didn't. . . . You do beautiful work. Really. I can see that." The subtlety of what she had created was almost as remarkable as the fact that she had done it at all. The kind of cheap vision-sensor she wore was barely enough to let most people find their way to the door. She must construct her masks by instinct and touch, as much as by sight. He wondered who she made them for. As far as he knew, Tiamatans didn't throw a lot of costume parties.

"You were looking for Inspector PalaThion, weren't you?"

"How the hell did you know that—?"

"Your accent." She smiled. "Other Police officers have been by here lately, bringing work to her while she recovers from her injuries."

"Oh." They both heard his sigh of relief.

Fate's smile widened. "The Inspector's apartment is upstairs over the import shop; it's the fourth doorway in from the storm wall. I know she'll be glad to see you."

He didn't answer, thinking the day the Warrior Nun was glad to see him would be the day she saw him in hell. "Thanks," he managed to say. "Nice meeting you, Fate." He headed on down the alley.

Jerusha PalaThion's apartment was just where the maskmaker had said it would be. Gritting his teeth, he climbed the flight of stairs, each step requiring more effort than the last. He rested for a long moment on the landing, until the pain in his side had eased enough to let him breathe again.

Facing PalaThion's apartment door at last, he took a deep breath, and knocked.

The door opened. PalaThion stood there, wearing a long, patterned caftan and a frown. He stared, unused to seeing her in anything other than a uniform—abruptly and disconcertingly reminded that she really was female, and not much older than his brother had been.

She stared back at him as if he were a total stranger. "Yes?"

He remembered that he wasn't wearing a uniform either, and looked like a mugging victim. "Officer LaisTree, Inspector." He straightened his shoulders, barely remembering not to salute. "Currently suspended from duty." He looked down, and let his protesting body slump back into the posture of a man who had recently had his guts restrung.

"LaisTree—" Surprise bordering on incredulity replaced the recognition in her eyes. "Come in."

He entered her apartment, swallowing his own surprise. He'd always heard that she was a ball-busting bitch; he and Staun had made a religion of keeping out of her way, afraid she'd report them if she ever thought twice about their names. He remembered then what Staun had written in his journal about her. . . . It only made the discomfort of standing here face-to-face with her worse.

"How are you doing?" she asked, with what sounded like genuine concern. "Gods, do your surgeons know you're out of bed?"

"I'm fine." He glanced away into the room, not letting himself think about them. Her common room held very little of the usual native furniture. Instead it was furnished with piled mats and folded rugs, decorated with woven and embroidered hangings, like the traditional Newhavenese homes he remembered from his childhood; the kind of home he had always wished he lived in. He looked back at PalaThion, down at the cast on her leg, and remembered again why she was wearing it. "You?"

"Fine," she said dryly, looking him over with a skeptical gaze. Her expression changed. "I'm truly sorry about Staun's death, Nyx. Your brother was. . . . I always felt that . . . he . . . was. . . ." Her voice faltered; the shadow of the Boatman's Hand seemed to pass over her, stealing the color from her face. "He was a good officer," she said faintly, at last.

A spark of unexpected emotion kindled in her eyes. It guttered out again before Tree could be certain it was actually grief . . . or even whether he'd seen anything at all. "You made a good team," she said, and there was only sympathy and respect in her gaze as she looked back at him.

His uncertainty choked off the sudden urge to tell

her how Staun had felt about her, and he said nothing.

And then the actual words she had spoken registered in his mind. "You knew?" he said, in disbelief. "You knew that we were brothers—"

"—and never reported you." She nodded. "Maybe I should have."

He looked down.

"What can I do for you, LaisTree?"

He looked up at her again. "I'm trying to find Sergeant Gundhalinu, Inspector."

"He didn't send you here—? No, of course not." Her gaze flickered to his bandages.

"No, ma'am. Why?"

"Damn it!" Her hand struck the open door, hard. "What the *hell* is wrong with him!"

Tree grimaced.

Rubbing her hand, she turned back and saw his expression. She drooped against the door frame as if gravity had suddenly increased in the room. "Probably just the same thing that's wrong with you . . . and me. He's 'fine,' too," she said, to his look. "You know what 'fine' means, don't you? 'Fucked-up, In-pain, Nervous, and Exhausted.' "

His grimace melted into a feeble grin. "So you were expecting Gundhalinu, but he hasn't shown up?"

"He knew he was supposed to go to the market for me. I'm all out of iestas, and this damn thing's got me under house arrest—" She nodded in disgust at her cast; her fingers rapped an impatient rhythm on the wall. "The meds keep telling me that 'next time' they'll take it off. Meanwhile, the Chief Inspector has dumped so much departmental shitwork on me that it'll take until the Departure to get caught up on my *own* shitwork. I swear by all the gods, this is starting to feel like a conspiracy—"

"Yeah, I know," he muttered.

"What?"

He shook his head, not meeting her eyes. Reaching into his pocket, he pulled out the crushed tin of Staun's bitterroot chews and offered it to her.

"Thanks, no." She shook her head. "They make my tongue bleed."

"Yeah, mine too. But Staun always . . . he. . . ." He pushed a chunk into his mouth as an excuse to stop talking, and put the tin away.

"What did you want to see Gundhalinu about?"

He glanced toward the door. "It's not important."

"Being on suspension must be duller than I thought," PalaThion said. "So dull that you've been searching all over the city, in your condition, for someone you barely know, just so you can talk to him about something unimportant . . . ?"

He looked back at her, his lips pressed together. "It's personal," he muttered, at last.

She stood gazing at him for a long moment. At last she sighed, and said, "Have you tried the Survey Hall?"

"No, I haven't." He straightened up. "Thank you, Inspector." He started past her; stopped, turned. "Inspector, I could go to the market for you, first—"

"No. Thanks." She smiled again, shaking her head. When she smiled, she was actually good-looking. "Just find Gundhalinu for me. And when you do, tell him to get the hell over here."

Tree grinned. "Yes, ma'am. It'll be my pleasure. *Sa mieroux*, Inspector." He murmured the traditional Newhavenese words of greeting and farewell almost self-consciously. The hand that would have saluted her pressed his aching side more tightly.

"*Sa kasse*, LaisTree," she said, adding almost inaudibly, as he went out the door, "May Saint Ambiko protect and guide you."

He looked back and nodded, swallowing the burn of bitterroot as he started down the stairs.

Tree made his way along the Street until he reached the Survey Hall. He glanced up at the star-and-compass on the painted sign above its door; stopped, staring. The lone static figure shimmered like light on water—bright/dark/*as fluid as a dream*/now/then/*as solid as the muzzle of a gun*—

He pressed his hand to his eyes. When he looked up again, the symbol, the sign, were nothing but paint on metal.

He forced himself to go in, under the shadowed portico, through the windowpaned doors, before another attack of vertigo left him puking on Survey's doorstep.

The hall's interior was dim and quiet. Its walls were paneled almost to the ceiling in dark wood; he breathed in a faint, oddly soothing odor of wood polish and age.

There were only a handful of people in the room, scattered among islands of comfortable settees and chairs. A few of them broke off their conversations to look up as he entered. They went on looking at him, with more than passing curiosity. He spotted a couple of uniforms, but neither one was Gundhalinu.

As he searched the rest of the room, someone who could have been Gundhalinu rose from a chair and headed toward the back of the hall. Tree started after him.

"Are you looking for someone—?" A hand reached out and caught his sleeve as he went by.

Tree stopped, looking down; seeing an offworlder,

probably just a trader. "Yeah. Gundhalinu."

The man shrugged, withdrawing his hand. "Don't know him."

Tree moved on, following the blue uniform's trajectory toward the rear of the club as the man disappeared through a doorway. He realized that the Hall had meeting rooms beyond the main room, and probably a full second story as well.

He went through the doorway. The dim corridor beyond it led to a flight of stairs. He started to climb.

The man he had followed—a lieutenant, he saw, and not one he knew—was suddenly at the top, blocking his way. "Are you a stranger far from home?"

Tree stopped, staring up at him. He laughed once. "Who isn't, in this place?"

The other man's face didn't change. He began to descend the stairs.

It was not a random question. Tree realized abruptly that he had just been tested; and that he had failed the test.

"Were you looking for the bathroom?"

"Uh . . . no."

"Are you a member of Survey?" The officer paused, just above the step where Tree waited.

"No."

"Did you want to join—?"

"No." Tree shook his head. "I'm looking for Sergeant Gundhalinu. I heard he might be here."

"He's not." The lieutenant descended another step. "And this is a restricted area in a private club. Since you are not a member, I have to ask you to leave." He came down another step.

Tree turned around and went back down, with painful slowness. The other man followed, step by step.

Tree hesitated at the bottom of the stairs as something caught his eye—something that shone against the blue of the lieutenant's uniform, as silverly elusive as the laughter of the gods.

He froze; words died in his throat.

The lieutenant looked down. "Yes," he murmured, "you know this . . . it's why they want to kill you. And it's why they haven't yet."

"*What the hell*—" Tree grabbed at the man's sleeve; the uniformed arm eluded his grasp like a reflection in water.

"You're out of your depth, LaisTree," the man said. "You can't even imagine the depths beneath you. . . . But not everyone wants to see you drown." His hand caught the silver star-and-compass pendant as if it were a fish and pushed it back inside his clothes. "If I were you, I would forget that this conversation ever took place. Just leave, now, while you still have the chance."

Tree backed up a dozen steps before he could force himself to turn and walk away down the corridor that led to the main hall. . . .

. . . He was walking down the middle of the Street.

He slowed, turning around to gape at the buildings on either side: He was still in the Maze, but nowhere near the Survey Hall.

The Survey Hall. He remembered going inside. He remembered that he hadn't found Gundhalinu there. And then . . . then . . .

Nothing.

He was standing in the Street. He looked down at his watch. *Half an hour.* Half an hour gone . . . lost. . . .

Gods, what had happened to him? Why couldn't he remember—?

He stared at the blank building faces, the empty-eyed windows staring back at him like his reflection in the shattered mirror on his bedroom wall. The crowd flowed around him as if he was inanimate, a stone in the middle of a stream. Time flowed on like a river, while he stood alone in the middle of the Street and covered his face with his hands.

14

By the time Tree climbed the ever-steepening steps to his apartment, the storm-gray sky at the alley's end was the color of his mood.

No one had seen Gundhalinu today; even his remote was off-line. It was as if he had disappeared overnight and no one had noticed. But a Hegemonic Police officer didn't just disappear without a trace, even in Carbuncle. Where the hell could he go?

And yet the surreal hangover of his day spent searching for Gundhalinu dogged his thoughts, whispering in his brain that everything about this city was an illusion and a deception, even the light of day . . . that Truth swallowed its own tail here, like the spiraling Street, where everything was always disappearing even as it reappeared. . . .

He looked back over his shoulder, half-expecting

to find Gundhalinu at the bottom of the steps, staring up at him. The stairwell was empty.

He reached the landing at last, and faced his apartment door. *He needed to start cleaning the place up; needed to clean himself up, get some fresh clothes, at least . . . needed to face the rest of his life, somehow. . . .*

A pot of home-cooked tapola from Nisha KraiVieux was waiting, as promised, on his doorstep. His sudden smile died as he saw the clay pot lying on its side, cracked open . . . as if it had been intentionally kicked over. The rich, mouth-watering smell of tapola filled his senses as he moved closer; he stood gazing down at the stain that soaked his doormat like blood from a wound.

At last he stepped over the rust-colored ooze; pressed his thumb against the door lock with what felt like the last gram of his strength.

The door swung open before he even touched the knob. He swore under his breath. A sudden surge of fear/fury/anticipation jolted his body to life; his hand groped for the gun he no longer carried, and tightened into a fist.

The interior of the apartment looked the same to his eyes, still in semidarkness the way he'd left it. He stayed a moment longer in the doorway, listening, until a series of unidentifiable noises told him that someone was in the common room, and not being quiet about it.

He kicked the door wide open, went down the hall and into the room without stopping. A man wearing a Police uniform stood frozen at its center, staring back at him.

"LaisTree, I—"

"Gundhalinu?" His fists knotted. "You stinking bastard!"

"Wait, I—"

He hit Gundhalinu with all his strength; Gundhalinu went down as if he'd been stunshot, and lay moaning on the floor. Tree crossed the room and jerked up the shades.

He turned around. Gundhalinu lay with his hands drawn up to his stomach, still making inarticulate noises of pain. Tree kicked him. "Get up, you fucking coward." He hauled Gundhalinu upright, propped him against the table, finally getting a clear look at his face. He saw fresh blood, vivid on Gundhalinu's chin . . . and rusty smears of dried blood, the purple stain of bruises that were already hours old.

The fist he had raised for another blow unclenched. He put an arm around Gundhalinu's waist and guided him to a chair.

"Ow . . . shit." Tree sat on the table, nursing his throbbing hand. "What the hell happened to you?"

Gundhalinu looked up at him out of one eye; the other one was swollen shut. "Four men hit me a lot," he mumbled.

"Who were they?"

"Offworlders, looking for the missing tech from the warehouse massacre. The same ones who searched your apartment before. I don't know their names." Gundhalinu wiped his mouth with a shaky hand.

Tree looked around the room, and grimaced. "Did they come here looking for me?"

"No. For me . . ." Gundhalinu said hoarsely. "I'm thirsty."

Tree went to the sink; he looked down in surprise at the floor. "Did you clean up the kitchen?"

"Yes," Gundhalinu muttered, as though he regretted it.

Tree brought him water, watched him drink. "What were you doing in my apartment, anyway?"

"Searching it, under orders from the Chief Inspector," Gundhalinu said, as tonelessly as he'd said everything else.

Tree's hands tightened. He saw a spark of panic show in Gundhalinu's eye . . . saw the dilated pupil. "Did they drug you?"

"Yes," Gundhalinu said again. "So I'd cooperate. But she didn't believe me when I told her I didn't know. She said I had to know, because I was 'a stranger far from home.' So they kept . . . hitting me. And—" He swallowed, looking down at his hands.

"Oh, shit," Tree breathed, seeing the swollen, unnaturally crooked fingers, two on one hand, two on the other. "I'll take you to the Med Center."

"No."

"You need a—"

"It's not safe." Gundhalinu shook his head.

Tree hesitated. "The station house?"

Gundhalinu shook his head again.

"Where, then?"

Gundhalinu shut his eyes, as if it was one more question he couldn't answer.

"We can't stay here," Tree said, trying to think beyond the obvious. "I know a place. Take your jacket off."

"Why?" Gundhalinu looked down at his uniform.

"A uniformed Blue who's had the crap beaten out of him walking up the Street in broad daylight is going to attract too much attention."

"You're saying a civilian who looks like that . . . won't?" Gundhalinu asked.

Tree laughed. "Happens all the time in the Maze, Sergeant. You should get out of the station more often."

He found patches of painkiller in the detritus on the bathroom floor. He applied two to Gundhalinu's

palms before helping him change out of his uniform
jacket and into a long, shapeless coat of Staun's. The
rest of the patches he used on the parts of his own
body that hurt the most. Gundhalinu's stunner still
lay where it had fallen, in the hall. Tree picked it up
and pushed it through his belt, covering it with his
jacket.

He pulled a knitted cap down over Gundhalinu's
head, disguising as much of his battered face as possible, before they went out to the Street and started
uptown. Gundhalinu walked stubbornly on his own,
doing a good imitation of a staggering drunk. Tree
adjusted their course when necessary.

As they entered the Upper City, Tree stopped at a
public access and put in a call to Devony. She gave
him the answer he needed; they went on their way
again.

She met them at the entrance to Azure Alley.
Gundhalinu showed no sign of recognition at the
sight of her, but Tree felt him stiffen when they
reached her door. He wondered how she had looked
when Gundhalinu was here yesterday, what kind of
fantasies someone like that kept hidden under all the
sanctimonious Technician propriety.

"Gods and Goddess . . . !" Devony murmured. She
stared at Gundhalinu, as Tree eased him into a chair
with a sigh of relief. "Did you do that to him?"

"No." Tree frowned. "I hit him once, that's all. He
was searching my goddamn apartment—!"

"Twice," Gundhalinu said. "You kicked me."

Tree made a face. "Somebody followed him there;
they did the rest. He still has a load of interrogation
drugs in his system."

"Drugs—?" she said. "He should be at the hospital."

"It's not safe," Gundhalinu said.

Tree shook his head. "He didn't want to go to Blue

Alley either. I didn't know what to do with him, at least until he's rational again."

"I'm perfectly rational," Gundhalinu said. "Don't patronize me, LaisTree."

Tree rolled his eyes. "Beg your pardon, Sergeant, sir. I seem to have mistaken you for the officer who was recently force-fed illegal drugs and beaten to a pulp, after breaking into my apartment." His expression sobered as he looked back at Devony again. "Dev, I. . . . Look, I don't have any right to involve you in this. If you want us to go, we'll leave."

She pulled her gaze back from Gundhalinu's bruised face, her hands pressing her own face in empathy. "I'm already involved," she said faintly. "I know what will help him detox, at least. Come on—"

She led them down a hall past closed doors, to a bath and dressing room. Beyond it Tree saw another door, its single transparent pane clouded with moisture. "Undress him." Devony began to take off her clothes.

"What?" Tree said.

"No," Gundhalinu said.

"The sergeant is on drugs. . . ." She faced Tree impatiently. "What's your excuse?" She gestured at the waiting door. "That's a steambath—a sweathouse, if you want the traditional term. Haven't you ever been to a public one, here in the city?"

"No," Tree said.

"No," Gundhalinu said.

She sighed. Turning back to Gundhalinu, she put her hands on his shoulders and said, "Sergeant, you need to get the drugs out of your system. This will help. Do you understand?" He looked toward the steamroom, and back at her. He nodded slowly. She removed his coat, and began to pull up his shirt.

"This is bloody humiliating!" Gundhalinu burst

out, his pale freckles flushing bright red against the
brown of his skin. "Don't you people have any sense
of decency—?" He shrugged her off, swearing as he
tried to remove his shirt by himself. When Devony
saw his fingers, her face turned white. Tree moved in
at her glance, to help him strip.

With practiced skill, she draped a bathsheet around
Gundhalinu, then finished taking off her own
clothes. Her sensenet gleamed in the light like the
scales of some fantastic sea creature as she turned
back, completely unself-conscious about her naked-
ness; the deep-red jewel of her necklace glowed softly
against her skin.

"You're beautiful . . ." Gundhalinu murmured,
awed; he turned his back abruptly, cursing himself
under his breath.

Devony stared at him for a long moment, her face
unreadable. Then she folded herself into a bathsheet,
and led him into the steam-room.

Tree took off his clothes, and put on a sheet.

He rubbed his eyes to clear his vision as he entered
the steamroom; inhaled and exhaled with a conscious
effort until his lungs accepted the startling density of
moisture, the strong, rich smell of herbs.

He sat down beside Devony on the lowest bench.
Gundhalinu huddled miserably in the far corner of
the chamber, eyes shut, taking slow, deep breaths. All
around them was glowing whiteness—the walls, the
ceiling, the floor were tiled in white, illuminated by
a lamp suspended above them like a fog-shrouded
sun. Tiny trembling stalactites of condensation clung
to the ceiling of this timeless pocket world; occasion-
ally one fell, in a slow, silent rain.

Tree pressed his hand to the wall beside him, studying the abstract pattern his fingers made against the
moisture-slick tiles, feeling the wall's soothing warmth

seep into his bones. He settled closer to Devony as his aching, exhausted body began to surrender to the steam's embrace.

She smiled at him, haloed by an aura of glowing mist. Gundhalinu stared at them from across the room as she began to gently massage Tree's shoulders, and he kissed her smiling lips.

At last she drew away and turned toward Gundhalinu. "Sergeant, the men who drugged you—who were they?" she asked. "What did they look like?" Tree glanced over at her in surprise.

Gundhalinu blinked as if he had been startled awake out of a dream. "One . . . one was Samathan, I think," he murmured. "The others . . . anybody's guess. They were just muscle, anyway. The Ondinean woman gave the orders. She drugged me. She asked all the questions."

Devony stiffened as Gundhalinu mentioned the woman. "You know her?" Tree asked, with sudden hope.

Devony shook her head. Her hand rose to touch the jewel that glistened like blood at her throat. "Just . . . how could she give the orders, and then watch them . . . do that to someone?" Something flickered in the depths of her eyes as she glanced at Tree— something he had seen too often, in too many eyes, since he'd become a Blue. He looked away uneasily.

"I thought you Tiamatans believed in complete equality of the sexes," Gundhalinu said; Tree wondered whether the irony was intentional. Devony looked back at him without answering.

"What did they want from you, Gundhalinu?" Tree asked. "What did they ask you?"

Gundhalinu shook his head, glancing away. "Where it was . . . what I knew about it."

" 'It' what—?"

"I don't know!" Gundhalinu said furiously; echoes assaulted them from every side. "If I knew what it was, don't you think I would have told her—?" His swollen hands rose in a spasm of futility; he let them fall into his lap again. "I think . . . I think that it has to do with that missing piece of evidence from the warehouse."

"What do you mean?" Tree leaned forward. "Why is that so important to you?"

"The Chief Inspector said . . ." Gundhalinu grimaced, fighting the drug-induced compulsion to tell them everything he knew, and losing, ". . . *bloody hell!* . . . the Chief Inspector said there was . . . stolen experimental tech from Kharemough involved . . . in a secret trade-off between the Source and Arienrhod, the night you raided the warehouse." He looked down. "It's missing."

"The stolen tech?"

"Yes!" Gundhalinu glared up at him. "Damn it, LaisTree! I'm not allowed to tell you this. Stop asking me."

"Not a chance," Tree said. "Why doesn't the Chief Inspector want me to know about it? Why doesn't the whole force know—?"

"It's a matter of Hegemonic security. You can't be trusted. The vigilantes must have been planning to steal the technology and sell it; that's why you were all there that night. The whole lot of you were corrupt—"

"That's a lie!" Tree said; his anger echoed off the walls. Devony put a hand on his arm as he rose to his feet. He sat down again, taking a deep breath. "We were just trying to bring some justice to this cesspit of a city—"

"Apparently you think 'justice' means 'breaking the law,' " Gundhalinu said. "The Chief Inspector believes you knew about the stolen tech, LaisTree. The

Ondinean does too. How can you be so sure it's not true? You don't even remember what happened."

Tree looked away into the surreal whiteness. Fresh steam, pungent with herbs, suffused the dripping silence.

"All the officers on that vigilante raid were Newhavenese. That's why the Chief Inspector doesn't want the whole force to know. He doesn't know who he can trust."

Tree looked back at him, his jaw tightening. "Oh, yeah, I guess we all look alike, to you."

"No," Gundhalinu said. "You all just act alike."

"At least we're not all dead from the neck down."

"I'm sure it's easier, being dead from the neck *up.*"

Tree made a rude noise. "I'll tell Commander LiouxSked you think so, Tech." He glanced at Devony as she put a hand on his arm again. "What kind of woman did he want to see, when he came here yesterday and questioned you?" He gestured at Gundhalinu. "Tell us your fantasies, Sergeant . . . what's your dream woman like? What do you imagine her doing to you . . . ?" He watched the smugness disappear from Gundhalinu's face, as the compulsion to answer took him by the throat.

"You don't have to answer that," Devony interrupted, before Gundhalinu could open his mouth. "You don't have to." She turned back to Tree, frowning. "Tell him."

Tree looked at her, at Gundhalinu; at his feet. "Don't answer. I don't want to know."

"Sergeant Gundhalinu," Devony said, "do you actually believe the things you said to Officer LaisTree, about Newhaveners?"

Gundhalinu looked surprised. "No. . . ." He shook his head. "I was just angry."

"Then I think you're making progress." She looked

back at Tree. "Now leave him alone," she murmured, "or leave the room."

"Why the hell should I?" he said sullenly. "They wouldn't leave me alone, those fucking Techs. Jashari wouldn't. Aranne wouldn't—" He pointed at Gundhalinu. "*He* won't! They'll never leave me alone, un-til—until I'm dead . . . as dead as my brother. . . ."

"Nyx, no!" Staun's cry of warning; an arm pushing him back out of Death's sight-line—

Tree rose slowly to his feet, caught in the crosshairs of eternity, as someone fired—vaporizing the wall of lies, releasing an unstoppable flood of memories.

"*Staun!*" he cried, deafblind in the echoing white-ness. "Oh, gods . . . no. . . ."

"You remember," Devony whispered, not even a question.

"They shot him! They shot my brother—" He shut his eyes, pressing his hands to his bandaged side, holding himself together. "But he saved me . . . he saved me. . . ." Water dripped from the ceiling, ran down his face like tears. "He saved me. . . ."

"You saw them?" Gundhalinu demanded, getting up. "Who were they?"

"Blues . . . uniformed Blues," he said brokenly, as image after image filled his head like a holy vision . . . *a Kharemoughi face, a Police uniform, a gun . . . Death . . . lies . . . betrayal—* "They weren't with us. They were already there. But somehow, they didn't trigger the hidden security. We did. . . ." He shook his head, trapped inside the coils of disjointed time. "And after the lasers hit us, they came into the tunnel, to make sure there were . . . no survivors. Cabrelle. . . ."

"Cabrelle?" Gundhalinu crossed the room toward him. "He was killed in the massacre. He was part of a covert team sent to retrieve the stolen tech—the mission the vigilantes interfered with. That was why everyone died." He shook his head. "Cabrelle wasn't trying to kill you. Wasn't he your unit C.O., for gods' sakes?"

"Cabrelle stood over me and stuck a plasma rifle in my face!" Tree shouted. "And the only goddamn reason he didn't pull the trigger was because somebody lobbed a grenade into the tunnel, and it blew him and those other bastards to hell first!" He shoved Gundhalinu roughly aside and stumbled to the door. He went through it and out into the cool, clear air.

He reached the washbowl and leaned over it, letting the water run, stunningly cold, down his hands and arms while he splashed his burning face. "Fuck you, Staun . . . fuck *you*! You promised, you *promised* me! You bastard, how the hell could you leave me behind, like *this* . . . ?"

He shut off the flow at last; watched his rage, his futility, his grief empty down the drain, like so much waste water. When he turned around again, Devony and Gundhalinu were standing across the room.

Drying his eyes, he met their somber stares. "I remember everything. . . . It *was* Blues that did it . . . other Blues. The only reason I'm alive is because my . . . my brother pushed me back. He took the hit . . . he pushed me. . . . But he *promised*—" His trembling hands balled into fists, closing over thin air. Devony came to him and put her arms around him; he clung to her until the reeling world began to stabilize.

"Father of all my grandfathers. . . ." Gundhalinu sank onto the blue-green surface of the bath enclosure. "The grenade that killed Cabrelle has to be the one that was pitched at us. They were trying to kill us, too. But the Inspector kicked it back into the tunnel," he gave a choked laugh, "and they were killed by their own grenade." He looked up again wonderingly. "What else do you remember? Do you remember everything that happened?"

"I—" Tree broke off, as anger closed his throat. "I remember you said you work for Aranne and Jashari, you spying bastard. Just like Cabrelle and that Special Ops team did."

"But that doesn't make sense. . . ." Gundhalinu looked down at his hands, shaking his head. "Nothing makes sense, anymore. Damn it, I don't even know why somebody wanted to drug me!"

Devony moved away from Tree's side to take first-aid supplies out of a cabinet on the wall. She carried them to the place where Gundhalinu sat.

"If you're not hiding anything, LaisTree, then why won't you tell me what else you remember?" Gundhalinu leaned to one side, holding Tree's gaze as Devony began to clean up his face.

Tree dropped his bathsheet on the floor. "Look at me." He gestured at his naked body—his side and arm, his leg, his face still covered with bandageskin and deadened by painkillers, still hurting with every breath he took, every move he made. "Don't look away, *look* at me, you fucking prig! I was the only one left alive in that tunnel . . . and that was an accident. Somebody wanted me dead, too. Somebody from Blue Alley, maybe even the Judiciate. The only reason I ever came out of a coma is because they think I can lead them to something they want."

Gundhalinu gritted his teeth and didn't answer; he made a choked noise as Devony forced a purple, unnaturally crooked finger straight, then splinted it.

Tree looked at Devony, her face no longer flushed from the heat but ashen as she straightened a second swollen, purple finger, and sealed another splint. "Devony . . . let me finish it—"

She shook her head, not meeting his eyes, or

Gundhalinu's as his breath caught on a barb of pain. "No," she said, her voice barely audible. "I will."

Tree picked up his shirt and pulled it on, wincing as the motion hurt his side. "How long do you think I'll stay alive, Gundhalinu, once you tell Aranne that I've got my memory back? If I'm lucky, maybe long enough for somebody to do to me what they did to you—"

Gundhalinu looked up at him, away again. Devony applied more painkiller derms to his wrists and palms. "Thank you . . ." he whispered. She nodded.

Tree finished dressing, and put on his jacket. "Forget about me. How long do you think you'll live, Tech, once Aranne learns what I've told you?" He pushed his hand into his pocket, felt the mesh of the missing headset cling to his fingertips.

"The top officials in the Hegemonic government and the Police are not part of some secret conspiracy," Gundhalinu said thickly. "That's impossible."

Tree took his hand out of his pocket, frowning. "Cabrelle put a gun to my head when I asked why he was there," he said, keeping his voice level with an effort. "He said, 'It's better for all of us if you don't know.' And then he said . . . he said, 'I'm sorry.' . . ." He took a deep breath. "You figure it out."

"That doesn't mean the Chief Inspector ordered it! You were in the wrong place, at the wrong time . . . for the wrong reasons. You made a botch of their mission. He had no way of knowing why you were there—"

"He spoke to me!" Tree said, his voice corroding with grief. "He knew who we were! They didn't want any witnesses. . . . Are you going to tell me the Hedge's retrieving some piece of stolen tech justifies killing his own men in cold blood? Is that what your fucking Technician code of honor is all about, Gundhalinu?"

Gundhalinu stared at his hands. "It's Carbuncle. . . ." he said at last. "It's like entropy. Everything breaks down, here. Nothing stays in focus; the meanings don't hold. . . ." He shook his head; when he looked up again, his eyes were filled with an old, deep pain. "I have two older brothers," he murmured. "They made my life hell. I used to wish they were dead, all the time. But now my father's dead . . . and they're alive. And I don't think they'll ever let me go home again." Tree stared at him, speechless. Gundhalinu looked away, his shoulders slumping.

Devony wiped wetness from her face, and finished dressing in silence.

"Devony?" Tree moved unsteadily back to her side. "Dev . . . you all right?"

She shook her head. "It's nothing . . . or it's everything. I'll be all right." She smiled, barely; her hand rose to the blood-red tear of her necklace. Abruptly she reached up and took the necklace off, moving away from him to place it on a shelf. Gundhalinu watched her put it down as if he were hypnotized.

"Why did you take your necklace off?" Tree followed her, brushing aside her hand to pick up the stone. "You always wear this. . . . Is it really an Old Empire artifact?"

"It looks like an artifact to me," Gundhalinu said. "The Snow Queen gave it to her."

Tree looked at him.

Devony shook her head as Tree turned back to her. "I think it's just a beach stone . . ." she said, glancing past him.

Tree laid the necklace on the shelf, keeping his frown to himself.

"What are you going to do now, LaisTree?" Gundhalinu asked.

"Start taking my goddamn life back." Tree raised his head. "Start acting like a Police officer, not a perp. Start *thinking*, like my brother would." *Like he always believed I could—* The wounds of memory bled endlessly inside his eyes now, where he couldn't look away. What had been unreachable had become inescapable, as if there was no middle ground. *No going back.* "I don't care who's involved, or what it takes. I'll find the Bluekillers who murdered him, and I'll make them pay. Or I'll die trying." He faced Gundhalinu. "What about you?"

"I want the same thing," Gundhalinu said.

Tree frowned. "Even if it involves top officials in the Hegemonic government? Other Kharemoughis . . . Technicians?"

"Yes."

"Even if you might die trying?"

Gundhalinu hesitated. "Yes."

"Are you sure?" Tree pointed at Gundhalinu's bloodstained clothes, lying in a heap on the floor. "You've been playing dress-up in that uniform until now, Blue boy. Do you have the stones to play for keeps? Because if you're not absolutely sure—if you have any doubt at all—I don't want you watching my back."

"I'm sure," Gundhalinu said, grimly and without hesitation. "It isn't an accident that we wear the same uniform, LaisTree. I chose to become a Police officer—just like you did."

Tree shrugged. "What about the missing tech?"

"I still want to find it. But not as much as I want to get the killers. The stolen tech was never really the point, for me; it was just a point of access, a way I could keep working on this case. Because I had to be part of the investigation." Gundhalinu's gaze darkened. "I *had* to—"

"Why?"

"Because I nearly died at that warehouse, too, damn you!" Gundhalinu said furiously. "And because I . . . I saw. . . . " He shook his head. "I saw them. . . . Now, every time I close my eyes that's all I can see: Blood and body parts." He looked down. "Gods, I feel like I'm losing my mind! I want *my* life back, too."

Tree nodded, his face easing at last. "Okay. . . . Are there any other leads, any suspects Aranne told you about, but not the rest of the force?"

Gundhalinu shook his head. "Three of the bodies in the warehouse weren't ours. They were offworlders, recently arrived on Tiamat. No prior histories, no ties to anyone established here . . . though they had to be involved with the Source on some level; it was his warehouse they were meeting in."

"The Source is involved in everything, at some level," Tree said. "He's the tapeworm in the guts of this city."

"I know." Gundhalinu nodded. "Do you remember anything else from the warehouse? Anything you saw, anyone, before—"

"No. It happened too fast." Tree shut his eyes. "Maybe Staun saw something; the rest of us never even made it through the door. We never hid any stolen tech, either. We never even saw it."

Devony glanced up at him from where she leaned against the wall, listening; he saw her expression, and looked away. "Everybody I talked to at the station house is ready to sell his soul for a lead," he said. "Word on the street is nonexistent; it's like everyone in Carbuncle has had their tongue cut out."

"Does that strike you as odd, considering the high profile of the crime involved?" Gundhalinu frowned.

"Yeah," Tree muttered. "I would say so."

"Only the Source has the kind of influence—"

"Or the Snow Queen. The Winters want to get their hands on proscribed technology as much as he wants the water of life." Tree glanced at Devony again, reluctantly.

Gundhalinu grimaced. "What the hell is the matter with these people—don't we do enough for them? Why can't they be content with what they've got—?" He broke off. "I wonder how far Arienrhod would really go to keep us from preventing this trade."

"What do you think?" Tree said bitterly. "We're only good for one thing, to the Motherlovers; we're as expendable to them as the mers are." He frowned. "Unless the coverup really is entirely on our end."

Gundhalinu's jaw tightened. "That's not—"

"You were the one who wouldn't go to Blue Alley. You said it wasn't safe, or the Med Center either. Why not?"

Gundhalinu rubbed his swollen eye, and swore under his breath. "Gods, I . . . when the Ondinean was questioning me, some of the things they said . . . there was no way they could have known those things without informants, or some kind of hidden surveillance." He sagged forward. "For all I know, there's hidden surveillance all over the city, and they're laughing at us right now."

Tree kept his eyes off Devony's face with an effort. "Yeah . . . well, you got us one new lead we can follow up."

Gundhalinu's mouth formed a painful smile. "The Ondinean."

Tree nodded. "I know some places where we can start asking around. But first we ought to—"

"First . . ." Gundhalinu said, in resignation, "will you help me get my clothes on?"

15

"Are you sure he's in any shape to do this?" Devony put a hand on Tree's arm, nodding at Gundhalinu, as they stopped in the doorway. "Nyx, are you—?" She put her arms around him, holding him, as though she would stop him physically from going out.

"Does it really matter to you?" he asked, hating himself.

She drew back, her face full of surprise and hurt.

"I'm sorry." He looked down, shaking his head. "I just . . . I'm sorry."

She kissed him. "Be careful," she said, the way she had said it the last time he left her; like a charm against bad luck. She glanced at Gundhalinu. "Both of you."

Gundhalinu smiled uncertainly, as if her show of concern for him was as hard to fathom as what the

Ondinean had done to him earlier. He lifted a bandaged hand in grateful acknowledgment as they went
out. They went back along the alley to the Street, and
headed downtown.

At the entrance to the next alley, Tree pulled
Gundhalinu to a stop.

"Why are we stopping?" Gundhalinu shook him off,
annoyed.

"There's something I need to find out." Tree
looked back toward Azure Alley.

"What is it?" Gundhalinu slumped against the
building wall, as if his body was just as happy for the
wait.

"I'll tell you when it happens . . . if it happens."
Tree paced restlessly back and forth, unable to stay
still. "What do you think of Devony, Gundhalinu?"

"What do I think of her?" Gundhalinu looked up
in surprise. "Do you mean her occupation?"

"I mean, what's your take on her?" Tree said impatiently. "What kind of impression did she make on
you yesterday when you questioned her, and today?"

Gundhalinu stared at his bandaged hands; his expression changed, and changed again. "Well . . . for
one thing, there aren't that many 'shifters in Carbuncle, because a sensenet is worth a small fortune. That
means she must have impressed Berdaz, or someone,
as being worthy of the investment. Personally, she
struck me as very intelligent, and . . . unnervingly perceptive, when I spoke to her yesterday. And she must
be a gifted actress—"

Tree stopped moving abruptly.

Gundhalinu looked down. "I only meant . . . that
she *convinced* me she was Kharemoughi, when I met
her. It wasn't just her appearance. Her whole manner
was perfect, if a little . . . forward. I never suspected,
until she—" He broke off.

Tree looked at his expression, and didn't ask. "She even knows enough Klostan to tell me when I'm being a real . . . jerk, in my own language," he muttered.

Gundhalinu's mouth twitched. "And she's Tiamatan, which means she had to pick it all up without ever having been offworld."

"She'd never even been off the farm, until about five years ago," Tree said.

"How long have you actually known her?"

"Only two days. . . ." Tree shook his head. "Three, if you count the night of the warehouse raid. We had one dance together, at the Closed Doors Club."

"I think she really cares about you."

Tree stared at him. "What made you say that?"

"You asked me what I thought."

"I mean, how do you *know*?"

"It's obvious. . . ." Gundhalinu shrugged helplessly. "It would be obvious to any trained observer."

Against his will, Tree felt a smile pry at the corners of his mouth. He became preoccupied with his coat pockets until he was sure his face was expressionless again. Then, looking up, he said, "Have you got a first name, Gundhalinu?"

"Of course I—" Gundhalinu broke off, looking embarrassed. "I mean . . . it's BZ."

"I have something for you, BZ." Tree pulled out the headset. "Is this the piece of tech you've been looking for?"

Gundhalinu's eyes widened. "Yes . . ." he breathed. "You had it, all along?"

"Only since last night." Tree frowned as he saw the sudden suspicion on Gundhalinu's face. "It was with the contraband that got diverted to the rec room. Now you know exactly as much about it as I do."

"You didn't see it before, at the warehouse? You didn't see who had it?"

"I told you the truth, damn it! The whole truth!" He looked away again, his throat working. "We weren't even armed. . . ."

Gundhalinu nodded, controlling his frustration with an obvious effort. "Why didn't you give it to me last night, then?"

Tree thought about it. "You didn't say 'please.' "

Gundhalinu pushed away from the wall, his fists clenching. "You honorless *idiot!* This could have been over, and I wouldn't have—I wouldn't—" He looked down, his face crumpling; slowly, finger by finger, he opened his hands.

"You wouldn't be alive, probably," Tree said sourly.

Gundhalinu leaned against the wall, frowning but silent.

"Besides, it's not over until somebody pays, remember?" Tree pushed the headset back into his pocket. *"Remember?"*

Gundhalinu nodded again, looking down.

"How did you track me, anyway? Am I marked?"

"Yes." Gundhalinu said, with glum reluctance. "Underneath the bandage on your side. But you weren't exactly secretive about your movements, anyway."

Tree pulled loose his shirt. He dug his fingers into the layers of protective film and peeled them back, fighting his body's sickening sense of violation as he exposed the wound to the air. He found the fingernail-sized patch of the tracer, among the sutures and the mottled expanses of skingraft that held the raw meat of his damaged side together.

Gundhalinu looked away. "They had every right to mark you," he muttered. "You were a suspect."

Tree picked the tracer loose and pressed the bandage back into place. Swallowing bile, he crushed the silicon patch between his fingers. "Fuckers. . . ."

"LaisTree—"

"*What?*"

"I'm sorry . . . about your brother." Gundhalinu looked up again, into the face of Tree's surprise. "I envy you your memories, Nyx."

"Thank you," Tree murmured, forcing the words out. "Sorry I hit you."

"No you're not." It was a simple statement of fact.

Tree burst out laughing, felt his surprise double as Gundhalinu unexpectedly joined him.

"Maybe . . . maybe I should have spent longer in that steambath," Gundhalinu mumbled, his freckles reddening.

Tree's mouth quirked. "I like you better this way."

Gundhalinu shook his head, and gave him a grudging smile in return. "There's an access across the alley." He gestured. "I'm going to check the starport immigration records. If the Ondinean's a recent arrival, like the ones who were killed at the warehouse, maybe I can find a lead that way." Tree nodded, looking up the Street toward Azure Alley again.

Gundhalinu was back in less than five minutes. "There's nothing that fits. I checked clear back to—"

"Son of a bitch . . ." Tree said.

Gundhalinu peered past him as a conservatively dressed Winter woman left Azure Alley, and started up the Street toward the palace. "What?" he said. "Do you know that woman?"

"Yeah," Tree muttered. "Or at least I thought I did. It was just another mask." He looked down. "You know her too. It's Devony. She's going to the palace, to tell Arienrhod everything she learned from us."

"Are you sure?" Gundhalinu turned back in disbelief. "How can you be certain?"

"Gods, I know the way she moves. . . ." Tree looked

away from Gundhalinu's expression, blinking. "I hate this fucking city. Let's go."

They went on into the Maze, more silent than strangers.

"Here." Tree nodded at last, and led the way down an alley. They stopped in front of a nondescript building entrance. "We can start asking questions in here."

Gundhalinu looked dubious. "What is this place?"

"A diveshop." Tree shrugged. "Sells any kind of mindbender that's legal somewhere . . . eat in, take out."

"What about the gaming hells? They're a lot bigger, with a lot more turnover than a place like this."

"And everything's automated, everybody's in their own private little world—it's so goddamn noisy that nobody can hear anything anyway. So nobody gets to know anyone else, nobody gives a damn. The little places are where people talk . . . and in places like this, they talk too much." He started for the door; turned back, putting a hand on Gundhalinu's chest. "Just back me up, for now. Don't say anything you don't have to. . . . Oh, and don't breathe too deeply." Gundhalinu frowned, and nodded. They went inside.

The small shop was cluttered with stools and tiny tables, most of them empty at this hour. It stank of incense trying to disguise too many less attractive smells. "Umthun—" Tree called, to the squat man stocking shelves and cases behind the counter at the back of the room. "I got an itch that needs scratching."

"What'll it be—" The man broke off as he turned around and saw them. "LaisTree? I heard you got busted off the force."

"Nah." Tree shook his head. "That's all cleared up."

He leaned heavily on the counter, trying to make the motion look casual. "I need one of those favors you owe me for not shutting you down, when me and my partner found that stash of *que'l* in your stockroom."

"When do they end, eh—?" Umthun waved his hand in disgust. "And I still say somebody planted that *que'l.*"

"That's what they all say," Gundhalinu remarked.

Tree glanced at him, wondering whether it was the man or the drugs talking now. "Give us some help on this one, Umthun, and I won't ask you again."

"Ya, until next time. . . ." Umthun muttered. "I don't know shit about what happened at that warehouse, LaisTree. I already told—"

"We're not here about that." Tree cut him off. "We're looking for somebody. Describe her, Sergeant."

"We want to find an Ondinean woman, around thirty standard years old," Gundhalinu said. "Black hair, black skin, dark blue eyes, and dresses like a laborer or a dockhand, not in *shadoudt.* Probably hasn't been on Tiamat long, probably working with the Source."

Umthun shrugged. "Maybe you should ask a Kharemoughi named Herne. He knows people. I think he might know her."

"Where would we find him?"

"Probably torturing cats," Tree said. "Or setting fire to some old burnout, just for laughs. I know him."

"Ask around, The Rack," Umthun said. "I hear he gets off on their new hunter-killer interactive."

"Great," Tree said wearily. "That's clear down by the Lower City."

"Do you have any stims?" Gundhalinu asked; Umthun nodded and pulled a sealed packet off the display wall. "And give me some iestas, too."

Umthun slid them across the counter at him.

Gundhalinu put the pack of iestas into his pocket.

"Let's go," Tree said, turning away. "Be seeing you, Umthun."

"Not for a long time, eh?" Umthun said.

"Not till at least next week—" Glancing back, Tree saw Gundhalinu pay for the stims and iestas before following him out.

Outside, Tree said, "You didn't have to pay for those."

"Yes I did." Gundhalinu gave him a look, applying a stim patch to his throat as they started back down the alley. "Did you plant the *que'l* you found in his shop?"

"No!" Tree frowned. "Why?"

Gundhalinu looked away, and didn't answer.

"You have a spare one of those . . . ?"

Gundhalinu passed him a patch, and he stuck it on. The mild buzz hit his brain within seconds, sharpening his perceptual and motor responses. He held up his hand; its telltale tremor said he was in no shape to be playing games with his nervous system. But the stimulant would give him the strength to keep moving—and he had to keep moving, had to keep thinking clearly. Because something was gaining on them. . . . He glanced at Gundhalinu's hands, and looked away again.

They continued their downward spiral until they reached the alley where The Rack was located. They stopped in front of the building entrance, and Tree looked up at its defiantly oppressive rusted-metal facade. "You ever been in one of these places?"

"Of course," Gundhalinu said impatiently.

Tree shrugged. Bracing his senses for a full-on frontal assault, he led the way inside.

Technically, The Rack was just another gaming

hell, but it catered to a rough trade, one that took the term "hell" seriously. Tree approached the gamers loitering in the outer gallery, wearing their hearts on their sleeves—in some cases, maybe literally—as they waited for pickups with similar interests.

Their tastes ran the gamut from fetishistic costumes to elaborate cicatrices and bioactive implanted body art, to basically nothing at all. When he and Staun were assigned this beat, he had been surprised by how quickly he reached the point where nothing he saw surprised him anymore. Behind him, he heard Gundhalinu's sharp, indrawn breath, and controlled his urge to smile.

Asking for Herne, he had to raise his voice over the indescribable sounds emanating from the bowels of the club. Someone gestured toward the dark sphincter of an access, and he went on through.

Gundhalinu followed close behind, keeping his mouth shut—or more likely struck dumb, after a person of indeterminate sex spotted the binders on his equipment belt and propositioned him. From the look on the sergeant's face, *one* was exactly how many of Carbuncle's hells Gundhalinu had been in before today . . . and one where the gaming losses were restricted to credit only. Tree was glad the more serious action here was confined to the private stalls.

"You looking for trouble, LaisTree?" Somebody the size of a transport, wearing full body armor, stepped into their path; his augmented voice boomed over the shrieks and sounds of destruction.

"Not me." Tree shook his head. "Already got more than I need."

"How 'bout him?" The bouncer indicated Gundhalinu.

"You wish." Tree grinned ferally. "We're looking for Herne. Where is he?"

"He was using a stall, but he left," the bouncer said. "He usually goes to Sestas—"

Tree nodded, struggling to control his gag reflex as he inhaled a stench like rotting meat. Gundhalinu recoiled as a random spray of something dark-red and viscous almost hit his chest. Tree caught Gundhalinu's arm, unobtrusively urging him back toward the entrance.

"Herne's at Sestas. It's an eatery down the block." Tree spat to clear the taste out of his throat as they emerged into the relatively fresh air. "The action must give him an appetite. You all right—?"

Gundhalinu shook his head. He leaned against the wall, pressing his mouth to his sleeve.

"It's virtual scenarios, interactives," Tree said harshly. "Most of what you see in there isn't even real. You *know* that."

"The players in there are real." Gundhalinu turned back, confronting Tree with his battered face and crippled hands.

"Well . . . at least nobody's in there who doesn't want to be," Tree muttered, looking down. "It's not our place to judge them."

"I know that," Gundhalinu said. "It just—" His eyes gleamed with sudden, unshed tears. "It reminded me of the warehouse."

Anguish drove into Tree's gut like a knife. He stood motionless, strengthless, waiting, until at last Gundhalinu said, "I'm all right. . . . Let's go."

They went on along the alley until they reached Sestas. Tree peered in through its wide front window, and saw Herne.

Herne looked up as if he could feel the pressure of their joint stare through the glass. Abruptly he got to his feet, and headed into the rear of the shop.

"Come on." Tree nudged Gundhalinu's shoulder, and started for the shadowy gap between the eatery and the building next to it. They arrived at the back door just as it slammed shut behind Herne, trapping him between them and a solid wall.

"Hey, Herne," Tree said agreeably, as they blocked his path. "Time to cough up another hairball."

"Eat shit, LaisTree." Herne looked him up and down. "You can't ask me for the time of day. You're busted, you vigilante cocksucker."

Tree shrugged, and indicated Gundhalinu. "He's not."

Herne glanced at Gundhalinu and his mouth curled, distorting a face that would have been handsome if there had been any recognizable human emotion in the dark, long-lashed eyes. "Sergeant Gundhalinu," Herne murmured. "What happened to you? Did PalaThion put you over her knee and spank you till your Technician butt was red, because you were a bad boy at court? I hear your mama leaves you home now, when she goes to see the Queen. . . ." He said something more, in a language that sounded like Sandhi, but not the way the Kharemoughis on the force spoke it.

Tree felt more than saw Gundhalinu go rigid. But Gundhalinu didn't respond, and Tree kept his eyes on Herne's hands, which were resting casually on his hips near a concealed weapon.

Herne's gaze moved between them, assessing the obvious damage. He settled his weight as if he was considering whether to take them both out with his bare hands.

Tree pulled the stunner from his belt. "Don't even think about it. Drop the weapons."

Herne removed a stun pistol from inside his coat,

dropped it on the ground and kicked it forward.

"You're not that glad to see us." Tree pointed at the unsubtle bulge in Herne's pants. "Lose the rest of the arsenal, or we'll do a strip search."

Grudgingly, Herne produced another stunner, a knife, and a heat pencil, and tossed them out.

"Sounds like you're well-informed, as usual. Tell us about the Ondinean woman who's working for the Source. What's her involvement in the warehouse massacre?"

"How would I know? What's the matter, LaisTree, you can't remember . . . ?" Herne sneered. "How come you were the only survivor, huh? Did you sell them out? Or maybe you're just a coward, maybe you let them down, and now you can't live with yourself unless you—"

"You son of a—"

"No." Gundhalinu caught Tree's arm, holding him back. "Don't. It's just what he wants."

Tree eased off, taking a deep breath.

Gundhalinu released him. Then he straightened his fingers, swearing under his breath. He fumbled with a pouch on his equipment belt, and brought out a small bottle. Holding it up, he said, "This is some of the drug the Ondinean gave me, to make me talk when she questioned me."

"How did you get that?" Tree asked, incredulous.

"She left it behind at your apartment." Gundhalinu smiled humorlessly. "Believe me, it works." He looked back at Herne. "I'm a Hegemonic Police officer, *mekru.* I'm addressing you without an intermediary, and without consequence, as required in the performance of my duty."

Tree remembered abruptly that *mekru* meant the bottom rung of Kharemough's rigid caste system; on his homeworld, a highborn like Gundhalinu was forbidden by law even to speak to a *mekru*. Gundhalinu opened the bottle with his teeth, and moved toward Herne. "Drink this."

Herne made a disgusted noise. "Make me, Tech."

"Oh, I will," Gundhalinu said, cold-eyed. "One way or another. Drink it yourself, or LaisTree will stun you and I'll pour it down your throat. Whether you talk to us or choke to death is of no real concern to me, or him." He paused. "Actually, I hope you choke. You choose." He held the bottle out again.

Herne snatched it from his hand and swallowed the contents. His face contorted and he spat, hurling the bottle away.

Gundhalinu came back to Tree's side, cradling the hand that had held the bottle; Tree glimpsed the fractures in his resolve.

"How long does this stuff take to work?" Tree asked.

Gundhalinu glanced at his watch; his face was under control again as he turned back. "Well, when the Ondinean drugged me, I think it took about two minutes. . . ." He studied Herne. "Not only couldn't I lie to save my life, I couldn't even stop myself from answering. I didn't know there *was* a drug that effective."

"The Police sure as hell don't have anything that good," Tree said, "or we wouldn't be having this conversation."

Gundhalinu grunted. He checked his watch again, looked back at Herne. "You're sweating, *mekru*. Are you nervous, or do you just wish you could puke it up? I felt like I'd swallowed toxic waste when they gave it to me. But I expect you know all about what happened to me . . . you seem to know everything else." He glanced at Tree. "You know, there might be other cases we could clear up while we've got him drugged. Hell, I could get another commendation out of this. You'd get back on the force, no question—"

Tree stared; Gundhalinu gave him a brief, urgent look. "Yeah," Tree said finally. "I like that. Sounds like a good idea. . . . So, where do we start, Herne? Who was the first person you ever killed? Or how do you know so much about the massacre . . . or about Arienrhod's court, for that matter?"

"I won't tell you anything, you dogfuckers. Except that you're dead men; they'll kill you no matter what you do!"

Gundhalinu glanced down at his watch. "Well, surprise." He smirked. "It didn't even take two minutes."

"Probably works faster on a small brain." Tree grinned. "So who are 'they,' Herne? Who's out to get us?"

"Fuck you, LaisTree! Everybody! There's nobody you can trust." His eyes were like coals. "If they don't get you, I will."

Tree glanced at Gundhalinu. "Of course, they did also beat the shit out of you, Sergeant. Maybe we need to shake his thoughts loose."

"That's assault, LaisTree," Gundhalinu said, frowning. "I can't—"

"What?" Tree demanded, turning to face him. "You want me to make it a fair fight—?"

Herne lunged. Tree swung back, his fist and the gun in it already on a collision course with Herne's skull. The force of the impact staggered him; Herne went down like he'd been pithed.

"Saint Phimas *wept*!" Tree shook out his hand. "Dam*nation*! . . . Is self-defense regulation enough for you, Gundhalinu—?" he gasped. "Fucker's skull must be made of composite. . . ."

"More like glass, I think," Gundhalinu said, staring

at Herne with a peculiar expression on his face.

Herne rolled over, groaning.

Tree put a boot on his chest. "Don't get up." He held out his hand to Gundhalinu. "Binders?" Gundhalinu passed them over; Tree dropped them on Herne's stomach. "Put them on." He pointed the gun at Herne's bloody head. Herne obeyed. "So what do you think was the most effective thing they did to you, Sergeant? Breaking your fingers—?"

Gundhalinu's mouth thinned. "Yes, definitely."

"You—" Herne snarled, raising his pinioned hands.

Tree shifted more weight to the foot on Herne's chest. "Should I immobilize the prisoner, Sergeant?" He nodded at the stunner.

"He might not be able to answer our questions then," Gundhalinu said.

"Yeah. And I'd have to break all his fingers." Tree shrugged. "I'd really hate that. . . . Why'd they only break four of yours, Gundhalinu?"

Gundhalinu looked down at his hands. "I passed out."

Tree leaned over Herne, taking hold of the binders. "This is it, Herne; truth or dare. For the first finger . . . who's the Ondinean?"

"Fuck!" Herne gasped. "Her name's Mundilfoere! She came here to get a piece of Old Empire tech from the Queen—"

"You mean the Queen wanted to get a piece of stolen experimental tech from *her*," Gundhalinu corrected gently. "And Arienrhod was willing to trade the water of life for it. Let's get the details right, *mekrittu*."

Herne flopped like a fish. "Who fed you that pile of shit? You've got it backwards! The Queen has some kind of functioning Old Empire tech to trade. This isn't about the water of life—"

Tree looked a question at Gundhalinu.

Gundhalinu shook his head; his eyes filled with sudden doubt. "What else?" he asked.

"The Source wants it bad. They set up an exchange that night at the warehouse. But the Blues got past the extra security somehow, and got the drop on us. They knew about the tech, they were going after it. Then the vigilantes broke in and triggered the system, and all hell—"

" '*Us*'?" Tree swore under his breath. "You said 'us'. . . . You were there?" He slid his foot up to Herne's neck. "Were you, motherfucker? *Were you—*?"

Herne made a retching noise. "Yes—"

"How many Blues did you kill? You shoot any Blues?"

"Nuh—no!" Herne gasped.

"Why should we believe you?" Gundhalinu demanded.

"You gave me the truth drug, you bastard! You think I have any choice? . . . I never got off a shot! I got grazed, stunshot; that's how I lost the goddamn artifact. I got grazed and my arm went dead!"

"So *you* ran. . . ." Gundhalinu smiled.

"I'll fuck you where you breathe, Gundhalinu! I'll kill you both—"

"You'll have to get in line," Tree said. "Who else was at the warehouse that night? Tell me all the names."

Herne began to spew names like spittle; Tree eased the pressure on his throat, but only a little. "You getting all this?"

Gundhalinu nodded, and pointed at the recorder on his belt. "Who do you work for?" he asked.

"For Arienrhod," Herne said.

"You, *mekru*?" Gundhalinu looked skeptical. "We're supposed to believe that it was you who delivered the

Queen's precious goods to the warehouse for her?"

"Yes!" Herne's eyes filled with hatred. "You wouldn't *believe* the things I do for her—"

"I'm sure you're right," Gundhalinu said acidly. He looked back at Tree, half frowning. "Arienrhod again. . . . What do you make of it, Tree?"

"If he's telling the truth, that would explain why he knows so much about what happens at the palace." Tree shrugged. "You know a Winter woman named Devony Seaward, Herne? She wears a sensenet; she's a—"

"A whore. Yeah, I know her. I hear you know her real well, LaisTree. . . ." Herne leered. "She's been real good to you, hasn't she, *shevatch?* Ever wonder what she sees in you—?"

"I figured it out." Tree leaned harder on his foot.

"So the Queen had possession of the tech in the first place?" Gundhalinu asked. "Where did she get it?"

"I don't know!" Herne gasped. "Maybe she found it in her closet; this whole fucking city's an Old Empire relic."

"And the equipment is Old Empire technology?"

"Functioning Old Empire tech. That's what I heard."

"What did it look like?"

"There was a piece of mesh . . . and some kind of synthetic jewel. It looked like crap. I think Arienrhod was putting something over on them—"

Tree looked at Gundhalinu.

Gundhalinu looked up, as if his gaze could penetrate the layers of the city all the way to Devony Seaward's townhouse, and the jewel lying abandoned on a bathroom shelf.

Herne bucked under Tree's weight, trying to throw him off. Tree staggered, and clipped Herne's jaw with a boot heel. "Not so fast, asshole." He replanted his foot. "Where can we find the Ondinean?"

"Why don't you try the palace?" Herne said sullenly.

"Maybe you'd like to come with us, so the Queen knows how cooperative you've been," Gundhalinu suggested. "Or maybe you want to give us another option."

Herne glared at him. "Find Humbaba."

"Who's Humbaba?"

"Drug dealer, from Ondinee. You can't miss him, he's got *i-shin* scarring . . . looks like he's wearing his guts on his face. He's here in Carbuncle on business."

"What's Mundilfoere got to do with him?"

"She's his wife."

Gundhalinu shook his head. "Gods . . . all in the family."

"Let's hope they don't breed." Tree took his foot off Herne's neck and stepped back, keeping the gun trained on him.

"I plan to make sure of that," Gundhalinu said. "Get up, *mekru.*" Herne climbed heavily to his feet, and Gundhalinu freed his hands from the binders. "Let's go, LaisTree."

"You're not taking me in?" Herne asked, frowning.

"We're on a clock. Some other time." Gundhalinu looked back at him. "The way I see it, if you tell anybody we had this conversation, you'll end up just as dead as we do."

Tree toed the empty truth-serum bottle. "Maybe we should keep this, get it analyzed."

Gundhalinu shook his head. "No point. It's a pretty simple formula. Anyway, you can always get more from the supply room."

"What?" Tree said.

"That was a bottle of surfactant. I was cleaning some equipment."

"*What?*" Herne said.

"You see, unlike some people, I actually learn from my mistakes." Gundhalinu smiled, glancing at him. "It'll give you a case of the runs, Herne, but that's about it. You told us the truth of your own free will." He turned his back on Herne's livid fury, and started away toward the open alley.

Tree followed him, looking back more than once.

16

"I can't believe he fell for that," Tree muttered, when they were safely on their way back down the alley.

"Why not? You did," Gundhalinu said.

Tree swung around in sudden anger.

"No—" Gundhalinu said hastily, raising his hands, "I only meant that Herne had no way of knowing it was a lie, any more than you did. And besides, he's a *mekru,* a product of his caste. No matter how tough or intelligent he is, deep inside he'll always feel inferior to a Technician. I assumed that would make him particularly susceptible to a psychological trick."

"So," Tree said finally, "I guess that would make you either a lot smarter than I figured, or a complete hypocrite."

"What are you talking about?"

"You lied, cheated, and intimidated to get that information out of Herne. Did you let me rough him up just because he's a *mekru*?"

"No!" Gundhalinu glared at him. "Sainted ancestors, it's bad enough that we did it at all!" They started on again; Gundhalinu's gaze turned bitter and distant. "My own brothers were proof enough for me that any 'genetic superiority' of the Technician class was a joke. . . . The social codes should be reformed. But on Kharemough, tradition is god. And no matter what your caste or rank, a god's hand. . . ." His voice faded; he bit his lip. "A god's hand can crush you like a fly."

"Then why?"

"Why what—?"

"Herne," Tree said irritably.

Gundhalinu stared straight ahead; Tree saw a muscle jump in his cheek. "Because he's a sadistic, psychopathic bastard, who would have murdered you and me and every other Blue at that warehouse, if he'd had the chance. . . ." His frown deepened. "And because right now we can't afford to go through the proper channels."

"Then I guess you are smarter than I thought."

Gundhalinu looked back at him. "Then I suppose I'd have to say the same about you." His pace lagged as they reached the alley's mouth; he took out another stim patch and stuck it on.

Tree pressed his arm against his side, his own burden of doubt and pain redoubling as the adrenaline of their encounter with Herne wore off. He took the fresh patch Gundhalinu passed to him without comment, and put it on. "Now what?"

"We go back to Devony Seaward's and get that other piece of tech from her," Gundhalinu said.

Tree looked at him; looked away again without saying anything. At last he asked, "And then?"

Gundhalinu hesitated, looking down. "We turn it over to the Chief Inspector, along with the names we got from Herne."

Tree caught Gundhalinu's arm, pulling him to a stop. "Are you crazy?"

Gundhalinu frowned. "No," he said. "Why, are you contagious?"

Tree swore. "I mean, you're going to trust Aranne with that? He lied to you about what it was! He's covering something up."

"I can't believe that." Gundhalinu shook his head. "There's some other explanation. And when I bring in the evidence, I'll find out what it is."

"I guess you are as stupid as I thought."

Gundhalinu jerked his arm free. "Then tell me who on the force *you* trust now—absolutely, unequivocally? Who can you swear to me hasn't been leaking information to the Source?"

Tree glared at him. "I don't trust anybody."

"Then what does it matter who we tell?" Gundhalinu said. He glanced restlessly up the Street. "We have to tell someone. If we don't get help, we're dead. And the information we got from Herne dies with us." He looked away again, raised his hand suddenly.

Tree saw a Police patrolcraft swerve toward them. "You called them? Why—?"

Gundhalinu turned a bleak stare on him. "Because we need to get back to Azure Alley, LaisTree. And I don't think I can walk uphill for half the length of the Street, in my present condition. And I don't think you can, either."

Tree watched in resignation as the patrolcraft settled on the pavement in front of them. Two Blues got out, KerlaTinde and another officer he knew . . . or hoped he did. He kept his hand on the grip of the pistol pushed through his belt, counting every second that passed without either of the officers pulling a weapon on them.

"Sergeant." KerlaTinde saluted Gundhalinu, looked him up and down. "You requested a patroller for a pickup . . . Are you all right?"

"Yes," Gundhalinu said brusquely.

"LaisTree, what are you doing here?" Both men looked at Tree, back at Gundhalinu, with more than passing curiosity.

Tree said nothing, relieved as Gundhalinu ordered the two men away down the alley to pick up Herne. "You think he's waiting around?"

"I don't care if he is or not." Gundhalinu's face pinched with self-disgust as he watched them go. "I needed to get them out of the way, for just long enough—Come on." He nodded at the patroller.

"No." Tree shook his head. "I'm going after Humbaba."

"LaisTree, do you have a death wish? You know we need to stick together now, more than ever—"

"I want the Ondinean more than I want that artifact. I thought you did, too."

"Or maybe you just don't have the stones to face Devony Seaward again," Gundhalinu said bluntly. He unsealed the patrolcraft's gullwing doors.

Tree swore. "Go fuck yourself, Gundhalinu. Or fuck her, if that's what you want—but make it fast, before she does it to you." He turned away, heading downhill.

"Did it ever occur to you that Devony could be in danger?" Gundhalinu called after him. "The Queen's using her . . . why the hell else would she have given Devony that necklace?"

Tree turned around. Gundhalinu sat behind the controls, waiting. Slowly, grudgingly, Tree started back to the patrolcraft.

Gundhalinu got out, looking relieved as he vacated the pilot's seat. "You drive." He held up his hands, and started for the far side of the craft.

Tree hit the flashers and took them back up the Street, scattering pedestrians like startled birds.

He was more than surprised when Devony opened the door to them—Devony herself, her face filled with sorrow and resignation, as if she read the future and the past in their eyes. She stood aside to let them in.

"Tree," she said. "Nyx—"

"Shut up." He felt his face burning as if she'd slapped him; his hands ached with the urge to hurt her back. He kept them open at his sides, forcing himself to remember that he was a Police officer, and not a *shevatch*. "Save it for your conversations with the Queen." He looked away from the pain he saw in her eyes, so that she wouldn't see the pain in his own.

Gundhalinu strode past her without speaking, heading down the hall toward the steamroom.

"What . . ." Devony murmured, as she watched him go.

"The necklace," Tree said. "We know what it is."

She looked at him blankly. "What is it?"

Looking into her eyes, he could almost believe she didn't know. "Bait," he said.

"I don't under—"

"Damn it!" he said furiously. "Don't lie to me anymore! Don't say anything, if you're going to lie to me!"

"I'm not . . ." she whispered.

He could have sworn there were tears in her eyes. "Oh, gods, you're good." He shook his head. "Are you telling me you didn't fuck me just to find out what I knew about the missing piece of tech?"

"That was never why—"

"And you didn't go to Arienrhod with everything I said?"

She looked away helplessly.

Gundhalinu came back into the room, the necklace dangling from his half-closed hand. "It's still here," he said, as if he was amazed at their good fortune.

Devony glanced toward him with brimming eyes as Tree said, "I guess we know now why you got your fingers broken, BZ."

Gundhalinu stopped, his gaze still on her. She looked down. So did he. Tight-lipped, he put the jewel into his belt pouch.

"Why are you taking my necklace?" she asked, almost angrily.

"It isn't a necklace," Gundhalinu said, "and it isn't yours. It's a piece of Old Empire tech the Queen was trading to offworlder criminals—the vigilantes walked in on them by accident and got butchered."

"It can't be. I don't believe you." She shook her head. "It was a gift; the Queen gave it to me! Why would she give it to me, then—?"

"Because you were seeing him." Gundhalinu nodded at Tree. "And he needed to remember."

She opened her mouth, closed it, looking back at Tree. The tears brimming in her eyes spilled out and down her face. He looked away; his own eyes felt like a desert.

"Arienrhod's gifts always have strings attached," Gundhalinu said.

"You don't know anything about our Queen!" Devony wiped her cheeks, her face reddening. "Arienrhod puts her world and her people first, when the Hegemony would put us last . . . Do you have any idea of how you sounded when the two of you stood in front of me today and told each other how the Hegemony had to keep technology from my people—as if I was too stupid to even understand what you were talking about?" Her voice rose. "What right do you have to treat me like that?" she demanded. "Or this world?"

"That has nothing to do with this," Gundhalinu said, frowning.

"It had everything to do with it!"

"And is that supposed to make everything *all right*—?" Tree shouted, in sudden fury. "My brother's *dead!*" He began to pace, caged in the space between her body and the door. "He's dead, because Arienrhod makes dirty deals with the kind of human garbage who'd do anything to anybody, even to you— even to *her*—to get what they want! You saw what they did to him," pointing at Gundhalinu, "and, and, *gods*, what they did to me . . . I trusted you, Devony! I told you all my . . . my . . . *everything*, because I thought . . . thought you—" He choked on the word, and spat it out. "Goddamn you, you bitch! You went to the palace as soon as we were gone!"

"You were watching me . . . ?"

He nodded, his face clenched.

She held his gaze, taking a long, slow breath; her fingers wove a lover's-knot in front of her. "Then you ought to know that I never went inside."

He stopped, staring at her.

"Why?" Gundhalinu murmured, finally.

"Because it was wrong!" Devony looked back at him. "When I saw what the Ondinean did to you, and I realized . . . This is all Mundilfoere's fault!" she said bitterly. "Arienrhod is still our Queen, and I've never regretted giving information to her. But this was *wrong*. I never meant to hurt you . . . either of you. Especially not . . . not you. . . ." Her voice fell apart as she turned back to Tree. "I'm sorry! . . . Oh, Nyx, please believe me, I didn't *know*. I'm so sorry, I'm so sorry about everything that happened," she reached out, trying to take his hand, "everything I did that—"

His hand made a fist, he jerked it away before it could crush her fingers. Glaring at Gundhalinu, he said, "Fuck you. Fuck me! Why the hell did I listen to you? Why did I even come here?" He swung around, heading for the door. "Why the hell did I *ever* come here—?"

"LaisTree!" Gundhalinu started forward. "Wait a minute, for gods' sakes—"

"Nyx, don't, *please*—"

He turned back, their voices drowning in the white noise of his blood. "I have to. I have to." He shook his head. "Just—just get her to someplace safe, Gundhalinu. Then do what you've got to do. . . .Because that's what I'll be doing."

He went out the door alone, slamming it behind him.

"Damn him!" Gundhalinu pressed his throbbing hands to his throbbing head as he stared at the door. "That stupid, stubborn—" He took a deep breath, letting his futile anger out in a sigh between clenched teeth.

When he felt able to face Devony's distracted gaze again, he turned back to her. "Devony, I . . . I mean we . . . we came back for you, as well as for the necklace."

"You're arresting me?" she whispered.

"No—" He shook his head. "No. I only meant protective custody. We were concerned about your safety. It's not safe for you to stay here."

She smiled, a kind of rictus, as she wiped the wetness from her face. "I'll be fine, Sergeant."

He studied the shadows in the corners of the room, the shadows under her eyes. "No," he repeated softly, "I think you won't be."

She glanced down. "There's nowhere I can go that's any safer," she said. "Not in Carbuncle. . . ."

"There is one person I still trust completely, though." He was only certain of it as he said it. *Jerusha PalaThion.* "Please, let me take you to her."

Devony nodded, finally, as if something in his expression had made her change her mind. Her body followed, metamorphosing within heartbeats into a Winter avatar he wouldn't have recognized, until he looked into her eyes again. And then she left the townhouse with him, leaving behind everything in it without a backward glance.

By the time they reached the Street, there was no sign of the patrolcraft, or of LaisTree. Gundhalinu sighed, and told himself that at least they would be walking downhill.

Tree took the patrolcraft down to the Lower City, to Sienna Alley—to the place where the Boatman had carried his brother and the rest across without a ticket, and left him behind, stranded on the shore of Life, forced to make restitution for all their souls before he would be allowed to follow.

Abandoning Gundhalinu and Devony hadn't caused him a moment of regret. *Fuck them both.* He hoped they spat on his grave. They meant nothing to him—an arrogant brass-kisser and a one-night stand—and there was nothing more he needed from either of them: No more truth, no more lies. . . .

Nothing, except for them to stay far away from him.

Because it might not be too late, for them.

They would try to save him, if they could . . . he knew it as surely as he knew that by now they'd be lucky to save themselves. He'd been a walking death sentence ever since the night of the massacre; with everything he knew, he was already as good as dead, and anybody who got too close to him was going to die too.

He wanted his brother back. He wanted his life back, and his badge—but he had no more chance of getting them back now than he had of seeing Staun's smile again, this side of the Beyond. There was nothing anyone could do to help him now; there was nothing left to save.

And nowhere for him to go, except down. No reason for him to still be breathing, except to deliver the Boatman's Due.

He abandoned the patroller at the mouth of the alley and walked in from there, having no more choice about that than he did about his destination. Sienna Alley was where Nhon, a trade broker, kept his office. Nhon's business was never as clean as he claimed, and the street Blues knew it. They let him go on making his deals, as long as he answered the occasional question about who was buying what, and when. If anybody in Carbuncle knew where to find Humbaba, it would be Nhon.

Tree kept his gaze fixed on the smothered darkness beyond the storm wall at the alley's end, barely glancing left or right. But still, he knew—even blindfolded, he would have known—exactly when he passed the featureless warehouse, the peeling door that had led the Nameday Vigilantes straight to hell on Saint Ambiko's Day. The place where his brother had died in his arms. . . .

It should have been him.

If it weren't for him, Staun would still be on Newhaven—safe, alive, married to Tarina. His brother could have had a real family, and a life of his own . . . a long, full, happy life; the one he'd deserved.

If it weren't for him, his brother would never have joined the Police. His mind hemorrhaged memories like blood, so much blood that he should have been weeping tears of it. . . .

No. His hands knotted into fists. His life belonged to the Boatman, now, the god of the street Blues— the god who only answered the prayers of the dying. And he swore by the Bastard Boatman, *this time it would be the killers who wept blood.* He kept walking, his vision hazed with red, not seeing how empty the alley had become, how unnaturally still, like the air before a storm. *He would stay alive long enough to send those butchers across without a ticket—to give the Boatman just due for his brother and his friends, blood for blood, so that when his own soul finally crossed over, it would be with a ticket honorably in hand. . . .*

"LaisTree!" Armed men suddenly blocked his way, as if he had conjured them up out of his own blood-red need for vengeance.

Tree pulled his gun and fired, dropping two of them, scattering the rest. As he turned and ran back toward the patroller, another cadre of armed strangers appeared, cutting off his escape route.

But before he had even reached the warehouse, someone behind him fired a stun rifle. The beam caught him full in the back, taking out his voluntary nervous system. He hit the pavement, hard.

He lay like a living corpse, waiting for them to come and get him. Fully conscious, but unable to do anything at all to stop it, he let the strangers gather him up like a corpse and carry him away.

*   *   *

The artificial energy of another stim patch was all that kept Gundhalinu moving as he led Devony Seaward into the Maze's bright anarchy, toward Jerusha PalaThion's apartment. She followed him through the evening crowds like an automaton, lost inside the labyrinth of her own thoughts.

"Devony—" He broke the silence between them at last, looking back over his shoulder as they climbed the stairs to the Inspector's flat. She glanced up, looking startled.

They stepped onto the landing; he gestured at the apartment door. "I just wanted to warn you not to shapeshift in front of Inspector PalaThion. It's not legal for a Tiamatan to be using sensenet technology." He glanced away as her expression changed. "The Inspector is usually more . . . tolerant of those things than I am. But even if she doesn't care," he looked up again, with a chagrined smile, "frankly, I'd never hear the end of it, if she found out *I* knew, and I didn't report you."

"Thank you, Sergeant," she murmured, smiling back at him.

"It's BZ—" he said. He felt himself flush as her expression changed again.

He knocked on the door, wincing as pain jagged up his arm; they waited together in awkward silence until at last PalaThion opened it. She stared.

"By the Boatman!" She motioned them inside. "BZ, what the hell happened to you?"

"Everything. . . ." For once in his life, only hyperbole seemed to describe his situation. Searching for the beginning, or even a stray end, in the tangled skein of events, he grasped the first coherent thought that came into his head. He pushed his hand carefully into his coat pocket, and pulled out the iestas he had purchased at the diveshop. "Here's that pack of iestas you wanted, Inspector."

"Thanks." She took the pack from his swollen, purple hand with a faintly incredulous look. "I can't wait to hear what kept you. . . ." She glanced past him at Devony. "Don't tell me you're married, Sergeant?"

"Gods, no!" His cursed freckles betrayed him with a hot rush of scarlet. "I mean . . . Inspector Pala-Thion, please meet Devony Seaward," he said, with a hopelessly belated gesture of propriety, "a . . . close personal friend of Patrolman LaisTree."

"*Sa mieroux.*" Denvoy bowed, speaking the traditional Newhavenese greeting. "Peace to you." She sent a bemused glance his way as she raised her eyes again.

"*Sa kasse* . . . Likewise." PalaThion nodded, studying her with frank curiosity. "So this obviously isn't a social visit." She moved away, tearing open the pack of iestas as she limped doggedly across her common room.

They followed. Bright-colored ovals of pressed glass hung in her windows, like the ones he'd seen in the windows of shops that catered to Newhavenese. Watching her pass through their radiant bands of light, he wondered whether they had some ritual function, or were purely for decoration.

Devony gazed around her in fascination, taking in the room the way he would absorb a datafeed. He realized that she might actually be recording it; realized too, with sudden insight, that her interest was genuine, and not merely a professional habit.

"No, Inspector, this is definitely not a social call." He sprawled on the quilt-covered mattress that served as PalaThion's couch, too exhausted and in too much pain to wait for an invitation. The Inspector seated herself uncomfortably in the single native-made chair, settling her cast-bound leg on a hassock, as Devony sat down beside Gundhalinu.

PalaThion shook out a small handful of iestas. "All right, BZ. Tell me what's going on. And this time, tell me everything." She put the iestas into her mouth, and began to chew.

He looked up at her, surprised, but only for a moment. "It's the warehouse massacre," he said. "Everything goes back to that night. . . . Maybe you ought to record this." This time he did tell her everything, beginning with Aranne's secrets and ending with Herne's, interrupted only by her occasional question, or by Devony's comments on the Ondinean and the Snow Queen.

". . . and that's why I brought Devony here." He nodded at her. "I'm sorry I couldn't tell you about any of this before, Inspector. And I'm sorry I have to tell it to you now, when it only makes you another target." He glanced at the cast immobilizing her leg. "But there's no one else I trust anymore."

"Being trusted with someone's life is an honor I'm not offered every day." She smiled wryly. "And being a target is what they pay us for. . . ." She stopped smiling. "If the killers really are some of our own, it only gives me more reason for wanting to help you bring them down."

He got to his feet again, swayed, suddenly lightheaded with relief—or something less reassuring. "That's two things off my mind, then. . . ." He glanced back at Devony.

"What are you going to do now?" PalaThion asked.

He looked down. "I'm going to make my report to the Chief Inspector and the Special Investigator."

Her face tensed. "Are you sure you want to do that? From what you've told me, you could be handing them your head on a plate."

He hesitated. "LaisTree has to be wrong about their involvement. They're Kharemoughis, Technicians, for gods' sakes! They have nothing to gain from some conspiracy to steal Old Empire technology, no matter how valuable it might be. If it's recovered, it will go to Kharemough for research and development anyway." He shook his head. "What would be the point?"

"Only another Technician could answer that." PalaThion shrugged. "Just keep in mind what Saint Arda once said: 'Unquestioning belief is not rooted in faith—but in doubt'."

" 'Carbuncle is like entropy,' " Devony murmured. " 'Everything breaks down here. The meanings don't hold.' "

Gundhalinu looked at her, frowning.

"You said that yourself." She held his gaze.

He looked down, trapped inside a moment of paralyzing self-doubt. "I. . . ." He shook his head again. "No. No, I didn't really mean that—" He glanced away, seeing PalaThion's troubled expression. "I won't tell anyone about either of you being directly involved in this. Inspector, you have the names we got from Herne. I'll be giving them to Aranne. But you could back me up by making sure they get into the databank at the station. If I—that is, in the unlikely event that I am wrong, I don't want that information buried along with me."

"Consider it done, Sergeant." She nodded. "What about LaisTree?"

He shrugged. "He went after the Ondinean. He's out there alone, he's not carrying a remote, and he's not wearing the tracer anymore. I don't know if that makes him safer, or just crazy."

"Moving targets are harder to hit . . . " PalaThion

said. She glanced at Devony's pale, silent face; looked down at her own cast-encased leg.

"I'd better get moving, then." Gundhalinu sighed. Straightening his shoulders, he smiled briefly at them both, before he crossed the room to the door.

──── **17** ────

The door of the windowless room opened at last. Tree stirred on the bare cot, where he had been unceremoniously dumped and left to recover. He struggled to his feet, barely able to remain upright as the aftereffects of stunshock harrowed his body's foundering nervous system.

The armed guards flanking the door glanced sidelong as Sab Emo Humbaba passed between them; their eyes came back to Tree at the sound of his indrawn breath.

Herne hadn't lied. Humbaba's ritual scarring looked like the result of a disemboweling. Tree bowed his head, unable to look at the man for long enough even to meet his gaze.

"I understand that you have been searching for me." Humbaba's voice was deep and resonant, perfectly modulated . . . completely normal. He seemed oblivious to the effect his own face had on the person he was confronting—which was probably the point. *I-shin* scarring was all about demoralizing your enemies. "But I gather it is really my wife you wish to see, Officer LaisTree."

Tree glanced up again, this time forcing himself to find two eyes somewhere in that mass of twisted flesh. "Yes," he muttered.

"What is it you want from her?"

"I want my brother to still be alive—!" The sudden, blinding pain of his loss rendered the hideousness of Humbaba's face meaningless, invisible. Tree went on, his voice steadying, his own face a mask of stone. "But I can't have that. So I want to see the ones who killed him dead."

Some seepage of emotion, rising from unseen depths, moved Humbaba's face; Tree had no idea what the emotion was. Humbaba merely shook his head, murmuring, "My wife observes the traditions of her people. She does not entertain uninvited guests. Not even those who come bearing gifts." He held up the mesh headset in one perfectly manicured hand.

Tree looked down at the floor again, twisting his bound hands until the knotted monofilament began to make his wrists bleed.

"Nonetheless, she feels indebted to you, for returning her property. She would have made an exception, in your case—"

Tree looked up in surprise.

"—And because she believes you know what's become of the rest of it, of course. . . ." Humbaba shrugged. "Regretfully she had more urgent matters to attend to. Her business associate will see you in her place. He is not fond of Police officers—even disgraced Police officers. If I were in *your* place, I would be . . . cooperative."

Humbaba turned and left the room, as abruptly as he had entered it. The two guards went out after him; the door locked behind them.

Tree felt his fleeting relief turn to incomprehension as he realized that the room was beginning to grow dark, the light leaking out of the space around him as inexorably as oxygen. He turned where he stood, filled with the sudden, irrational fear that it actually was becoming harder to breathe. *Her 'business associate'—*

"Oh, gods," he whispered, almost a prayer; he dropped onto the cot again as his knees buckled. He knew the rumors on the street. He had thought he was simply a walking dead man, but he'd gone one step beyond even that, into the real heart of darkness. *. . . He had reached the Source.*

The blackness around him was total now. All that he could hear was his own heartbeat, the rasp of his frightened breathing. *Or was it . . . ?* He held his breath.

The sound of labored breathing went on.

Gundhalinu entered the Chief Inspector's office, barely able to keep from glancing left and right, up at the ceiling, down at the floor, as if his presence might trigger hidden weapons. "Sir?" he said, forcing his gaze to stay on Aranne's face.

Aranne looked up from his work; his expression was exactly as startled as it should have been. "Gundhalinu—?" he said.

Gundhalinu made an awkward salute, hoping his own expression looked convincingly open and forthright.

Aranne rose to his feet. "Gods, what happened? Where the hell have you been?"

"I went to search LaisTree's apartment, sir. Somebody jumped me there. They seemed to think that I knew something about the . . . the missing prototype."

"You? Why?"

He shook his head. "Maybe because I was also at the warehouse that night. And because I asked questions about this." He pulled the necklace out of his belt pouch and laid it on Aranne's desk. "Chief Inspector, is this part of the missing tech you were looking for?"

Aranne's jaw dropped. "Yes! By all the gods, be careful with that." He took it into his hands as if it were the dust of his ancestors. "Where did you find this?" He looked up again, his face filled with disbelief.

"The Snow Queen gave it to the woman LaisTree was seeing. Arienrhod must have hoped it would trigger his memory. It didn't, because he never even saw the missing tech. . . ."

Aranne went on staring at him for what seemed like an eternity. At last he said, "Shut the door, Sergeant."

Gundhalinu obeyed, cutting off the umbilical of noise and activity from the station house beyond. Turning back, he had the sudden unnerving sense that he had cut his own lifeline. He caught hold of a chair, supporting himself as another wave of dizziness broke over him.

"Sit down," Aranne said, with a frown of concern, "and tell me everything you know about this."

"What about Special Investigator Jashari?"

"Jashari is in a meeting," Aranne said impatiently. "I will keep a full record of your report for him."

Gundhalinu sat down. "Sir, about the necklace—"

Aranne still held it in his hand, as if he was afraid

it would vanish if he lost contact with it. "You got this from the shapeshifter? And she got it from the Queen?"

"Yes, sir."

"So Arienrhod had possession of it all along. But she doesn't have the headset?"

"No, sir. LaisTree—" He broke off.

"LaisTree what?"

"LaisTree . . . and I questioned a man named Herne, who admitted he was at the warehouse that night."

"You and LaisTree? Together?"

"Yes, sir." Gundhalinu pressed on, before Aranne could ask him more questions. "Herne claimed that the Queen had the tech in the first place, that the Ondinean—"

"What Ondinean?"

"A woman named Mundilfoere, who's working with the Source. She and four others were the ones who . . . questioned me, at LaisTree's apartment."

Aranne stiffened. "What did they ask you?" The monitor screen in the surface of his desk sent an eerie play of light and shadow over his features as he leaned forward.

"They asked me what I knew about the missing tech—which was nothing, at that point. They didn't believe me. . . . " He looked down at his hands. "And they kept saying that I was 'a stranger, far from home.' " He shook his head. "I don't know what that means, but it seemed to mean something to them."

Aranne muttered a curse; he looked down at the techno-jewel in his hand. "And they just left you there?"

Alive. Gundhalinu glanced up as he caught the unspoken coda to Aranne's question. "Yes, sir." It only occurred to him now to be surprised that they had let him live. "Maybe they heard someone coming. . . . LaisTree found me there."

"And LaisTree has finally remembered everything that happened at the warehouse?"

"Yes, sir, he has." Gundhalinu nodded, reminded with sudden stomach-knotting vividness of the reason LaisTree's memories had shaken them both so badly. His bandaged hand moved unthinkingly to his holster, found it empty. Wincing, he forced his hands to lie still in his lap. "The vigilantes never had a chance to see anyone in possession of the tech, let alone take it for themselves, before they triggered the hidden defenses."

"You believe that?" Aranne said. Gundhalinu wasn't sure whether it was a question or an assertion.

"Yes, I do." His answer was the same, either way. "I was there when his memory came back. I believe him." He took a deep breath, forcing his mind to seek a quiet, focused center. "Sir, he saw the Special Ops team you told me about; he recognized Captain Cabrelle. . . ." He broke off as his resolve faltered.

"Yes—?" Aranne said.

"Chief Inspector, he said Cabrelle tried to kill him—*would* have killed him, in cold blood, if that grenade hadn't gone off."

Aranne stared at him. "What are you saying?"

Gundhalinu looked down, away, at the wall. "Maybe they thought the vigilantes were a threat . . . but LaisTree said Cabrelle *knew* him. Added to the kinds of questions the Ondinean and the others asked me, and what we got from Herne—" He looked up at Aranne again, searching the Chief Inspector's impassive face, his impenetrable eyes. "Sir, I believe that someone on the force is in collusion with the killers, and maybe worse. And furthermore, the information you gave me about the missing tech does not jibe with what Herne told us."

"Explain." Aranne sat back, his face grim.

"Herne told us the missing tech is actually a functioning Old Empire artifact of some kind, and that he was delivering it *to* the Ondinean, for Arienrhod; not the other way around."

"He was lying, obviously."

"No, sir, I don't think so. He believed we'd given him a truth drug." He explained, briefly.

Aranne shook his head, with a reluctant smile. "That was uniquely resourceful, Sergeant." His expression sobered. "Then perhaps he was telling you the truth. But as you say, it doesn't match what you— or I—believed was going on that night at the warehouse. In which case, I am as concerned as you are about getting to the real truth." His frown deepened as he stared at the displays flickering over and through his desktop. Abruptly he shut off the access; the terminal went dark, metamorphosing into a plain metal surface. "What else did this Herne tell you?"

"He gave us the identities of the other offworlders who were at the warehouse that night. He mentioned the names of the men whose bodies were identified, so I believe he was also telling the truth about that. I have his entire testimony on tape."

"Father of all my grandfathers, why didn't you say so!" Aranne leaned forward again, his eyes shining. "Input it into the system directly. We'll finally be able to nail those bastards who cost us many good men. Good work, Gundhalinu. Excellent work!"

Gundhalinu settled back in his chair, feeling the tension in his shoulders and neck loosen as he activated the data transfer from his remote. *He had been right. Aranne couldn't be corrupt; he cared too much about the men under his command to ever betray them.* He rubbed his eyes, praying that now, finally, he would be able to sleep again at night.

"What else did you and LaisTree find out from this Herne?"

LaisTree—Gundhalinu looked up again. "Herne described the missing tech. That was enough for us to recognize that the necklace was part of it . . . and that LaisTree had the rest of it."

"What?" Aranne said, in disbelief. "You have the headset too? Why didn't you tell me?"

Because I didn't know whether I could trust you. Gundhalinu looked down. "LaisTree has it, sir. He took it with him."

"Where is he?"

"Pursuing a lead on the Ondinean."

"Why the hell didn't you take the headset from him first?"

Gundhalinu stared at his feet. "Sir, I didn't get the chance. He was upset and angry. He left me behind—"

"Never mind, Sergeant." Aranne took a deep breath. "You've obviously been through an ordeal. So has he. Neither one of you should be faulted for errors in judgment. But he shouldn't be out there alone, for gods' sakes, with that piece of equipment or without it. Do you know where he went?"

Gundhalinu shook his head. "He has informants all over the Maze."

"But he's still wearing the tracer?"

Gundhalinu grimaced. "No, sir. He removed it."

Aranne swore under his breath. He stood up and moved out from behind his desk. "Let's give the men those names, at least. They'll want to be out there hunting down the suspects . . . and I want them searching for LaisTree too, as quickly as possible."

Gundhalinu forced his reluctant body up out of the

chair, fighting the gravitational drag of his exhaustion. He followed Aranne toward the door.

Just as he reached it, his remote began to buzz. He glanced down, stopped dead as he saw the caller ID.

It was LaisTree.

"An old superstition on Newhaven says that perfection attracts the Evil Eye. . . ." Jerusha PalaThion limped across the common room toward her desk. "So there's always a flaw somewhere in a weaver's design, if you search for it long enough."

"Selfish pride offends the gods . . . the Goddess." Devony nodded, forcing her thoughts to wander as randomly as her fingers roamed the surface of the antique carpet that hung on PalaThion's wall. "So the weaver made a mistake in the pattern, on purpose. She believed that doing it would keep her . . . safe." Her voice faltered as she suddenly found the flaw. She pulled her hand away, folded it into a fist. The rug's intricate pattern blurred into pools of formless color in front of her eyes. "But believing she could control fate that way . . . that's just another kind of arrogance, isn't it?" She shook her head.

PalaThion was silent for a long moment, as if she was trying to think of a response that wasn't simply a platitude, or a lie. At last she just took the pack of iestas from her caftan's sash pocket without answering, and turned back to her monitor screen. "Damn it!" she murmured. She dropped awkwardly into her desk chair.

"What—?" Devony crossed the room to look over her shoulder. The other woman's hands moved over the touchboard too rapidly for her to follow the results. "What is it? What happened?"

"I've been monitoring Gundhalinu's remote,"

PalaThion said, frowning. "He just got a call from
LaisTree, on the Police band." Words began to ap-
pear on the screen as she tapped into his communicator line. She activated the port's speakers.

"—*where you are?*"

"*I don't know . . . I mean, just listen—*"

Devony froze as she heard their voices in the room,
speaking as clearly as if they were standing next to
her. "But that's good, isn't it?"

"No." PalaThion canceled the sound. "LaisTree
doesn't carry a remote since his suspension. He
didn't make this call on his own, and I doubt he
made it willingly. He must have walked straight into
a trap after he left your place. The Ondinean, probably—which means the Source. They've got the headset now. They're trying to pull in Gundhalinu, and
the necklace." She shook the pack of iestas; three
fingernail-sized pods dropped into her hand. She
shook the pack again, then crumpled it into a wad.
"Shit. . . ."

"It's my fault." Devony turned away, sick at heart.

"How do you figure that?" PalaThion spat a pod
into a bowl on the desk.

"He would have listened to Gundhalinu, he wouldn't
have gone off on his own, if . . . if he hadn't. . . ."

"If he hadn't found out you were telling everything
to Arienrhod?"

Devony nodded; her hands closed over the back of
the common room's single chair until they whitened.

"You really care about him, don't you?" PalaThion
said, surprised.

"I barely know him—" Devony broke off as her de-
fensiveness sublimed, suddenly becoming another
emotion entirely. "I've never met anyone like Nyx.
Never. . . . He really wanted *me*. . . ." She pressed her

hand to her lips, without actually touching her own flesh; her eyes burned with unshed, wholly unexpected tears.

PalaThion sighed. "Devony, it's not your fault that he made a bad decision. He let his emotions cloud his judgment. He's a Blue; he's trained to know better."

"He's not a Blue!" Devony said sharply. "Not anymore. They took that away from him too—after he lost his brother."

PalaThion looked down, grimacing. "It still isn't your fault," she said. "And it isn't really his, either. The only ones to blame, for everything that's happened, are the killers." She gestured at the monitor; her hand tightened into a fist. "Gundhalinu's at the station house. He'll know the call is a setup; they'll find a way to get LaisTree back—"

"I wouldn't be too certain of that, Inspector," a voice said, from somewhere behind them.

Devony turned and her breath caught as PalaThion said, "Who the hell are you?"

"Mundilfoere . . ." Devony murmured, both a question and an answer.

PalaThion reached for the gun lying on the tabletop beside her.

"Don't bother with that, Inspector." Dressed in black, Mundilfoere crossed the room like a shadow dancing with light. "There is no need, and there is no point." Something glinted as she raised her hand.

PalaThion turned away from the stunner, leaning back again in her seat with a casualness that belied her expression. "How did you get in?" she asked, as if she honestly wanted to know.

Mundilfoere gave a fluid shrug. "It's a gift," she said, smiling faintly. "You Police take too many things for granted. That is far more dangerous than this is—"

She nodded at the object she held in her hand, then tossed it out suddenly. It arced through the air into PalaThion's startled grasp.

PalaThion made a disgusted noise as she looked at it. "A subdermal infuser?"

"I used it to drug your sergeant earlier today," Mundilfoere said. "I truly regret that I couldn't afford to take his honesty for granted. He actually *was* as innocent as he seemed to be."

The stunner was in PalaThion's hand between blinks of an eye; she fired.

It had no effect. Mundilfoere smiled, not even slowing down as she finished crossing the room. "Your poor sergeant." She nodded at the monitor screen. "I see he has insisted on taking Aranne at face value after all, in spite of LaisTree's warning, and everything we let him overhear during the interrogation. . . ."

"Cut the crap," PalaThion said. "What do you want?"

"She knows what I want—" Mundilfoere turned back. "Don't you, Devony Seaward?"

"The necklace," Devony said softly. "But I don't have the necklace anymore. Gundhalinu took it. The Police must have it by now."

"Obviously," Mundilfoere said, as if that fact was no more than a tiresome detail. She glanced at the monitor again. "But all stasis is flux at heart. Tell me, Devony, what did Nyx LaisTree mean to you?"

"*Did?*" Devony whispered, and the unguarded grief in her own voice shocked her. "Oh . . . oh, gods, no." She sank into the chair that was suddenly the only thing supporting her.

"That's what I thought," Mundilfoere said, with a brief, oddly sympathetic smile. "LaisTree is still alive,

Devony. . . . What would you do to keep him that way?"

Devony stared at her, dazed. "Anything I have to," she said, at last.

Mundilfoere nodded, as though she had anticipated that reaction as well. "I need your help, then. Will you come with me?"

Devony got up and crossed the room to her side.

"Wait a minute—" PalaThion pushed to her feet, swore as the abrupt motion threw her off balance and she banged her hip against the desk. She stood glaring at them, as conscious as they were of her helplessness. "Devony, don't be stupid," she said. "You don't really believe that woman needs your help. Even if LaisTree's not dead, do you think she'll let either one of you walk away from this—?"

"You underestimate Devony's resourcefulness, Inspector," Mundilfoere said, "and also her gifts, because you don't really know her. I have genuine need of her help." She locked eyes with PalaThion. "And you know nothing about me. I learned at an early age that I had to make my mind large, like the universe is large, in order to make room for all of life's paradoxes . . . especially the paradoxes in my life. I let your sergeant walk away, today. Do you think Aranne will be as generous to him, or to LaisTree?"

"Aranne has no reason—"

"You know that is always an unwise assumption to make . . . Inspector." Mundilfoere glanced at PalaThion's helmet and uniform coat hanging by the door. "Especially when you serve on this world. Every time you peel back the layers of meaning around a word, or think you see what lies behind someone's smile—or even imagine you've fathomed the reasons for this city's existence . . . you only strip away one mask to find another. When we speak of gods, and say that to gaze on them naked would be suicide, what we really mean is Truth. If you're weak, it will destroy you. But look away at your peril. . . . Your position is precarious enough. Be sensible."

PalaThion didn't answer, but Devony saw the frustration that burned in her eyes, the subtle movement of her head that said accepting the Ondinean's words would mean committing suicide, for a man she barely knew.

"I chose the life I lead because everything happens in Carbuncle, Inspector," Devony said quietly. "I just never really realized what 'everything' meant, until now."

"This is the real world we're talking about, damn it!" PalaThion said angrily. "The rules apply to you, too."

Devony canceled the sensenet's image, abruptly showing PalaThion her real face. "I make my own rules—"

PalaThion's eyes barely flickered at the transformation. "And you're the one who just told me how arrogant it was to believe that."

"You're forgetting one thing, Inspector," Mundilfoere said. "We're in Carbuncle. 'The Rules' are suspended for the duration. Making your own rules, and living by them, is an act of self-preservation here. Isn't that true, Geia Jerusha . . . ?" She raised her eyebrows. "Saint Geia, your namesake, is the protector of innocents, is she not?"

"The protector of fools," PalaThion muttered.

"It's all in how you translate it." Mundilfoere shrugged.

"I am a Hegemonic Police officer. I obey the Hegemony's rules."

Mundilfoere laughed. "And Arienrhod makes a mockery of them. So whose rules are you obeying, really? And what is it you've been risking your life for all these years—?" She gestured at PalaThion's cast.

PalaThion looked down at her injured leg. Then, slowly, deliberately, she picked up the stunner again, and took aim at Devony. "It's my duty to protect all the Hegemony's citizens—even from themselves, if necessary. Nobody dies on my watch . . . not if I can prevent it. I'll stun her before I'll let you take her away from here, Mundilfoere. Drag her dead-weight down the stairs if you can, but she won't be much use to you . . . if that's really why you want her."

Devony stiffened, looking from PalaThion to Mundilfoere.

"Fire the gun and you've killed your sergeant," Mundilfoere said. "Nyx LaisTree, too. I swear it—" Something in the woman's voice stopped Devony's breath in her throat. "*They* will not be temporarily inconvenienced. And if that happens, you and Devony will be the next victims. There will be no way you, or anyone, can prevent it."

"So you'll guarantee that, too," PalaThion said, with deadly spite.

Mundilfoere shook her head. "It will be out of my hands by then. Whether I live or I die, Inspector, I simply won't be here after to-night. . . . The time to stop the inevitable is before it starts. For once in your career, you have the chance to live up to your name, Geia Jersuha PalaThion. Will you take it? Isn't it better to face the truth unafraid, to live honestly even for a day, than to surrender your entire life to a lie?"

PalaThion stared at her for an endless moment. Then, slowly and deliberately, she put the gun back on the desk. "Saint Geia, protect us all . . ." she muttered, looking down.

Devony glanced back as she followed Mundilfoere out the door. PalaThion stood staring at the monitor screen, her face clenched with silent pain.

As they walked down the alley toward the Street, Devony finally let herself ask, "What is it you expect me to do?"

Mundilfoere glanced over at her. "I expect you to help me be in two places at once, of course. Do you think you can do that?"

Devony returned her smile like a steel mirror. "I think you've given me enough motivation for the performance of a lifetime."

"I don't doubt it." Mundilfoere's amused smile turned sardonic.

Devony frowned, stopping.

"You're in no danger from me," Mundilfoere said mildly. "I need you. And I never burn my bridges behind me, unless the enemy is at my back. I've always preferred to keep my options open." She started on with an impatient motion of her hand. "I'll tell you the details as we go. Time is short."

A vacant Police patrolcraft was waiting for them at the entrance to the alley. Devony felt something drop sickeningly inside her as she realized where the patroller had come from.

Mundilfoere opened the doors and reached in. "Can you use one of these?" She handed out a stun rifle from the rack behind the seats.

Devony took it, checked it. "Yes."

Mundilfoere raised her eyebrows.

"I grew up in the outback," Devony said, shrugging. "I could pick off thieving nomads with a pellet gun before I could spell my own name . . . And target practice became a hobby of mine, very soon after I moved to the city."

"Well, then," Mundilfoere smiled, "welcome to the League of Competent Women." She got in behind the controls.

Devony got in beside her, and the doors closed. "Where are we going?"

Mundilfoere started the power unit. "Down," she said, as the patroller rose over the stream of pedestrian traffic. "Into the underworld. . . ."

18

Gundhalinu walked alone down the ramp that gave access to Tiamat's omnipresent sea, and to the sheltered moorage that lay among the city's massive support pylons. Darkness rose to meet him, all the more unnerving for his having grown used to Carbuncle's endless day. The hour was well into graveyard watch, as it had been on the night when he had so stubbornly begun this fool's progress into the abyss.

During the day, this ramp and the harbor below swarmed with activity: Winter dockhands using imported servomechs to move offworld shipments coming in from the starport; traders and sailors bringing local goods from down the coast. But at this hour, he could see no one on the ramp or on the docks below. Here, where the natural world was still accessible, old customs and diurnal rhythms held sway, and people slept the sleep of the weary, if not the just.

He stopped at the bottom of the deserted ramp, looking back over his shoulder before he looked out across the harbor. The moorage was randomly illuminated by lights strung high in the dripping entrails of the city, among the chains and pulleys twenty meters above. A fog-hung forest of masts and rigging extended as far as he could see, making his vision as uncertain as his judgment suddenly seemed.

He pulled the technojewel from inside his shirt, letting it hang suspended in plain sight around his neck. He turned right, following LaisTree's instructions, and started down the pier into the creaking, sighing wilderness of vessels. LaisTree's captors were asking for a simple exchange, they claimed: LaisTree's life, for the artifact Gundhalinu had. He had no illusions about whether they planned to keep their part of the bargain. The cold wind out of the icebound north set his body crawling with gooseflesh; or maybe it wasn't the wind, only the cold awareness in the pit of his stomach that no matter how empty this gelid underworld seemed, hidden eyes were watching him, and hidden weapons had him in their sights.

Every breath he took filled his head with the pungent smell of the sea, as well as stranger, less appealing odors; every time he exhaled, his breath frosted in front of his face. His hands were getting numb, although for once that was only a relief. He had helped himself to a fresh round of painkillers before he left the station, but they barely muffled the complaints of his mistreated body. He hadn't needed another stim patch; his fear was more than enough to keep him alert.

He sealed the flapping edges of LaisTree's coat, and considered with fleeting irony that he was used to thinking of Carbuncle as cold. The city suddenly seemed like a haven of warmth and light, compared to the forbidding Winter world beyond its walls.

He peered out into the forest of ships and shadows again, and glimpsed open water; he was nearing the end of the docks. Either something was about to happen, or he would have to start swimming. . . . The wind off the icy sea gnawed his bones, and he began to shiver.

"Gundhalinu—"

He stopped, as a voice he wasn't sure he recognized called his name.

A shadow-form emerged from the deeper darkness beneath a ship's looming hull and moved haltingly toward him. As the man entered the light, Gundhalinu saw the gleam of the headset suspended from his jacket front.

"Nyx. . . . ?" he whispered in disbelief. He saw the raw, half-healed flesh on the side of LaisTree's face, where someone had ripped off the bandages; looked into LaisTree's swollen, red-rimmed eyes, and cringed.

"You came?" LaisTree mumbled. He shook his head, his arms pressed against his side. "It's a trap, BZ. Oh, gods, I thought you'd know. . . ."

"I did," Gundhalinu said.

"Then, why—?"

Gundhalinu glanced again at LaisTree's oozing face. He looked down. "We started this together, that night in the warehouse. We might as well finish it together." He shrugged. "It seemed better than dying alone."

LaisTree's throat worked; for a long moment, he said nothing. At last he whispered, "I'm sorry."

Gundhalinu looked down at his own bandaged hands. "I understand," he said softly, as the circle of armed men closed around them like a noose.

Surreptitiously he searched the restless underworld for a trace of other motion, for any sign of his promised backup, while strangers searched him for weapons; but it was impossible to make out any detail.

"Sergeant Gundhalinu." Mundilfoere appeared in front of him, all in black, darkness incarnate. "Always so punctual." She reached toward him with a knife in her hand. "So reliable—"

Gundhalinu stumbled back; the muzzle of a gun dug into his spine, stopping his retreat.

"Don't cringe, Sergeant." She reached out again; her fingers brushed his cheek gently. "I'm not going to hurt you. You simply have something that belongs to me." She caught hold of the necklace. He couldn't keep himself from wincing as she cut the silken cord and pulled the jewel free.

"Thank you," she said, with a mocking smile. She stepped back through the circle of armed men, turning to LaisTree.

"And thank you—" a voice from the outer darkness said, "for underestimating us so profoundly." Gundhalinu gaped, as incredulous as anyone around him, as Aranne suddenly materialized on the empty pier, flanked by a squad of body-armored Police. "Drop your weapons," Aranne ordered.

Someone in the ring of offworlders swore loudly; weapons clattered to the wooden planks of the dock. The sounds echoed and re-echoed from random surfaces all around them. Gundhalinu put out an arm to support LaisTree, who suddenly swayed, weak-kneed with relief.

They watched silently, neither of them quite believing their eyes, as Aranne came forward and took the necklace from Mundilfoere. She made no resistance while he pinioned her hands. The officers with him put binders on her men and herded them to-

gether. Gundhalinu took a deep breath as Aranne
held up the necklace; he realized that he had been
afraid, in some part of his mind, that Mundilfoere
might throw it into the sea as a final act of spite.

"Sir—" he said, reaching out as Aranne turned
back.

"In a moment, Gundhalinu." Aranne shrugged off
the contact that proved his reality. He studied the
piece of mesh dangling from LaisTree's clothing, and
looked toward Mundilfoere. "Is this how you handle
the greatest resource the Old Empire has left us?" he
asked sourly. He reached out to unfasten the headset.
"This had better still be functional."

"Don't be concerned, Aranne," Mundilfoere said.
"The Founders would hardly be so careless as to make
something that was intended to last millennia so fragile. . . . And I am not careless, either."

"Really?" Aranne laughed. "My compliments on
your clever planning."

"On the contrary," she murmured. "I should compliment you on the constancy of your hubris." She
called out, suddenly and sharply, in a language Gundhalinu didn't recognize. All along the pier, dark
forms rose from the sea.

Before he could even react, weapons-fire tore open
the night; around him, bodies scattered like water
molecules in a boiling pot.

"LaisTree, come on!" Gundhalinu tugged Lais-
Tree's shoulder as he dove for the shelter of the nearest gangplank. He rolled under cover, only realizing
as he looked out again that LaisTree hadn't followed
him.

LaisTree stood on the pier, weaponless and alone,
his transfixed face limned by the incandescence of
weapons-fire as he screamed, "Come on, you bastards,
do iiitt—!"

Gundhalinu pushed out into the open and dragged him bodily down. Half-shoving, half-bullying LaisTree under cover, he held him there; LaisTree curled into a fetal ball, crying someone's name over and over. Even deafened by the senses-searing discharge of energy weapons and the cacophony of agonized screams, BZ knew who Nyx was crying out for.

A body and a section of pier exploded in front of them where they lay. Trembling uncontrollably, unable even to turn his face away, Gundhalinu shut his eyes as the burning wave of heat washed over them, searing his exposed flesh. He bit down on his coat sleeve and did not cry out, because he had never had anyone in his life that he could trust that way: *who would always be there to hold him; who would always answer, when he cried out in the night . . . who would never let him fall. . . .*

A falling weapon slammed into the gangplank, almost within reach. Gundhalinu jerked upright, shocked out of his paralysis. He pushed forward, dragging the gun back under cover. Nearly half the shooters on each side were out of the fight already, he realized, either down or fled. Mundilfoere's second wave of attackers were firing indiscriminately on the Police and the prisoners, using heatseekers and plasma rifles, cutting down their own helpless, unarmed allies as ruthlessly as they slaughtered any Blue who gave them a target.

He was so far beyond his own understanding of terror now that his mind seemed suddenly, preternaturally clear. He checked the stun rifle's charge, hefted its weight, solid and real. *He was a Police officer: He knew what he had to do—*

Crawling out from under the gangplank, he began to fire. One of Mundilfoere's men went down, and then another, and another, before someone suddenly

turned to fire at him. Gundhalinu flung himself backwards; the heatseeking projectile struck the gangplank above his head, shattering wood, exploding his
consciousness—

Tree stirred, dragging his battered senses out of the
black pit where his mind had taken refuge when
nightmare and reality merged. Slowly he became
aware that all motion, all commotion, had ceased;
that the underworld was still and silent, and somehow
he was still alive. . . . *Because of Staun; Staun would always take care of him.* He rolled over and nudged the
unresponding body beside him. "Staun—?"

But it was Gundhalinu who lay unconscious there,
not Staun. *Not Staun. Staun was dead.* Tree raised his
head, swallowing a stone of grief as he looked out on
the moorage, the docks, the aftermath of slaughter.
Dimly he remembered that it was Gundhalinu who
had come after him, dragging him down; saving him
when he wouldn't save himself.

Gundhalinu had been right all along. Aranne wasn't
corrupt; these were the Police he had always known,
and trusted.

Rubbing his eyes clear of their double vision, he
saw Aranne's men moving like specters among the
dead and wounded. He could still barely believe that
the faceless, uniformed figures were not the spirits of
the dead—not his own butchered comrades, come
back to claim their revenge—as he remembered how
they had appeared around him out of thin air. But
they looked solid enough now, as they rolled bodies
over and checked them for signs of life.

Which meant they must have been wearing stealth
fields. None of the patrolmen he knew even had access to that kind of technology. Maybe a Special Ops

team might have the resources to requisition something like that. That must be who these men were, how they'd done it; the same way the team at the warehouse must have gotten through the Source's backup systems on the night of the massacre. . . .

A plasma rifle, in the hands of a uniformed Blue . . . a target beam that kissed the fragile kill-points of his head and heart, slid down his body like the touch of a betraying lover. . . . The image strobed suddenly in front of his eyes, forcing him to look away.

"BZ." He shook Gundhalinu gently, and then more insistently, until Gundhalinu groaned and began to stir.

"Easy—" Tree put a hand on his arm as he tried to sit up.

"Gods . . ." Gundhalinu mumbled, "gods. . . ." He tried again, floundering until his sense of balance finally reintegrated.

Tree struggled to his feet in the smoldering ruins of the gangplank, shaking off bits of charred wood.

"Wait—" Gundhalinu said, his voice slurring.

"S'all right," Tree muttered, his own voice not in any better shape. "We won." The knowledge left him curiously unmoved, as if the return of a terror so profound it made everything else meaningless had stripped him of the ability to feel.

Some of the Blues glanced his way; their headlamps pinpointed his motion as he helped Gundhalinu stand up.

"Chief Inspector—!" someone called.

Aranne came toward them through the smoke and bodies, his flash shield up, a smile of vast relief on his face.

The sound of a plasma weapon being fired tore apart the darkness behind them. Tree jerked around as someone's choked cry of protest ended with another sense-ripping burst of *lightheatsound*.

"They're killing the prisoners. . . ." Gundhalinu mumbled.

"What?" Tree saw someone in a night-black diver's suit crawling toward the edge of the pier; watched a uniform move in on him and fire, point-blank, reducing the wounded man to a mass of charred meat.

The Blue kicked the remains off the pier; Gundhalinu made a small, sick noise far back in his throat.

Tree turned away, his eyes crushed shut.

"Sir," Gundhalinu said desperately as Aranne reached them. "Are you killing those men? Why are you killing them? Chief Inspector—?" Aranne pushed past him as if he were mute.

Tree froze, barely even breathing, as Aranne stopped in front of him. With infinite care, Aranne unfastened the piece of mesh hanging from Tree's jacket front, then stepped back. Taking the Queen's necklace out of a belt pouch, Aranne held the artifacts side by side almost reverently. His face filled with the awe a man might feel who was about to witness the literal conjoining of the past and the future, the interlocking halves of which he held in his grasp. He stood, waiting. . . .

The anticipation faded from his eyes as nothing continued to happen. He swore suddenly, furiously, turning away. "You miserable bitch—!"

Tree tracked his motion; saw Mundilfoere lying on the pier, moving feebly, as if she'd been stunshot. Aranne pushed the artifacts back into his belt pouch before he crossed to her and hauled her to her feet. She clung to the railing of the pier as if she could barely stay upright.

"It's ruined!" he shouted at her. "Useless! Do you realize what you've done? What you just made me do—? And all for *nothing*!" He struck her with a gauntleted hand, staggering her.

And then he leaned down and picked up a plasma rifle. His eyes were dark with grief and rage as he turned back to face Tree and Gundhalinu.

Gundhalinu raised his hands in a gesture that was both pleading and warding, his expression stripped naked by the utter finality of Aranne's betrayal.

Any emotion—any response at all—struck Tree as beyond futile, now; beyond even absurdity. The scene unfolding around him had become so surreal that he could feel Time itself winding down, as logic and Order were overthrown at last by entropy and Chaos. . . .

He watched, empty-eyed, as the Chief Inspector took aim at them . . . felt his eyes widen as Mundilfoere surreptitiously gathered herself behind Aranne, and launched her body away from the rail.

Registering Tree's reaction Aranne turned, just as Mundilfoere collided with him. Throwing her arms around him, she wrenched the gun aside, but not out of his hands.

Aranne shoved her away, turning the gun on her. Tree lunged, jerking the barrel off-target just as Aranne pressed the trigger. The gun fired; the white-hot shock wave from the plasma stream punched Tree backward into the railing of the pier.

Aged, weather-worn wood cracked and split; he screamed as the sutured ligaments and muscles tore in his unhealed side. But Mundilfoere's sudden, piercing scream drowned out his own. Trapped in a weir of splintered rails, he watched ghostfire spread over her body as she fell back onto the pier. Still screaming in agony, she . . . changed.

"Dev—?" Tree cried, his voice raw with disbelief. *"Devony!"* He tried to pull himself up the mooring post. The move drove a spine of broken rail into his back like a spear into a frantic fish; he collapsed, tasting blood. He could only watch, helpless, as spasms racked her body, until at last she lay still and her staring eyes closed.

Aranne crouched on the dock, still agape at her transformation. Gundhalinu staggered to his feet and picked up the fallen plasma rifle. "Get your hands up," he said, his voice deadly.

Aranne turned his incredulous stare on Gundhalinu. Slowly he put up his hands.

"Look out—!" Tree gasped, as a uniform farther down the pier suddenly raised a stun rifle. Gundhalinu swung around, too late. Aranne's man fired, and Gundhalinu went sprawling as the glancing hit took his legs out from under him.

The Chief Inspector kicked the gun out of reach as Gundhalinu tried to drag himself after it; stood gazing down at him, almost in sorrow. "Your performance in this investigation surpassed all expectations, Gundhalinu-*eshkrad*," Aranne murmured, his voice as bitter as the wind. "You will never know how profoundly I wish that it had not." He glanced away along the pier littered with lifeless bodies. His gaze was a dead man's as he turned back again. "You asked me before why we were killing the prisoners, didn't you? We did it for the same reason that I have to kill both of you, now. We answer to a higher calling—"

"You mean the gods?" Gundhalinu raised his head with an effort, contempt smoldering in his eyes. "Or the honor of your sainted ancestors, Aranne-*eshkrad*? Or did you simply mean greed, or power?"

"Don't look at me like that!" Aranne's face mottled with sudden fury. He moved toward the spot where his weapon lay. "Jashari was right; you couldn't even begin to comprehend the choices we are forced to make. . . . Do you think I *want* to do this?"

The *crack* of a stun rifle sounded again, followed by a hoarse shout. Aranne turned away, startled, as one of the anonymous Blues inexplicably fired three more shots in rapid succession, dropping the last members of the renegade special ops team who were still on their feet.

"Do you want to do it—?" The real Mundilfoere raised the flash shield of her Police-issue helmet as she turned to face them, pointing the stun rifle at Aranne. She came toward them, picking her way deliberately through the obstacle course of bodies. "That's not the right question, Aranne. It will never be the right question. You know that."

"You—?" Aranne breathed.

"Give me the artifact," she said, aiming the gun at his chest. Fired at close range, a stun rifle would paralyze both voluntary and autonomic nervous systems, killing a man almost instantly.

He grimaced. "There's no point. The reader device is ruined. It's not responding. After all this. . . ." His mouth twisted.

"Perhaps that's because it isn't the real device." Mundilfoere held something out: a curving piece of mesh that shaped itself to her fingers as if it were a living thing. "We didn't put the real one on LaisTree. Did you honestly believe we were that stupid?"

Aranne glared wordlessly at her. And then, suddenly, he laughed out loud.

Beyond Mundilfoere, one final ghost in a uniform materialized out of thin air. "*That* was the wrong question. Drop it—" Jashari said, training his gun on her. Slowly, reluctantly, she let her weapon fall.

"Now," Aranne said, putting out his hand, "give me the reader."

Mundilfoere averted her eyes as she held out the headset, as if his smile of triumph was too humiliating

to bear. Through a deepening slurry of shock and
pain, Tree saw her averted gaze glance off Devony's
motionless form, off Gundhalinu lying helpless beside the shattered gangplank . . . until finally she was
looking straight at him.

She nodded slightly as she saw him respond, and
glanced toward his feet.

He followed her gaze, and saw Aranne's plasma rifle lying almost within reach. A sudden surge of
adrenaline cleared out his head; he looked up again,
but her gaze was back on Aranne. Setting his jaw,
Tree watched her peel the headset from her outstretched fingers and shake it free.

He could never clearly describe, afterward, what
happened then—whether the headset actually leaped
across the gap into Aranne's hands, or whether Mundilfoere had thrown it at him. Because what happened then—the burst of dazzling darkness, as the
headset and the technojewel made contact at last—
defied all description.

Aranne made a strangled noise and stumbled back,
dropping them both on the dock.

"What—" Jashari began furiously.

Mundilfoere twisted like a cat, driving her elbow
into his jaw. Jashari's weapon flew up in a reflex motion; the barrel cracked against her skull. He hit her
again as she fell, clubbing her to her knees.

Aranne ducked down to pick up his own gun.

Tree pushed away from the railing, jerking his body
free as he fell forward to grab the rifle first. He swung
it up, praying more than aiming, and fired.

The plasma beam caught Aranne point-blank, and
blew him through the rail on the far side of the dock,
into the dark, waiting sea.

Tree struggled to his knees, gasping with the effort

it cost to keep his eyes and his weapon tracking Jashari. "Drop . . . the gun. . . ."

Jashari laid his gun down, kicked it away, raising his hands. "LaisTree," he murmured, sounding oddly surprised. "You don't understand—"

Tree made a sound he didn't recognize as a laugh. "Bullshit," he whispered.

"Listen to me," Jashari said, holding his gaze with a fevered intensity. "You must believe that there are some things more important than loyalty, or honor— or even our individual lives." Slowly he began to move forward, holding out his empty hands. "All our lives are meaningless, compared with what this discovery could mean to the Hegemony. . . ." He leaned down, reaching for the fallen headset, and the necklace.

"Back off!" Tree said raggedly. "Shut up! Gundhalinu . . . pick them up." He jerked his head at the artifacts.

Gundhalinu dragged himself forward and collected the pieces of tech carefully, one at a time. He rolled onto his side to look up at Jashari. "You're under arrest," he said, his voice flat.

"No. . . ." Tree shook his head. The itch of blood crawling down his back made a maddening counterpoint to the brutal agony of every breath he drew. "No—" His hands tightened on the gun.

"LaisTree is right, Sergeant." Jashari smiled faintly. "No one will believe you if you report what really happened here tonight. I'll deny everything, and since LaisTree is already under suspicion—" He shrugged, his eyes lingering on Gundhalinu's face, gauging his reaction. "Aranne had great faith in you, Gundhalinu. Cooperate with me. Back me up in the official report and you can both be heroes, instead of pariahs. . . . After all, thanks to you, the ones who were really responsible for the warehouse massacre are already dead, or being arrested as we speak—and we've kept an invaluable artifact out of the hands of the Hegemony's enemies. . . ."

Tree began to cough; blood dripped from his lips onto the planks of the pier.

Jashari looked back, his smile widening fractionally. "You understand what I'm saying, don't you, Lais-Tree? You knew it all along, instinctively. You and your friends became vigilantes when you realized that the law, by its very nature, can never contain Chaos. Humanity has always needed its Sin Eaters: those of us willing to break the rules, to risk condemnation— to sacrifice our souls, if necessary—in order to defeat Chaos on its own terms." He spread his hands. "Who else is there to protect the truly innocent, or to defend the truly irreplaceable, from the monsters who walk among us, passing for human. . . ."

Tree swayed, putting a hand down to support himself. He felt the gun shift in his grip; his vision began to blur as Jashari's words muddied the clarity of his anger.

"LaisTree!" Gundhalinu shouted.

Tree lurched upright as Jashari drove at him and seized the barrel of his gun. He struggled desperately to keep his hands on it, felt the stock slipping—

Mundilfoere picked herself up from the dock, and fell against the back of Jashari's legs. Jashari pitched forward onto his knees, and Tree wrenched the gun free.

And then somehow he was standing, with his body braced against the rail, gazing down into Jashari's stunned face. "That's it, fucker," he said. "You're dead."

"LaisTree, don't!" Gundhalinu said. "It's—"

Tree shut his eyes, and fired.

"It's . . . it's. . . ." Gundhalinu murmured, staring.

"No," Tree whispered, shaking his head. The gun fell from his nerveless grip. He pressed his hands against his side; blood leaked through his fingers as he looked up into Gundhalinu's unforgiving eyes. "It was justice. . . . And you know it."

He watched, feeling neither surprise nor alarm, as Mundilfoere got painfully to her feet and moved to pick up her own weapon. Blood gleamed on her face and in her hair. She crossed to the spot where Gundhalinu lay and said, "Give me the artifacts." Gundhalinu glared up at her, making no move to hand them over. She smiled at him as if he were a child, or an idiot.

"Give them to her," Tree mumbled.

Gundhalinu looked at him, away again, as if the sight of him was as painful as the knowledge of what he had just done.

"Do you honestly believe Jashari would not have killed you both, Sergeant?" Mundilfoere said. She glanced at the smoking hole in the pier. "If not tonight or tomorrow, then in a week, or a month, from now. . . ?"

Gundhalinu looked up at her, his eyes desolate. Slowly, reluctantly, he pulled the headset and the jewel from their hiding places in his clothing and handed them to her. She put them carefully, separately, inside her own clothing.

"What are they for?" Gundhalinu asked, at last. "What do they do?"

She shook her head. "Nothing that will ever affect your life again, Sergeant Gundhalinu."

Tree pushed away from the rail and staggered to the place where Devony lay. He fell on his knees beside her, cradling her head in his bloodied hands. "Devony . . . why . . . ?"

She opened her eyes; her lips formed words that

he could barely make out: "You made me . . . fearless." Her eyes closed.

"*Dev?*" he cried. "No. . . . Don't be dead . . . not for me, please, no . . . not for me. . . ." He touched her face; his own face contorted with pain. "Gods, *please—*"

"Help is coming, LaisTree," Mundilfoere murmured. He thought that sorrow, regret, even admiration, showed fleetingly in her gaze as she looked down at Devony lying in his arms, crimsoning with his blood. "The Police will be here soon."

Tree looked up at her again, his eyes clouded.

"The Police you know . . . the Police that you can trust," she said, almost gently.

She turned back to Gundhalinu. She tossed the gun away with a grimace and showed him her empty hands.

"Why . . . ?" Gundhalinu murmured.

"Perhaps because I want you to spend the rest of your life trying to answer that question." She smiled faintly. "Or perhaps simply because Carbuncle knows how to keep secrets."

Tree held Devony in his arms as he watched Mundilfoere walk away, leaving them there like stormwrack on the shore of an alien sea . . . the living among the dead, strangers far from home and strangers to each other. She walked slowly, as though it hurt, but steadily, until she was no more than a shadow moving in the depths of night, the sound of water lapping, a memory. . . .

19

Arienrhod stood alone in her private study, in the topmost room of the palace—at the very pinnacle of Carbuncle, the apex of her power. Looking out through the transparent walls, she gazed at the perfectly cloudless night sky. A clear night on Tiamat was like a blazing chandelier of stars, so many of them that they dimmed the face of the full moon. Their light refracted eerily from the distant icebound peaks of the interior, even now, when the approach of High Summer had already freed some of the lower slopes from Winter's burden of snow.

Closer in, the dome of the offworlders' starport mocked her, and her people. The port complex glowed independently, with light generated by the same self-contained power source that controlled the landing grids. The starport was designed to be as immune to meaningful interaction with the world it served as the Hegemony itself was; even though the complex lay so close to the city that any native could walk out and challenge its security fields, if they dared.

That forbidden gateway to the stars was the chink through which Mundilfoere had slipped last night, vanishing back into the infinite universe. . . .

Looking down again, Arienrhod saw Carbuncle spread below her, its gleaming folds like a mountain of glass: ageless, indestructible, and inscrutable.

Beyond that, there was only the sea, as eternal and elemental as a goddess . . . as the universe. She knew those black depths waited for her—waited for one false step—silently, patiently, beneath the deceptive film of light that mirrored the unattainable stars.

She turned her back on them all, moving across the pale carpet to the jewel-framed mirror that sat on a table at the room's center. She studied her reflection in its surface, touched it lightly with her fingers. The same ageless girl's face gazed back at her, just as it had every day, year after year. But still she scrutinized the image, searching for any trace of time's corruption—as always, finding none. Never seeing how the gaze itself had changed: how the sly accretion of time, the corrupting, self-indulgent manipulation of power, had clouded the depths of her agate-colored eyes.

Impatiently she touched a pearl on the mirror's base, and her static reflection became a monitor screen. Images of the palace's interior, of the streets of the city and even certain critical buildings in it, passed before her eyes like the fragments of a dream. Along with her network of informants, she had unsleeping electronic eyes planted throughout the city, enabling her to watch its citizens—and especially its visitors—at any time she chose, undetected, to a degree they would find appalling if they ever suspected. . . .

The screen abruptly showed her an image of Starbuck—returned at last from his latest Hunt—as he made his way upward through the palace toward her sanctuary. She wet her lips observing him, watching him come to her. When she heard his heavy tread climbing the circular staircase that led to the study, her hand moved to the monitor's base again. At her touch, it become once more a mirror on a table, containing only her reflection.

Starbuck rapped perfunctorily on the door frame, as if it was his unquestioned right to be here; but he entered the room, and her presence, almost tentatively. She allowed him the privilege of access to her in this private sanctuary only after a successful Hunt.

His bloodstained clothing told her that this Hunt had been very successful, despite the dwindling mer population. She smiled, starting toward him with outstretched hands. The spined helmet dropped from his black-gloved fist as he took her into his arms, hungrily claiming his reward—her lips against his mouth, her body pressing up against his with equal urgency.

She released him from her kiss at last, her smile returning as she watched the effect it had on his dark, handsome face—the way that she alone could bring his expression alive, bring real emotion into his eyes, which usually reflected only death, or nothing.

"Well, Herne. . . ." She stroked his bloodstained sleeve, calling him by his real name, as she did when there was no one to overhear. "A good Hunt . . . a fitting end to the day."

He half frowned. "Mundilfoere's gone offworld with the artifact—I thought you'd be furious."

"Why?" She raised her eyebrows.

"Why—? Even the Blues were slaughtering each

other over that fucking thing; and now they're purging their ranks. . . . The Source must be shitting his pants, if he does shit." Herne shook his head. "Why all of that, if the artifact was really nothing, a useless piece of crap?"

"The Source lives in darkness," she said, her voice casual, insouciant. "It tends to limit his perceptions. And the Police are only men, after all." She shrugged, and smiled, as she saw that Herne didn't, or didn't want to, grasp her implications. "Like Mundilfoere, I refuse to let any object, or any individual—or even the Hegemony itself—limit my vision. Yes, Mundilfoere is gone with the artifact . . . something I had no use for anyway. And that has cost my two worst enemies dearly, while costing me nothing . . . just as she promised."

He gave a skeptical grunt, as though he thought she was lying, simply to save face.

Her expression turned brittle and byzantine, like a frost-covered windowpane. "There might have been something more that passed between us, Herne. . . . But that was not, and is not, your concern—fortunately. So at least I don't have to wonder if you told *everything* to that suicidal renegade, LaisTree, and that insufferable, arrogant boy, Gundhalinu."

"How did—" Herne's face flushed as the words stung him like sleet.

Glimpsing his barely controlled rage and humiliation, she added, "Just be glad they didn't ask you who Starbuck was."

She saw murder come fleetingly into his eyes; but he only looked away, still frowning. "You'd have a hard time finding someone to replace *me*," he said bitterly. "Especially now. . . ." But it was an empty threat, and they both knew it.

His fists tightened at his sides. "Those fucking Blue bastards . . . they actually survived the warehouse *and* the docks. I'd like to know what devil in what hell they sold their souls to."

"Perhaps it was a goddess who answered their prayers. . . ." Arienrhod looked out at the sea. Her smile mocked them both as she turned back again. "And perhaps she preferred them."

For a moment something incomprehensible filled Herne's eyes: something far more terrifying, and more agonizing, than simply death, or even the fear of death.

But then his bitter smile returned. "How does it make you feel, Arienrhod, to know your loyal bitch Devony preferred that Hegemony *shevatch* over you?"

She looked down at the tabletop beside her, at the various objects lying on its surface. "Devony played her part, and served her purpose," she said impassively. Her hand drifted across the table, pausing, moving on, as if the ornaments were game pieces on an offworlder's *tan* board. "Exactly as I meant her to."

"You're telling me this all went exactly like you intended?" He shook his head. "Bullshit."

She glanced at the mirror—where so much lay hidden, beneath the reflecting surface of her smile. "Of course not. Don't be a fool. No one controls fate. But I am more than satisfied—for now. As for the future—we'll see." She selected something from the table at last: A pendant set with a solii dangled from the chain looped over her finger.

Herne frowned. "A Survey charm? Not much of a trade. Maybe the solii's worth more to you than that crap you gave Mundilfoere, at least—"

"Did I say this was an article of trade? . . . Don't try to outthink me, Herne; no one on this planet has lived long enough to do that." She shook her head.

"A Winter laborer brought this to me, early today. He found it on the docks near the site of last night's bloodbath. Mundilfoere had one exactly like it, which she always wore, yet kept hidden. Odd, don't you think? . . . I don't know what this is, but I intend to find out. I have a feeling that the Source may know. That should be worth something to me, at least. . . ."

Herne rubbed his eyes, fatigue settling over his sullen features. He grimaced as though he had given up, for tonight, trying to pursue her through the labyrinth of her relentless plotting.

Her face softened with satisfaction, as she realized that she had won. She put down the pendant, and picked up the vial containing the water of life. Wordlessly, she offered him the first dose. He opened his mouth as hungrily as he had for her kiss; received its blessing in a burst of heavy silver spray. He passed the vial back to her, and she took its precious essence into her own body the same way, like a sacrament.

A dazzling sense of well-being swept through her, like a warm wind sweeping away fallen petals, leaving behind a pristine clarity of mind like nothing else; filling her with the endless wanton joy of youth. She reached for him, gazing up into his eyes. "It's late," she murmured, "isn't it . . . ?"

He pulled her roughly against his body, running his hands over her; his fingers tangled in her hair as he crushed her hungry lips in a deep, lustful kiss. "Let's go to bed . . ."

The memorial service for the fallen officers was held in two separate locations, because there were so many dead to be remembered, following the bloody night in the warehouse and the bloody night on the docks below the city. The Kharemoughi dead were honored at the Survey Hall, the Newhavenese in a public hall rented from local Winters.

Tree sat between KerlaTinde and TierPardée, his head bowed, his eyes too full of unshed tears. He stared fixedly at the reliquary box resting on his knees, while friends and relatives of the deceased officers took the stage one after another, paying tribute, sharing memories.

Commander LiouxSked spoke first, giving a eulogy that actually sounded sincere, before he left the hall discreetly but hurriedly to attend the Kharemoughi service.

The rest of the ceremony ran longer than Tree had expected, but despite his physical discomfort he felt no impatience for it to be over. He needed all this time, and more, simply to comprehend the immensity of the hole that had been torn in his life. Coming to terms with all he had lost was going to take him a lifetime. . . .

He looked down at his dress uniform, at his fingers fidgeting aimlessly with the fringe of the red mourning scarf, which he wore over the sling that protected his arm and side. At least they had finally given him back the right to wear the uniform that had cost him so dearly—doing it as much, he suspected, because he had agreed to keep his mouth shut about what he'd seen on the docks that night as because of his part in tracking down the murderers.

The Police Commander and the Judiciate officials had appeared to take his accusations seriously; the fact that Gundhalinu had told them the same story, and Gundhalinu was a Kharemoughi, hadn't hurt. But whether the brass were really resolved to root out corruption on the force, or only giving lip service to a further investigation because Aranne, Jashari, and the rest were conveniently dead, he had no idea . . .

any more than he knew why Gundhalinu hadn't told anyone how Jashari had died.

In the end, it was impossible to be certain of anything. In the end, it hadn't really mattered. He had gotten the ones who were actually responsible for Staun's death, and that was all he needed to be sure of.

Whatever the truth, the Commander had been desperate to avoid another scandal, especially one so closely associated with the warehouse massacre. The force was still reeling from that blow, he said; they were already undermanned and demoralized. The killers had been brought to justice. Why cause more grief for the families of those involved, or spread more suspicion among the men who had served under them or with them for so long . . . ?

Gundhalinu had gotten a medal out of it, for "service above and beyond the call of duty." Tree had not attended the ceremony. It was enough simply that he had been given back his rightful place on the force . . . Staun's final legacy to him.

Haig KraiVieux, who was leading the memorial service, spoke Staun's name and then Tree's. Tree wiped his eyes, and got up from his seat. Clutching the reliquary, he limped stiffly down the aisle to the front of the hall. He climbed the steps at the side of the stage, one at a time. Passing through the symbolic wall of greenery—none of it any species he recognized—he followed the path lined with lanterns substituting for the luminaria that should have guided him to the altar.

Two potted trees, their branches lashed together, formed a living portal above the altar set up at the front of the stage . . . creating a space that by tradition lay neither *here* nor *there*; a place where the membrane between the world of the Seen and the world of the Hidden was most tenuous.

He set the reliquary on a small table covered with the altar cloth from the watch chapel, where he had spent the past two nights alone with his memories. The cloth was embroidered with idyllic vistas of the Beyond. He knew every stitch on it by heart now; though he was no more certain that it was anything besides a piece of cloth covered with pretty scenes of a place that looked too much like his homeworld.

A bowl, filled with water flowing perpetually over stones, sat on the altar. Alongside the bowl were a single unlit candle, and a holographic image of his brother. He stared at the image for a long moment, oblivious to the expectant rustling of the crowd.

At last he looked up from his brother's face to the sea of faces that filled the hall. He saw the men Staun had served with and been friends with—the ones who were still alive—and the families of the men who were being remembered here today. He was surprised by the number of Tiamatans in the crowd. Some of them were wives or lovers; the others, he realized, had simply come to show their respect for the Hegemonic Police, whose duty it was to keep other offworlders from doing them harm.

As he realized it, a clenched fist of bitterness deep in his chest suddenly released its hold on his aching heart. He took a long, full breath, and the air he inhaled was sweet with gratitude and release.

The murmuring crowd grew hushed as he lit the Candle of Life, and the sweet scent of blooming sillipha began to fill the air. He picked up his brother's picture and held it in trembling hands. Only Staun, of all the men who had died at the warehouse, had not had the Words spoken for him in a traditional prayer service.

He should have been there to speak for his
brother, at the proper moment, in the proper way;
not here like this, not in a rented hall. . . . But
whether he blamed the gods or the brass or himself,
that perfect moment was gone, and he would never
get it back. He glanced over at KraiVieux with a brief,
grateful smile. KraiVieux had insisted he go through
with this, had made certain that he would have the
opportunity to speak the Words in the presence of so
many witnesses.

He looked down again, concentrating on his
brother's face until the hall and its occupants became
a radiant field of light. As he felt their focused life-
energy breach the intangible membrane between
Staun's future existence and his past, Tree began to
recite the Words, calling on his brother's grieving,
exiled spirit to come and put a seal on the cruelly
unfinished business of his life.

The sound of his own voice speaking his native
tongue fell strangely on his ears. He remembered the
last time he had spoken this much Klostan, the last
night he had spent at home with his brother and a
handful of friends . . . remembered suddenly that all
of them were dead, their deaths as brutally senseless
as his lone survival.

Staun's image blurred out of focus. Tree's voice
faltered, panic rising in him as his memory tried to
tell him it had forgotten the order of the prayers—

He shut his eyes, and found a thousand images of
his brother's face, heard the echo of Staun's speech
in his every spoken word. . . . Blind faith, and a luminaria of unbroken memories, showed him the path
through the trackless void of loss; the patterns of
prayer began to flow easily again. He finished the ritual of opening, without dropping a single fragile
strand.

KraiVieux came to join him; and then others, climbing up the steps from the audience. Each one in turn placed some small token in the open reliquary, reciting the Words with him, or responsively: asking forgiveness and granting it; speaking of loss, of grief; swearing the pledge that any family Staun had left behind would never want for the basic needs of life. . . .

". . . that your life was lived with honor, and your death was not meaningless."

Tree glanced up at the unexpected valediction, spoken in flawless Klostan, and found BZ Gundhalinu standing in front of him. Gundhalinu nodded in silent acknowledgment before reaching up to unfasten the medal he wore, that he had been given only yesterday. He placed it in the box, and moved on.

Tree looked down at Staun's picture, his gaze clear again, and his voice steady. ". . . And that you now can rest in peace," he murmured, "because I paid the Boatman's Due, Staun. I paid for all of you . . . I got the killers." He laid the tin of bitterroot chews in the box. "I love you. I miss you. I'm sorry. I forgive you. . . ." He took a deep breath. "I set you free." He placed his brother's picture in the box, and closed the lid. "Let nothing hold you here: not pain, not regret. The veil is torn; pass through." He blew out the candle.

He did not raise his eyes as the other mourners filed away, leaving the stage, merging into the rustling flow of departure as the crowd began to rise and stir. He looked up again only when the scent of sillipha in a whisper of smoke had faded, like the sound of the crowd going out from the hall.

"Thanks, Sarge," he murmured, as KraiVieux returned to his side. KraiVieux nodded, waiting while Tree took the reliquary from the altar, before he began to gather up the ritual objects and the cloth.

Tree descended the steps with painful care. As he reached the bottom, he stopped and gazed around the nearly empty room. Gundhalinu stood midway up an aisle, waiting for him. The few Newhaveners still filing out glanced at Gundhalinu with looks that ranged from surprised to resentful. He only moved aside, to let them pass, his attention fixed on Tree.

Tree walked up the aisle to meet him. They had barely spoken three words to each other since that night on the docks; yet it seemed completely fitting and perfectly logical that Gundhalinu should be waiting for him today. "Is the Kharemoughi service over already?" he asked, stopping by Gundhalinu's side.

"I didn't go. I've been here all along."

"Why?" Tree asked, surprised.

Gundhalinu only shook his head. "Loyalty, and honor . . ." he said at last, the words barely audible. "I guess they had more in common than I realized." He turned away abruptly as his composure began to slip. "Someone wants to see you—" He gestured toward the rear of the hall, glancing back at Tree as he started up the aisle.

Tree walked with him; Gundhalinu's stride slowed to match his halting pace. "Any news on Mundilfoere?" Tree asked, falling back into the familiar patterns of duty and routine with a profound sense of gratitude.

"She got away clean. She's gone offworld." Gundhalinu sounded almost relieved; although maybe it was just his own relief at finding the conversation back on safe ground. "Word has it that she screwed both the Queen and the Source out of that Old Empire tech, as well as us." He made a disgusted face. "I suppose it's comforting to know there's someone out there who can do it to them . . . since we never will."

Tree grunted. "And we never even got to thank her."

"For what? For almost killing us?" Gundhalinu flashed him a gallows grin. "Or for saving our lives . . . ?"

"Take your pick," Tree muttered, and Gundhalinu began to laugh in earnest. Tree laughed with him, simply because it was better than the alternative. "What the hell do you think that was all about, anyway?"

Gundhalinu stared at his feet, watching their steady forward motion. "I don't suppose we'll ever know," he said at last, shaking his head. He gestured at Tree's side. "How are you doing?"

Tree looked down at the sling, at the red scarf. "All right, I guess." His gaze lingered on the reliquary, held against his heart. "At least one of us has found peace." He smiled painfully. "How about you?"

"Finally getting a little sleep. . . ." Gundhalinu still wore splints on his fingers, but most of the bruises were gone. "I'm doing all right—considering the alternative."

Tree nodded. "Yeah. Considering the alternative." He glanced down again, seeing only his uniform this time. "Gundhalinu?"

"What?"

"Why didn't you tell them? About Jashari."

Gundhalinu's shoulders tightened imperceptibly. "I told them everything I knew."

"No you didn't. You didn't tell them that I—"

"It was self-defense."

"I shot him in cold blood. You saw me do it."

"LaisTree—" Gundhalinu broke off, shutting his eyes. "It was justice."

"But can you live with it . . . ?"

Gundhalinu took a deep breath. He nodded, looking out across the empty hall. "When the 'truth' is a barefaced lie, what does a lie become?" He looked back at last. "The case is closed, Nyx. It's over. It's over . . ." he repeated softly, almost to himself.

Jerusha PalaThion stood waiting for them by the exit.

"Inspector." Tree came to attention and saluted, more because it felt good having the right to than because she was expecting it.

"Welcome back, LaisTree." She smiled, returning his salute, and glanced to one side before stepping through the doorway into the room beyond.

Following her glance, he found someone else sitting in the shadows in the last row before the door.

"Devony . . . ?" he murmured in disbelief. He had been told that she would not be allowed to leave the hospital for another week.

He sat down in the seat next to hers and touched her cheek, gently, uncertainly—touching the slick surface of bandageskin that still covered most of her body, in the aftermath of the energy backwash that had shorted out her sensenet. The doctors had promised him that her burns would heal well, without scars.

She smiled at him. "I wanted to be here," she whispered. "I have to go back soon."

He nodded, and looked down. He had spent as much time at her bedside as her doctors and his would allow before she had regained consciousness. Since then, he had been to see her only once.

Glancing up, he held out the reliquary, passing it into Gundhalinu's safekeeping. He turned back again, putting his good arm around Devony with infinite care. Shame caught him by the throat as he

tried to speak. He held her close until he could man-
age words. "Dev . . . gods, I've missed you. Oh, gods,
I'm so sorry—" He felt the wetness of tears on her
bandaged cheek; dried them as gently as she had
once dried his own. At last he helped her to her feet,
guiding her slow, awkward steps through the doorway
and out of the auditorium.

Gundhalinu stayed close on her other side, shielding her from careless passersby, as they made their
way through the crowd that still lingered in the outer
hall over drink, condolences, and cakes.

PalaThion was waiting outside with a patrolcraft, to
take Devony back to the hospital. Tree looked up the
Street toward the Medical Center and Blue Alley, trac-
ing the profiles of building facades—all the ancient,
seemingly distinct structures that were really no more
than a superficial intaglio impressed on Carbuncle's
seamless, ageless singularity. He saw how their patterns merged as the Street's inexorable spiral folded
them back into the tesseract that was the city. He
looked the other way, seeing the same view . . . realizing how many things always lay hidden in this place
where it was always day. Carbuncle kept its secrets, as
it had since the beginning; it kept them very well.

He helped Devony settle into the back seat of the
patroller. She clung to his hand as he straightened
up again. He glanced at PalaThion long enough to
say "I'm going with you," before he looked back, not
letting his eyes leave Devony's face until he saw her
smile.

Then he turned one last time to Gundhalinu, who
stood waiting, watching the two of them together.
Gundhalinu offered him the reliquary with a look
that was equal parts melancholy and satisfaction.

Tree took the box and smiled. "Thanks." He
glanced down at his uniform. "For everything."

"Likewise." Gundhalinu's empty, bandaged hands dropped to his sides. "We worked pretty well together. I learned a lot."

"Yeah." Tree grinned, suddenly remembering Herne's face at the moment of truth. "Yeah, me too." He hesitated. "You ever like to go out for a beer, BZ? Or play interactives?"

Gundhalinu shook his head. "No. Not really." Then, slowly, almost uncertainly, he began to smile. "But ask me sometime, will you, Tree? I think I should get out more. . . ."

"You should." Tree's smile widened. " 'Never' is not often enough."

Gundhalinu grinned briefly, putting his hands in his pockets. "I don't know if you heard, but Mantagnes will be the new Chief Inspector."

Tree nodded. "Yeah, I heard. What's he like?"

"I don't know him, really. The Inspector says he's a tightass; but then—" Gundhalinu made a wry face as he glanced toward PalaThion, waiting in the patroller. "You know. . . . Have you heard anything yet about who your new partner will be?"

"KraiVieux's still working on the roster; he's got so many goddamn holes to fill. . . ." Tree looked down. He looked up again. "Why? Do you actually want permanent street duty?"

"Well, I thought. . . ." Gundhalinu pulled his hands from his pockets, and stared at them. "No," he muttered. "No. I just wondered. . . ."

"Yeah, I would. Take you on as a partner." Tree shrugged, smiling, as Gundhalinu looked up in surprise. "Just in case you ever change your mind. You're greener than sweetgrass; but gods, we must be each other's luck. It's a miracle we're still alive—and we actually get to go on doing what we both wanted to do all along."

"Luck. . . ." Gundhalinu glanced up the Street toward Blue Alley. His smile faded. "It's going to take more than that."

Tree followed his glance. His own smile disappeared, as he looked back and met Gundhalinu's gaze. He opened his mouth, closed it, shaking his head. He got into the patroller beside PalaThion, and the gullwing doors dropped down into place.

He turned in his seat, looking over his shoulder as the patrolcraft rose effortlessly above the crowd, beginning the short journey up the Street to the Med Center. Devony's smile was waiting for him; he smiled back at her. But for just a moment, his eyes moved past her, to the place where Gundhalinu still stood, watching them go. *Watching their backs.* "Likewise . . ." he murmured, as he reached out to take Devony's hand.

ABOUT THE AUTHOR

Joan D. Vinge has been described as "one of the reigning queens of science fiction," and is renowned for creating lyrical human dramas in fascinatingly complex future settings. She has won two Hugo Awards, one of them for her novel *The Snow Queen,* which began the series that includes *Tangled Up in Blue.*

Vinge is also the author of the bestselling *The Return of the Jedi Storybook, World's End,* and *Psion. Kirkus* called her novel *Catspaw* "complex, deftly woven . . . an engrossing and satisfying read." *The Summer Queen,* a sequel to *The Snow Queen* and a Hugo Award nominee, was published in 1991. *Dreamfall,* which *Publishers Weekly* called a "richly detailed and suspenseful sequel to *Catspaw,*" was on the *Locus* 1996 Recommended Reading List.

Most recently, she wrote the *Random House Book of Greek Myths.* She lives in Madison, Wisconsin, where she is currently writing a novel set in the Bronze Age.